MIDNIGHT AMBUSH

The night was black as pitch. Sheriff Billy Walker turned south, his feet going uphill now, and the ground was hard as concrete. Stepping carefully, he climbed to the top of a granite slab. Then he stopped. Ears straining, he listened. For a full minute he heard nothing but the breeze sighing through the pine tops.

Then he heard something else. Something ahead of him had thumped the ground. A horse shifting his weight from one hind foot to the other.

Billy started forward, measuring each step. What, he asked, was he going to do when he found them? Shoot it out? All right, he decided, the thing to do is cut their horses loose. Leave the killers afoot. They couldn't get far that way.

That's what Billy was thinking when an angry hornet whined past his ear. At the same instant he heard the ear-splitting *pop!* of a gun. Whirling, he saw the flash of gunfire and another bullet ricocheted off the rocks.

He hit the ground rolling, his Colt in his hand.

ASHES
BY WILLIAM JOHNSTONE

CATCH THE ADVENTURE
FROM THE VERY BEGINNING!!

DOYLE TRENT
DEAD MAN'S BADGE

ZEBRA BOOKS
KENSINGTON PUBLISHING CORP.

ZEBRA BOOKS

are published by

Kensington Publishing Corp.
475 Park Avenue South
New York, NY 10016

First printing: October, 1991

Printed in the United States of America

"My name is Bill Walker. I'm kind of mean when I'm drinking and I drink a little all the time."

With that, Billy Walker dropped onto a wooden bench and stared at the gathering of citizens in a back storage room of the Lake Mercantile. Only a handful of people were there, a few seated on whatever chairs they could find and some standing, leaning against the walls.

For a long moment, no one spoke. Come on, Billy Walker muttered under his breath, somebody object. Damnit, somebody say something.

"Uh-hum." County Commission Chairman Hiram Jackson stood and cleared his throat. "I move we appoint Mr. Walker sheriff of Concha County. Does anybody second the motion?"

Aw, for crying in the street, Billy Walker thought.

Finally, after a long silence, a woman stood, an elderly woman, thin, round-shouldered, with a long nose and straggly gray hair. "Well, it seems to me that we could find somebody that's sober. Youall heard him say he drinks. The last thing we need is a boozer for a sheriff."

With a glance at Billy Walker, Chairman Jackson said, "Has anybody ever seen Mr. Walker drunk? So he imbibes now and then, he's been a deputy sheriff for two months now, and I've never heard of him being drunk."

"Well," the woman said, "we ought to find somebody that don't drink likker."

"All right," Chairman Jackson said, "do any of you commissioners want to make another motion?"

Silence. They looked at each other.

"Do any of you citizens want to make a motion? This meeting is open to the public, and we'll be happy to listen to anything youall want to say."

More silence.

"All right, there's a motion on the table." There was no table, but Chairman Jackson pretended there was. "Do any of you commissioners care to second the motion?"

It was Bill's former boss, Samuel Price, who seconded the motion.

Thanks for nothing, Bill thought, but he didn't say anything.

"All right, then, the motion has been seconded. There are four of us duly elected commissioners present. That's enough for a quorum. Are we ready to vote?"

"Are we to understand," the woman said, "that this appointment is only until the elections this fall?"

"Yes, Mrs. Tooly. Concha County can't afford a special election so we have to appoint somebody to take the late Sheriff Koen's place until the regular county elections. Deputy Walker seems to be the most likely."

"Well, are we to understand that if he doesn't do his job we—you commissioners—can fire him?"

"I believe that is correct, Mrs. Tooly."

"Well, I guess we have to have a sheriff. Lord knows there's a lot of killin' and robbin' and stuff goin' on. What we need is a bunch of U.S. Marshals."

"I've inquired about some help from the U.S. government, but I haven't received an answer."

"Well."

Silence. Then, "Are we ready to vote on my motion?"

No one spoke.

"All right, those of you commissioners who favor my motion raise your right hands."

Samuel Price's hand went up. Then slowly, another hand was raised. Chairman Jackson raised his hand. "The motion carries."

Aw . . .

"Now then, Mr. Walker, you are the official sheriff of Concha County until the regular elections next November. Your salary will be sixty dollars a month. The county will provide saddle

6

horses and their care and feeding according to state law. The county will also provide a room for an office, the county jail, and a room for you to live in at the back of the jail."

"Humph," said Bill Walker.

"You are entitled to one deputy. Choose whoever you like, as long as he has resided in Concha County for one year or longer."

"He hasn't been here that long," the woman said, pointing at Billy Walker.

"Yes, Mrs. Tooly, we are aware of that, but the board of commissioners can make an exception on a unanimous vote. That's what the law says."

"Well."

"This is a special meeting of the County Commission of Concha County in the state of Colorado. Now that our business has been conducted, this meeting is adjourned."

"Humph."

Still grumbling to himself, Billy Walker stomped in his flat-heeled boots through the front of the general store owned by Hiram Jackson, outside onto a new plank sidewalk, past two vacant lots, and on down a block to the combination sheriff's office, jail, and living quarters. It was midmorning and the July sun felt good on Billy Walker's back. The Concha County sheriff's building was made of heavy timbers hauled down from the Wet Mountains and slabbed at the sawmill just west of town. It was believed to be escape-proof. After unlocking a big padlock on the door, the newly appointed sheriff plopped into one of two chairs and grumbled under his breath. How in hell did he get into this jackpot anyway? The last thing he wanted to be was a badge-toting lawdog. Hell, he'd never trusted the law or its enforcers.

It was Captain Koen who'd talked him into it. Captain Koen had saved his life twenty years ago in the battle of Shy's Hill.

When Captain Koen needed a favor, Billy Walker couldn't refuse.

"If you think the war was hell," Captain Koen had said, "you ought to be sheriff of this goddamned territory. There's every kind of lawlessness and meanness you can think of around here. If it ain't the rustlers, it's the goddamned road agents that will kill any man who looks straight at them, and if that ain't enough, the railroad's getting so close that the track builders are coming to Concha Lake to do their drinking and carousing and fighting. I need a dozen deputies, but the county can only pay for one. You've got a good head on your shoulders, and you're good under fire. I remember when we had to retreat you walked backward so you wouldn't be found with a hole in your back. What's equally important for a lawman is you're even-tempered. There ain't a man in the world I'd rather have on my side."

So he was sworn in by the circuit judge of the sixth judicial district in the young state of Colorado. He read the one law book the sheriff had and learned what he could about the job, but he'd never felt comfortable wearing a badge. And then Sheriff Bert Koen went and got himself killed.

Well, all right, he owed it to his former battalion commander to finish what he'd started. But damn, he wished he was back driving the six-ups.

While Billy Walker was grouching to himself, heavy boots came pounding up to the open door. He could tell by the quick steps they meant trouble.

"Deputy." The man was breathless from hurrying. He wore baggy wool pants held up by a tight belt. His cap was the kind with earflaps that most men wore in the winter. "Somebody's gonna git kilt. They're drunker'n the lord and they're bettin' who c'n shoot the straightest."

Billy Walker heaved himself up. "Where, at the Pink Lady or the Longhorn?"

With a gulp, the man said, "The Pink Lady. It's some a' them railroaders. Ever' one of 'em is packin' a shootin' iron, and they're lookin' for somethin' to shoot at."

"Aw, goddamnit," Billy Walker grumbled, pulling his dirty gray hat down tighter on his head and shifting his gunbelt. He walked swiftly out onto the plank walk and down a block to a long log building with a wide open door. Maybe just the sight of an officer of the law would stop trouble before it happened. That's what Billy Walker hoped. But just as he started to step inside, two shots boomed. "Aw goddamnit," he groused again.

Inside, the bartender, a round-bellied man with no neck, was pleading, "Go somewhere else, will you. Why don't you go outside to do your target shooting?" He saw Billy Walker and complained, "They've shot two bottles of good bourbon off the bar and they're fixin' to shoot some more."

Four of the dirty ragged railroad laborers were standing at the rear of the long room, behind six card tables. They wore bill caps, lace-up shoes, and bib overalls. "Whooee," bellowed one, holding a long-barreled six-shooter. "Got it right in the middle. Watch me . . ." Then he saw the badge on Billy Walker's shirt pocket, and clamped his mouth shut.

But another pitched in, "Well, lookee here. It's a shurff, or some kinda law. Wonder can he shoot."

"Shit, whar I come from we feed shurffs to the hawgs. Hey, Shurff, wanta bet I cain't hit that there bottle?"

"Haw-haw."

For the dozenth time since he'd been sworn in, Billy Walker remembered advice from Sheriff Bert Koen: Don't get mad. Keep a cool head. Keep your gun in its cradle until you have to use it. Moving slowly, trying to be nonchalant. Billy Walker hooked his left elbow on top of the long polished wood bar and studied the four men. "What I'd like to know," he said, trying to sound pleasant, "is what you fellers are doing here this time of day. Did they quit building a railroad?"

"Haw-haw. Wouldn't you like to know?"

"I take it then that you were, uh, relieved of your duties?"

"Relieved of our duties? Haw. We was fired."

"For beatin' up the godamned foreman."

"Yeah. He looked a lot like you."

"Well, I'll tell you, gents, now that you've got time on your hands, you don't want to spend it in the calaboose, do you."

"Haw. We ain't about to."

"Weel, now, I'd say you're definitely headed in that direction. Of course if you were to pay this man for the damage you did, and keep peaceful while you're here, then you can go on about your drinking until you get ready to go."

"What if we don't."

Billy Walker shook his head sadly. "I hate to see it come to this, but if you don't, somebody's going to get hurt. Maybe killed."

"There's four of us."

9

"Yeah, there is. But look at it this way, I can shoot one or two of you and the county will pay me for doing it. If you shoot me, all you'll get is a hangman's noose."

Their faces sobered while they pondered that. Then one of them, a red-faced man with narrow shoulders and a big hogleg pistol in his hand, stepped around the tables and sneered. "Shit, I never seen the law I'd run from. What if I was to shoot a hole in that tin star?"

It was suddenly quiet in the Pink Lady saloon. The next move was up to the sheriff. Three of the four men had suddenly sobered, and were standing like statues. The third one was still sneering, holding his hogleg pistol down at his side, ready to snap it up and fire. Forcing himself to stay loose, cool, Billy Walker sighed and took two steps toward the sneering one.

"I'm asking you kindly to put that gun away."

"Shit."

Two more steps. While he moved, the lawman was concentrating on his own gun, a Navy Colt in a low-cut holster. Since he'd been appointed deputy sheriff, he'd practiced the fast draw, and he was fast. He watched the sneering man's eyes, and concentrated. Then he was standing in front of the man. His heart was pounding in his chest, and he could only hope it wasn't heard. Speaking slowly, he said, "Give me the gun."

The sneering eyes moved down to the lawman's gun in its holster, then back to the lawman's face. "Try and take it."

Billy Walker moved his left shoulder just enough to prompt a reaction from the man facing him. When the long-barreled gun was snapped up, Bill grabbed at it, got his left hand around it before the hammer was cocked. At the same instant the Navy Colt jumped into his right hand. Bill didn't cock it. Instead he swung it upside the man's head. Swung it hard. The man staggered, but didn't go down. Bill hit him again. The man dropped to his knees and fell over on his face. His bill cap rolled across the floor. Bill twisted the hogleg out of his hand, then thumbed the hammer back on the Colt and covered the other three.

Ordering his heartbeat to slow down, Bill drawled, "Now what do you gents want to do, hand your pistols to the barkeep and stay peaceful or go to jail?"

It took them a moment to realize what had happened. Finally one spoke, "Well, uh, we didn't mean no harm."

"Lay your guns on the bar."

One by one they did. "Now," Bill said, still trying to keep calm, "pay the man for the damage you did."

"Well, uh, how much is it?"

Glancing at the bartender, Bill said to him, "Be honest about it now. Don't cheat these gents. They're going to behave from now on. Give them back their guns when they're ready to go."

Moving fast, the bartender grabbed the pistols and put them under the bar. "It's a buck and a half a bottle," he said.

"Well, gents?" Bill said.

They looked at each other a moment, then dug into their pockets and laid some coins on the bar.

"That one," Bill said, "prob'ly won't need a doctor, but if he does, there is one in town. You boys can drink yourselves silly if you want to but don't bother anybody." With that, Bill spun on his heels and stomped out the door.

Back in his office, Billy Walker dropped into his desk chair, let his breath out with a long sigh, and leaned back. How many of these fracases could a man survive? Captain Koen, how in hell did you ever survive? Hell, come to think of it, you didn't. Why in hell did a man who fought in a long bloody war get himself killed trying to track down cattle thieves? With another long sigh, Billy Walker put his hands behind his head, stared at the ceiling, and reminisced.

It had happened just beyond Quaker Ridge about two miles east of the newly incorporated town of Concha Lake. Out there on the Circle J. That woman, Angelina Peterson, had come loping into town straddling a horse like a man and bellowing at the sheriff to come and see for himself how the cattle thieves were about to drive her out of business. Sheriff Bert Koen told Bill to stay in town, and he'd go see what there was to see. Bill waited until daylight the next morning then rode out to the Circle J. The woman said the last time she saw the sheriff he was headed back to town. She sent one of her cowboys to show Bill where she'd seen him last.

They cut his sign a mile east of Quaker Ridge, out there where a glacier about a million years ago had pushed granite rocks as big as bushel baskets downhill and scattered them over a four-mile-wide valley. First it was the horse, saddled, grazing on the spring grass. Then the man, crumpled on the ground like something wadded up and thrown away. Two bullets had hit him, one in the left shoulder and the other in the center of the chest. Rigor mortis had set in, and they had to get a wagon from the Circle J headquarters to carry the body to town. Sheriff Koen was a bachelor like Billy Walker so his funeral was quick and tearless. Then Commission Chairman Whatisname slapped Bill on the shoulder and told him he was in charge of the sheriff's department until further arrangements could be made. Now further arrangements had been made.

"Goddamnit," Billy Walker muttered, parking his boots on top of the sheriff's desk. He wanted to be a hundred miles away from Concha Lake, two hundred, maybe five hundred. Anywhere. Billy Walker a county sheriff? Hell's hooks.

Well, when he thought about it, he had no choice. Sure, he could saddle his horse, a good big bay gelding, and put a lot of miles between him and this log-and-tarpaper town before anyone knew he was gone. He didn't owe this county anything. But damnit, he did owe Bert Koen. And he did take that oath. Some town. A man could stand on any corner and spit across the town limits. Still, the few merchants had somehow talked the state's General Assembly into incorporating it and designating it a county seat. Hell, they didn't have the money to build a courthouse, a town hall, or anything. They couldn't even hire a town marshal and they left all the law enforcement up to the sheriff.

"Goddamnit," Billy Walker said out loud, and wished he hadn't. That woman was standing in the open door.

"So you're it," she said, looking at him as if he were to be pitied. "You surely haven't got time to sit with your feet on the desk. We cattle growers are paying a nickel a head tax so the county can have a sheriff's department."

Angelina Peterson didn't look tough. But when her husband was shot out among the jagged hills of eastern Concha County, she had taken over management of the Circle J, the biggest cow outfit in at least a hundred miles. She was a smallish, slender woman, about thirty-five, who might be pretty if she wanted to, but would rather go around in men's baggy clothes and a floppy black hat. A few strands of brown hair sneaked out from under the hat and more brown hair curled around her ears. Otherwise she could have been mistaken for a man. Well, no, not exactly. She had a smoother complexion than a man and the high cheekbones and oval face of a woman. And the full mouth. And the gray eyes. But when she hollered "Frog," she expected everyone to jump, and everyone generally did.

She didn't holler "Frog" now, but the gray eyes were boring into Sheriff Billy Walker. "I want you to get on a horse and

13

come with me. I'm going to show you just how vicious these cattle thieves can be."

"I know they're vicious. That's why I'm sheriff and no longer a deputy." Billy Walker's feet came down with a thump, and he stood, standing a little above her. He was only average in height and weight. In fact, he was only average in just about everything. Even his age was average, middle thirties. If folks were asked to describe him, they'd be at a loss for words. All that set him apart from most working men were the badge pinned to his shirt pocket and the pearl-handled Navy Colt in a holster made for a fast draw.

Angelina Peterson turned and walked out, expecting him to follow. He pulled his hat down again, the dirty gray hat with a rolled-up brim, and followed. But he said, "If you think I'm gonna walk, you're mistaken. I've got two horses in a feedlot behind the mercantile. Where do you want to meet?"

Whirling, facing him, she snapped, "On the road east of town. We'll be waiting. Don't be long." Whirling again, she stomped down the plank walk. The seat of her baggy pants waggled and the spurs on her boots rang with every step.

Goddamnit, Billy Walker said, but this time he said it under his breath.

At the corral reserved for the county sheriff, Billy Walker started to catch a roman-nosed dun gelding, one of two horses the county furnished for the sheriff's department, then changed his mind. The dun had ankles and pasterns like fence posts, and his trot would jar a man's bones loose. And when he broke into a run, he always threw his head back in his rider's lap and tried to stampede.

"Not today, ol' buddy," Billy Walker said. Using some fast footwork, he cornered his good bay horse and slipped a bridle over its head. "I didn't hire out here to educate spoiled horses."

Saddled, he rode out to the edge of town, where Angelina Peterson and two armed men sat their horses waiting for him. Without a word they took off at a fast trot, which seemed to be the favorite gait of cowboys going somewhere, and Bill followed. Billy Walker never pretended to be a cowboy, and he was more comfortable on the high seat of a stage coach or a freight

14

wagon than on a trotting horse, but he had covered a lot of miles on horseback, and he kept up with them.

While they rode, he studied the two men. One was middle-aged with gray hair around his ears and on the back of his neck, and a thick gray mustache over a wide mouth. He carried a walnut-handled six-gun in a holster that was cut so low he had to loop a leather thong over the gun's hammer to keep it from falling out. He also had a Winchester repeating rifle in a boot under his right leg. The other man was big. About six-two and an axe handle and a half across the shoulders. He wore a battered, sweat-stained brown hat and denim pants with red suspenders. His six-gun was in a deep holster, not made for a fast draw. Bill guessed his age at around twenty-five. They sat their saddles as comfortably as Bill sat in an easy chair.

They quit the road and took to the rocky hills, covering another four or five miles without speaking. The only sounds were the horses grunting and blowing through their nostrils. Finally, on top of a boulder-strewn hill, they reined up. The big man pointed down to a line of willows about two miles away. And then they were plunging down the hill. The horses slid on their hind feet in places, and Bill feared his three-quarter rigged saddle was going to crawl up onto the bay horse's neck. But he was still on horseback when they reached a shallow draw at the bottom. He was grateful when they booted their horses into a slow gallop. Bill's bay horse swung along easily, allowing him to relax in the saddle.

The big young man reined his horse to the right and everyone followed. When they stopped near the line of willows, they were looking down at a longhorn cow. A dead cow.

"Shot," the big man said. The horses were blowing hard from the run.

"And," the woman added, "whoever shot her was ready to shoot a man if one came along. Just like he shot the sheriff."

3

The big man dismounted and walked, dragging his spurs through tall swamp grass. He looked even bigger on foot. Bill guessed he was six-four and all muscle. Narrow in the hips, big in the shoulders.

Angelina Peterson said, "Tell the sheriff when you found her, Eddie."

"This mornin'," the big man said, squinting up at Billy Walker. He pointed at the willows. "There's another'n over there across the crik."

"Show us, Eddie."

Eddie swung into his saddle and led the way. The horses were up to their knees in a bog and had to hump and buck to get across and into the willows. There the men and a woman ducked their heads to let their hats take a beating from willow branches while they pushed through. They splashed across a shallow creek, pushed through more willows and found another dead cow.

"This 'un was shot too," Eddie said.

Angelina Peterson's gray eyes turned to Billy Walker. "So what do you think, Sheriff?"

Bill dismounted and dropped the reins. He walked around the cow. "I'd guess she was shot day before yesterday, wouldn't you?"

For the first time, the other man spoke, "Why would you think that?"

"Rigor mortis has come and gone. The eyes are dry and sunk. It's been hot and dry the last couple of days."

16

"So tell us something else, Sheriff," the woman said.

"Like what?"

"Like why was she shot?"

All Billy Walker could do was look down and shake his head. The cow was shot just above the left eye. She was looking at whoever shot her.

"Well?"

"I don't know," Bill admitted, looking up.

"Eddie?"

"Wa-al." Eddie spoke with a drawl as broad as Colorado. "It's purty plain to see. Look here." He squatted and pointed at the cow's udder. "She's got a calf. The calf's been suckin'."

When he looked close, Bill could see that the hair around the teats was curled, an indication that a calf had nursed and slobbered. But why was she shot? Then he knew. He'd heard Sheriff Bert Koen talk about how the ownership of unbranded calves was determined by the brand the calves' mothers wore. That's why cattlemen went together on the spring calf roundups, to make sure nobody put his brand on another's calves.

Pushing his hat back, wiping his forehead with a shirt sleeve, Bill said, "Somebody stole the calves and didn't want the cows following and bellering."

"So tell us something we don't know, like who."

"Mrs. Peterson." Bill reset his hat and squinted up at her. "I'm no cattleman and I don't pretend to be. But even I know you can't drive two calves away from their mamas on horseback. Either they had a wagon or they shot the calves and carried their carcasses on a horse. And right now I don't know who." He walked, studying the ground. Tall swamp grass hid any footprints that might have been left here. He walked through the bog and beyond, getting his boots wet. On dry ground he found the wagon tracks. Eddie was behind him on horseback, leading the bay horse.

"Eddie," Bill said, "did you follow these tracks?"

"Yessir, Sheriff. I follered 'em plumb out to the Notch Road." Eddie had a weathered but pleasant face.

17

"How far is it to the road from here?"

"I'd cal'clate four, maybe five miles."

"And I'd guess there were other wagon tracks on the road."

"Yessir, Sheriff. I couldn't tell one wagon track from another."

"When they joined Notch Road, which way were they going?"

"East."

"Hmm." Billy Walker hooked his thumbs inside his gunbelt and studied the horizon. "Hiram Jackson's outfit is almost straight south of here and there's some little homesteads east of there along Concha Creek." Squinting up at Angelina Peterson, he asked, "How far east does your country go, Mrs. Peterson?"

"Only about four miles from here. We go about ten miles north, and south to the Notch Road."

"Any idea how old those calves are—were?"

It was the other man who answered. Bill knew of him. His name was Jeff Overton, and he was foreman of the Circle J. Supposed to be. It seemed to Bill that Mrs. Peterson gave all the orders. "The thief wants 'em to add to his herd or to butcher. He can't steal calves to raise if the calves are branded. That means we missed these two in the roundup." He shifted in his saddle, leaned forward, and crossed his arms on top of the saddle horn. "All of which means if the thief wants 'em to raise, they gotta be old enough to wean without bein' dogied. And he's gotta slap his own brand on 'em." He squinted at the sheriff. "You can tell a new brand from one that's a couple months old, can't you?" Without waiting for an answer, he added, "And if he wants 'em to butcher, they gotta be big enough to pack some beef." He shifted his gaze from the sheriff to the horizon and back. "That might give you some idee of what to look for."

With a wry grin, Bill said, "Yeah. I noticed your longhorn cows are just about every color in the rainbow. I don't reckon you'd know what color those calves are?"

The woman answered, "They're part shorthorn. We've got

18

twenty-six shorthorn bulls, and some of this year's calf crop is the first of their get. They're a little beefier than longhorns, but"—she shook her head sadly—"they could be almost any color."

Billy Walker took the bay's reins from the big man and stepped into the saddle. "Well, all I can do is go east on the Notch Road and see what I can see. Some days there's considerable traffic on the road and maybe somebody saw something."

"Not much daylight left," the foreman said.

"I'll do what I can before dark, and if I don't learn anything, I'll try to get back to work on it in the morning."

"It was one of the squatters," the woman said. "They think because we've got more cattle than we can count they ought to be able to help themselves to free beef."

"They ain't about to butcher one of their own when they can steal somebody else's," the foreman said.

Billy Walker pondered that. "I can't help thinking it's not the farmers. Look at it this way—they drove a wagon across four miles of Circle J country. You've got more country and cattle than you can keep an eye on, still there was a chance they'd be seen."

"And," the woman finished, "if Eddie or any of my men happened to come along, we'd be looking down at his dead body."

"Yeah. That's why I don't think it was one of the squatters. Those farmers are all family men, and while they might steal a beef now and then, I don't think they're killers."

"Anybody would kill to keep from being hung for cattle stealing."

"We don't hang folks for stealing. Not anymore."

Angelina Peterson's gray eyes bored into Bill's. "Maybe you don't, but we will."

The way she said it was a challenge, and Billy Walker knew it. His throat tightened, and he came close to saying something insulting. But he held it back. "Mrs. Peterson," he said, speaking slowly, "you know . . . if you did that, I'd have to arrest you."

The eyes were hard. They didn't waver. "You could try." She reined her horse north, and the two men followed.

Yeah, Billy Walker muttered to himself as he watched them ride away, I could try. If I could find an army to help me.

By the time he got to the narrow, rocky road known as Notch Road, the sun was close to top of the Wet Mountains. He rode east, hoping to meet a farmer, a rancher, or a freighter. By the time he came to the first set of wagon tracks leading off the road, the sun was sitting on the horizon. He followed the tracks to Concha Creek and a one-room log shack with a tarpaper roof. A three-sided stock shelter was near the shack and two heavy harness horses stood in a log corral. Only one cow was in sight. A man in bib overalls was squatting on a one-legged stool under the cow's right flank, squirting milk into a galvanized bucket he held between his knees. He didn't hear Bill ride up.

"Evening," Bill said.

The man jumped up so fast he dropped the milk bucket. Quickly, he righted it before all the milk spilled out.

"Didn't mean to spook you," Bill said, trying to sound pleasant. "I'm Sheriff Walker, and I thought you might be able to help me."

"Huh? Help you with what?" He was short, with a square face and a week's growth of whiskers. He was not carrying a gun.

Bill took a long look around. A few acres of meadowland had been plowed behind the shack, and some kind of row crop had grown about four inches above the ground. A light wagon was parked near the corral. He looked for the milk cow's calf, but didn't see any other livestock. Glancing at the shack, he saw a woman's face peering through a glass window. He forced himself to smile.

"I was wondering if you happened to be out on the Notch

Road day before yesterday and if you saw a wagon about the size of yours with stock racks or a tarp over it."

"Ain't been nowhere. Didn't see nothin'.."

"Where's her calf?" Bill nodded at the cow.

"He was stole. We was figgerin' on butcherin' 'im next fall."

"Any idea who stole him?"

"Nary a one. Him and her was grazin' over yonder close to the road. Somebody come along and caught 'im."

"Did they kill him where they found him?"

"Didn't see no blood."

"Did the cow try to follow her calf?"

"Couldn't. We got a fence over there."

"Was the calf branded?"

"Naw. Where we come from folks don't brand their stock."

Bill didn't ask where they came from. Instead, he said, "Well, I'm looking for a cattle thief, or thieves, and I believe they hauled two calves or their carcasses east on the Notch Road day before yesterday. If you see anything suspicious, come to town and tell me."

"Shore."

"How far to the next homestead?"

"East or west?"

Glancing at the sun, now sinking below the Wet Mountains, Bill said, "West, between here and town."

"It's 'bout a mile and a half to the Widder Osborne's place. Next to the crik. She's got a bunch of kids to feed. She could of done it."

"Much obliged."

It was dusk and rapidly turning darker by the time he got to the next homestead. They saw him coming, and two boys, about ten and fourteen, came out of the two-room log cabin to meet him. The oldest one wore shoes that were about to fall off his feet. The other was barefoot. Both wore pants that had been patched at the knees.

"Evening," Bill said.

The oldest boy spoke. "You the sheriff?"

Another forced smile widened Bill's mouth. "Yessir, I am. What's your name?"

"We're the Osbornes. My ma is in the house. She said to tell you to come in."

Bill dismounted. The younger boy reached for his bridle reins. "I'll put 'im in a pen out back. We ain't got much hay, but I can feed 'im a little bit."

"You don't need to feed him. I'll be going back to town in a few minutes."

Inside the cabin, two coal oil lamps were putting out a dim light. Something that smelled good was cooking on a wood-burning stove. Three youngsters, a boy and two girls whose ages ranged from three to thirteen, gaped at him. A plump woman in a shapeless dress and a long apron greeted him. "I'm Mary Osborne, Mr. Sheriff. You're just in time for supper."

"Well, I sure do appreciate that, Mrs. Osborne, but I've got to get back to town. I'm, uh, I'm looking for cattle thieves and I thought you might have seen someone or something suspicious."

She had a tired but pleasant face and dark, gray-streaked hair combed back and tied in a knot. Glancing around, Bill saw two wooden bunks covered with patched quilts along the far wall, and a homemade table with six chairs in the center of the room. The room was neat and clean. Bill remembered how the woman's husband was killed two years ago in a wreck with a stage coach. They had both worked for Samuel Price's stage and freight line.

"We heard about Mr. Worster's milk pen calf being stole, but we didn't see anything."

"Did any of you happen to be out on the Notch Road day before yesterday?"

"Nossir. Won't you set and have a cup of coffee? I was to town, to the store, this morning with some baked goods, but we didn't go anywhere day before yesterday. We've got a right nice little apple orchard out back that'll bear fruit in another year, and we've got some spuds and carrots planted and we've

22

got some chickens to take care of, and we're baking for the store, and we keep busy. Set and eat. I'll put another plate on the table. Did I hear once that you was working for Mr. Price?"

"I was before I pinned on a deputy's badge. I knew your husband."

"He drove a Concord over the notch and on to Fordson and back. Handled a six-up as easy as most men handle a two-horse team. If a big boulder hadn't a rolled off the mountain on top of him, he'd still be a drivin'." The two older boys came back in but said nothing, only listened.

"I've handled a six-up through the notch," Bill said. "I know what it's like."

"Well, the railroad'll soon put Mr. Price out of business, I reckon."

"Prob'ly will. Mrs. Osbborne, I appreciate your hospitality, but I have to get back to town. If you see anything suspicious, I'd appreciate it if you'd get word to me."

"I surely will. Are you sure you can't stay for supper?"

Riding back to the road in the dark, Billy Walker shook his head. With five kids to feed, how could she be so hospitable? Whatever she had cooking sure smelled good, but if he'd had supper with them, the kids would have had that much less. The Widow Osborne couldn't have any grub to spare. Well, back to the Home Café and Old Lady Witter's greasy fried spuds and tough steak. Wish to hell she'd do something with spuds once in a while besides fry them.

Fumbling in the dark, Billy Walker unsaddled the bay in the pen behind the mercantile and carried in three armloads of hay from a stack just outside the pen. Feeling tired and discouraged, he walked stiff-legged to the sheriff's office. On his way he passed the Home Café, saw it was crowded, and decided to come back later. He also passed the framework of a hotel going up. The two-story building would be the only hotel in the town of Concha Lake. Hiram Jackson owned it

23

too. Inside his office, Bill struck a wooden match and lit a lamp. The pale light illuminated the desk, one wall, the jail door, and that was all. Before he sat, Billy Walker went over to the steel jail door and slammed it shut. He didn't lock it. It was empty. Then with a sigh, he dropped into the desk chair and parked his boots on top of the desk. Tomorrow he'd go back east on the Notch Road. Maybe he'd be lucky and find someone who'd seen a buckboard with stock racks and two calves in it. Naw, that would be expecting too much. Whoever stole those calves wouldn't be seen with them.

Billy Walker was thinking about that and wishing he were somewhere else when he heard heavy boots running on the plank walk outside. They were coming his way. "Aw for . . . goddamnit," Billy Walker muttered. Then a man was standing in the door, out of breath from running.

"Sheriff." He gulped for breath. "Sheriff, better get over to the Longhorn. Somebody's been shot."

4

The plank walk rattled under Billy Walker's boots as he hurried to the Longhorn Emporium. Damned stump-head town, he muttered under his breath, only one general store, one blacksmith, one laundry, one greasy spoon café, one livery barn, no hotel, but two goddamn saloons. The best business in the whole goddamn territory was the saloon business.

The Longhorn was exactly the same kind of enterprise as the Pink Lady in the next block, with a long polished bar and tables. Here, the tables were across the room from the bar instead of at the end of the room, and the Longhorn had pictures on the wall, a pot-bellied stove, cold now, a brass footrail and spitoons. It once had sawdust on the floor, but that had been tracked outside or pushed into the corners. Bill had to elbow his way through a crowd to the far end of the bar where everyone was looking down at a man.

"Give me room," Bill said. "Step back, please." He squatted over the man, who looked to be a sawmill worker in baggy denim pants and a red plaid shirt. He was husky with big shoulders and arms and a heavy black beard. The hole in his stomach had stopped bleeding. His eyes were open but sightless.

"He's dead, Shurff," someone said.

Bill put his ear against the man's chest and heard nothing. He felt for a pulse in the man's wrist and felt nothing, but he wasn't sure he knew how to find a pulse.

Standing, feeling weary, Bill looked at the faces surrounding

25

him. Working men's faces, some bearded, some mustached, some smooth. All hard. "Did anybody go for the doctor."

"Yeah, but he ain't showed up yet."

"Too late anyhow."

"Well," Bill said, "don't everybody talk at once, but tell me what happened."

"It was one a them railroaders. There was four of 'em. One of 'em had a lump on the side of his head and he was madder'n a crow on a wet nest and lookin' for somebody to take it out on."

Another added, "He said it was you that slugged 'im, and he said he was gonna shoot your goddamn head off when you got back to town."

"Them others was tryin' ta talk 'im into leavin', but no, he just had to shoot somebody."

Bill looked down at the dead man and asked, "Who is—was—this gentleman?"

"I know 'im—knowed 'im. Andy Watkins was his name. An off-bearer at the sawmill. Liked his likker, but a good worker."

Bill was afraid to ask, but he had to, "Did he have a family?"

"A wife and a kid, a little girl. They live over west by the sawmill in a wood frame house."

Bill groaned, "Aw, goddamnit." Someone had to break the news to the new widow. It would have to be him.

"May I get through, please." A little man in a finger-length black coat, a dirty white shirt, and a long sad face was pushing his way to the body. He carried a small black leather satchel.

"It's too late, Doc," someone said.

Dr. Hadley knelt beside the dead man, felt for a pulse in the neck, felt of the wrist, and closed the eyes. Standing, he turned toward Billy Walker. His breath smelled of bourbon, and the little thin mustache over his upper lip quivered. "I'm sorry I didn't get here sooner, but it wouldn't have made a difference. Immediate medical attention wouldn't have saved this gentleman."

"Yeah," Bill said, "you can go back to your libation now. Unless you want to go with me to break the news to the widow."

Dr. Hadley's face grew even sadder. "I'd, uh, rather not. Unless you need me."

"All right," Bill said glumly, "I know who shot him. That is, I've seen the gent, although I don't know his name. Did the four of them leave together?"

"Yup. Took out a here like their asses was on fire."

"On foot or horseback?"

"On foot. I don't think they had hosses. I seen 'em git off a railroad's work wagon this mornin'."

"Which way did they go?"

"They was runnin' east last time I saw 'em."

"Did anybody else see or hear them?"

"Yup. That's the way of it."

"Are you goin' after 'em, Sheriff?"

Studying his boots, Bill allowed, "I don't know. I'd never find them in the dark. On foot they could hide anywhere. I guess the best thing I can do, the best thing youall can do, is warn everybody to keep an eye on their horses tonight. If those four are afoot, they'll be looking for a chance to steal some horses."

Someone said, "Yup, yup, sounds like a good idee."

"Will somebody go over to Price's barn and tell them about it?"

"I'll do 'er, Sheriff." A bearded man left, walking rapidly.

"Meanwhile," Bill went on, "will some of you gentlemen carry this man to the shed? Cover him up and lay him out the best you can. I'll, uh, I'll have to go see his widow. Will" — Bill gupled — "will somebody show me where she lives."

Billy Walker hated himself for being so helpless. All he could do was stand just inside the cabin door with his hat in his hand and mumble something about how sorry he was, and ask if he could do anything for her. Yes, ma'am, he'd show her where the body was laid out, and yes, he'd go fetch her neighbor.

The neighbor woman was full of sympathy for the widow, but not for Billy Walker. "Seems to me we need more law and order around here," Mrs. Tooly snapped. "What's the use havin' laws and law enforcers if people can't live without fear. Why don't you shut down them terrible saloons where men drink and kill one another? Why don't you order all them hooligans out of town?"

All Bill could do was gulp and say again that he was sorry.

But the woman was someone for the widow to lean on, a shoulder to cry on, and for that Bill was grateful. He carried the little girl as he and the two women walked to the shed, a one-room shack used as a morgue. The child knew something was wrong and she whimpered all the way. Bill wished he knew how to talk to her, but he didn't. Inside the shed two candles had been lighted, one at each end of the body where it lay on a wooden bunk, illuminating the face. That brought on another outburst of tears from the widow as she knelt and touched her husband's hair. The newly appointed sheriff of Concha County couldn't stand it. He had to turn away.

Later that night, he lit the lamp in his own room at the rear of the sheriff's office and jail, wearily pulled off his boots, and lay on his back on a narrow spring bed. He didn't think about the supper he'd missed. He didn't think about how tired he was and how he could never be sure he'd get to sleep the night through without someone hollering for the sheriff. He didn't think about how hopeless his job was. All he could think about was the new widow and the mistake he'd made that day. A terrible mistake.

If he'd locked up those four hoodlums as he should have, Andy Watkins would still be alive.

Billy Walker was up at dawn, throwing hay to the horses in

28

the feed lot reserved for the sheriff. He cooked his own breakfast on the one-burner combination space heater and cook stove in his room at the back of the sheriff's office and jail. He could mix flapjacks, fry bacon, and boil coffee as well as Old Lady Witter at the Home Café. Deciding what to do that day was not easy. He ought to get on a horse and try to find some trace of the killer and his three cohorts. At the same time he ought to try to find out who was stealing and killing Circle J livestock. At the same time he ought to be in town keeping the peace. And in case anyone had anything new to say about the stage coach robbery last week, he ought to be where he could be found.

All right, he decided, chewing rapidly, wanting to get started, the killer and his pards probably went east. West, they would have a long walk over the Wet Mountains to the town of Fordson. East, they could go to the railroad work camp and maybe bum some grub and a ride to the town of Rosebud. The best thing for him to do was head east on the Notch Road and try to find a clue to the identity of the cattle rustlers. He'd go as far as the end of the railroad, hunt up the bosses, get the names of the four troublemakers, and telegraph ahead to Rosebud. While he was at it he'd send another telegram to Fordson. He'd been told that Fordson had a telegraph which worked most of the time in the summer but not always in the winter when snow and ice broke the wire. With the killer's name and description telegraphed all over the west, he'd be caught. Sooner or later.

Then Bill would have to go and get him and bring him back.

He wished to hell he had a deputy. The county board was prepared to pay for a deputy, but who could he get? Not just anyone would make a good deputy. And what fool would want the job?

Mounted on the hard-trotting dun, Bill stood in his stirrups to take up some of the shock and even tried posting, military style, as he left town and started up the Notch Road. The horse was glad to be out of the pen and going somewhere, and it repeatedly threw its nose up, wanting to run. "Better slow down," Bill said, "you'll have all the traveling you want before we get back." He passed the Widow Osborne's place, saw one of the boys herding a milk cow near the creek, waved, and figured the family was safe. Four more miles out of town he met a light wagon carrying a man and a woman going toward town. He raised his right hand, signaling that he wanted to talk to them, and stopped the dun.

"Morning," he said, forcing a smile. "Pretty day."

"Shore is," the man said, "but we could use some rain. This damn climate, if it don't rain twice a week, the grass quits growin' and the country dries up. Where you headed, Sheriff?"

"Up the road," Bill said. The man was rawhide lean. He wore high-heeled riding boots and a flat-brim hat. "Are you folks from the Double O?"

"Yup. We hold down the Concha Creek Camp. Goin' to town to see the boss and pick up some chuck."

"Were you out on the road a couple of days ago, let's see, three days ago?"

"Naw."

"Well, I don't know if you've heard, but somebody stole some calves and shot their cows over yonder on the Circle J. Left wagon tracks. A light wagon. I don't know whether they shot the calves and were hauling their carcasses or had stock racks on the wagon or what. If they went very far up the road, somebody should have seen them."

"We lost some too. Only ours was big steers."

The dun was shifting its feet, pulling on the bit. "Is that so? When was this?"

"Don't know exactly. Alls I know is eight or ten head of prime beefs are missin'." The man pointed to the southwest. "They was in the Blue Spring pasture. It was before the last rain. There ain't no tracks."

"Got any ideas? Any suspicions?"

"Nope. Wish I did. The boss is gettin' mighty unhappy about these damned thieves."

"Your boss is Hiram Jackson?"

"Yup. He's your boss too, I reckon."

"Yeah, in a way, I guess he is. Only the board of commissioners can fire me, but he's the head duck on the board." Glancing at the sun, Bill knew he had no time to waste. "Well, got to get going. If you see anything suspicious, let me know."

"Shore will, sheriff." He clucked to the two-horse team, and the wagon pulled away.

Standing in his stirrups, posting, Bill rode to the next farm, saw a man working in a field, and went on. At the other homestead, he saw no one at first, and feared the four hooligans were there. Cautiously, he approached the cabin door, stopped, dismounted, and keeping the horse between him and the cabin, yelled, "Hello." When he got no answer, he yelled again. the door opened and a woman came out.

"Good morning," Bill said. "I'm Sheriff Walker. Are you alone here?"

"Yessir, Mr. Sheriff." She was well fed and pregnant. "My husband is working in the potato field."

"You're Mrs. Worster, ain't you? Reason I stopped here is four men are running from the law and I was afraid they'd been here."

"We ain't seen 'em."

"Well, be careful, will you. Be better if Mr. Worster stayed closer to the house today."

"I'll go fetch 'im."

Riding on, climbing the long hill up Dynamite Ridge, Bill met the stagecoach coming down. Six horses pulled the Concord coach, and they were coming at a high trot. Bill wanted to question the teamster, but he didn't want to stop the coach on the downside of the hill. The teamster was Charlie Lupkin, a man he'd worked with. Bill waved and hollered, "Morning, Charlie."

But Charlie stood on the brake handle and "Whoaed" the team anyway, bringing the coach to a stop. Four passengers were inside, three men and a woman. Another man sat on the high seat outside with a double-barreled shotgun between his knees. The men inside stuck their heads outside the window to see what was happening. They were nobody that Bill recognized.

"Billy," the teamster said, stretching the fingers that had been curled around the driving lines, "I heered you was the sheriff nowadays. Any idee who stuck us up last week?"

"No idea at all. Got any ideas yourself?"

"I'm bettin' they come from back there at Rosebud. If they was from Concha Lake, we'd prob'ly recognize 'em by the clothes they wore or the horses they rode."

"You could be right."

"You headed for Rosebud?"

"Naw, just to wherever the railroad's come. There was a killing in Concha Lake last night and I'm sure it was some railroaders."

"Some a them track layers are a tough bunch, all right. The laws at Rosebud are mighty happy they're movin' this way." Charlie pulled a biscuit watch from a shirt pocket, snapped the lid open, and allowed, "We're right on time. Keep your eyes peeled, Billy. Hit up thar, Duke. Prince, hit up thar."

The next traffic Billy Walker saw was six big freight wagons pulled by four-horse teams. They were hauling lumber from the railhead to the hotel under construction at Concha Lake. Bill hailed the lead wagon and asked questions. The teamster had seen nothing suspicious. Another mile, and he came to the notch.

It was on top of a high rocky ridge, named Dynamite Ridge, because it had taken two wagon loads of giant powder to blast a road through it. A steep granite cliff rose straight up on the south side of the road, and boulders as big as houses lined the other side. The road was so steep, and a curve through the notch was so sharp, that stage coach drivers took no chances and unloaded the passengers here. Bill had done it himself. "Sorry, folks," he remembered saying, "for your own safety I have to ask you to get out and walk till we get around the curve. Hope you don't mind."

Some passengers grumbled until they got out and saw the curve. Then they quit grumbling and were happy to walk. Samuel Price, owner of the stage line, often advised his teamsters to unhitch the lead team until they got around the curve. "Be sure to scotch the wheels when you get down and hitch 'em up again," he'd said. Bill had never done that. Neither had Charlie. Neither had the Widow Osborne's late husband.

The dun was sweating and blowing by the time they got to the top of the notch. From there, Bill could look east across a broad plateau, bare of timber, bare of nearly everything except tall bunch grass. Cattle got fat up here in the summer, and traveling was easy. The cold, snowy winters were something else. Looking out across the miles of flatland, Bill saw the railroad. A steam engine stood idle with a string of rail cars behind it. The cars were mostly flat, carrying railroad ties and rails. Five cars had windows. Bill guessed they were bunk cars for the laborers. There was a caboose. Just ahead of the steam engine, men were working, shoveling dirt, swinging sledge hammers, driving spikes. They were a good two miles away, but Bill could hear the ringing of the hammers.

He let the dun blow awhile before booting it down out of the notch. The horse's trot was even rougher traveling downhill, the forefeet striking the ground harder. A mile east of the ridge he passed the stage relay station. The relay man was a grizzled old buzzard named Luke Somethingorother. He held court over a long, low cabin made of two-inch planks hauled from a sawmill over by Rosebud, two pole corrals, a stack of mountain hay, and twenty horses. Grouchy and grizzled as he was, he knew his job and did it well. Bill rode past at a trot. It was already noon, and he had things to do before he got back to town.

Most of the track builders straightened their backs and watched him ride up, then bent to work again when a man bawled, "Awright, awright, you ain't gettin' paid for staring out yonder. Get hot on them shovels."

The man who did the bawling was average height, with a round red face, a handlebar mustache, and a flat-brim engineer's hat. He watched with a suspicious eye as Bill rode up.

"Howdy," Bill said, forcing a smile.

"Huh," the man said, eyeing the silver star. "Who you lookin' for? My men ain't been to town for a spell."

Without waiting for an invitation, Bill dismounted stiffly. "The men I'm looking for have been here. They worked here. Four of them. Quit or were fired early yesterday. Remember them?"

"I bet I know exactly who you mean. What'd they do?"

"One of them shot a man at Concha Lake last night. They ran off on foot. I'll know them if I see them again, but I don't know their names."

"I know 'em, but I can't r'call their names offhand. Too many men come and go here. But Mr. Chance can look 'em up. He'll remember 'em. They beat 'im up before they left. He's over in the waycar."

"I don't reckon you've seen them today."

"Nope. They ain't welcome here."

"Thanks."

At the waycar, at the end of the line of cars, Bill tied the dun to an iron ladder on the side, climbed the iron steps, and knocked on the door. The man who opened the door had a black eye and a split upper lip. He was stout with a smooth-shaven face, a stiff white shirt collar, and wool pants with creases down the front. He, too, eyed the badge. "Yes?"

Forcing a smile, Bill said, "I take it you are Mr. Chance. Are you the superintendent?"

"Yessir, I am."

"I'm Sheriff Walker of Concha County. I would like to learn the names of four of your track workers who quit or were fired yesterday morning. Do you know who I mean?"

"I can guess. Come in and I'll hunt up their names. Are they in trouble with the law?"

"Yes, they are. One of them killed a man in Concha Lake last night."

"Which one?"

"He was the skinny one. He needed a shave but he had no beard or mustache."

"John Wicher. The four of 'em hired on about a week ago. They come from Denver, they said. We wouldn't let them carry their guns at work, but they were carrying pistols when they left."

Looking around, Bill saw a desk and chair, a wall covered with pigeon holes, all stuffed with papers, a few chairs against another wall, and another desk at the far end of the car with a man in a green eyeshade listening to the clickity click of a telegraph key.

"Can I get their names and send some telegraphs to the sheriffs at Fordson and Rosebud?"

"You can. I'd like to see those bastards caught and sent to the pen where they belong."

Nodding at the end of the car, Bill said, "That telegraph is the best invention ever for a law officer. I've got a hunch they're headed for Rosebud and then Denver, and a telegraph will get there a lot faster than they will."

"There'll be other messages ahead of yours, but yours will be there within a few hours." The superintendent reached into a pigeon hole, pulled out a sheet of paper and read four names to Billy Walker.

"Thanks. Now how do I send a telegraph?"

"Just write it down and he'll send it."

Bill composed a short message, asking all officers of the law to be on the lookout for the four below-named men, especially the one named John Wicher. The sheriff of Concha County had warrants for their arrest. He didn't, but he believed he would have within a few days when the circuit judge made his rounds.

"What are you gonna charge them with?"

"That will be up to the prosecuting attorney at Rosebud. I'll recommend murder for John Wicher and accessory for the others. Wicher will be convicted. There were all kinds of witnesses."

Bill's stomach reminded him it was afternoon, and that reminded him of something else. "I take it your men, your workers, get their beds and grub along with wages."

"Yes, we've got four bunk cars and a cook car."

"I reckon you get your grub from Rosebud."

"Yes. Except for fresh meat. We buy that from a rancher at Concha Lake."

"You do? I didn't know that. What's his name?"

"Jackson. Hiram Jackson."

"Oh, him. Well, tell me something, have you bought any beeves lately, say in the last few days?"

"We bought six calves day before yesterday. Our cooks butchered one the same day and another this morning."

"You do your own butchering?"

"Meat spoils too soon in the summer. We keep the cattle in a pen and feed them hay until we need meat. Then our cooks butcher one."

"And you bought these calves from Hiram Jackson?"

"Two of his employees. They drove them here on horseback."

"Hmm. Let's see, Jackson brands a double O, I believe. Did you notice the brands?"

"They're branded with a double O."

Bill studied the floor a moment, then, "I'd like to see them."

"I can show you. They're only a short walk from here. Can I ask why you're so interested?"

"Two calves were stolen from the Circle J outfit, just north of Hiram Jackson's Double O. There've been cattle stolen from other ranchers and farmers."

"I see. Well, I'll show you where we keep them." The superintendent took a narrow brim hat from a peg on a wall, slapped it on his head, and went to the door. Bill followed. The wire pen was about two hundred yards back down the track. Four longhorn calves were munching hay. Bill guessed they were early spring calves, big boned but thin. They wore fresh brands. All Double O. The two Os overlapped. Bill had heard a cowboy in one of the Concha Lake saloons refer to the brand as the "Double Asshole."

He could find nothing wrong here, but he was puzzled. "Why," he asked, "do you buy calves? Most ranchers would rather let them grow and sell them by the pound."

Shaking his head again, Mr. Chance said, "Usually we buy grown steers and heifers, but the cowboys said these calves were, uh, I believed 'dogied' was the word they used."

"Yeah? Well, could be, I guess. I'm no cattleman, but I've seen calves smaller than these cropping the grass. But—

come to think of it — I believe they were nursing the mother cows too. Yeah, I guess they could be stunted from losing their mothers too young. Did the other two look like these?"

"They looked the same to me. They wore the same brand."

Bill nodded, then gazed at the eastern horizon, deep in thought. The calves wore fresh brands, but that was to be expected. Fresh brands were wounds that turned to permanent scars in time. Hair grew over them. Old brands were sometimes hard to see. Brands could be altered with a hot iron, but doing that would cause a fresh brand, and a fresh brand on anything other than a calf would be suspicious. A fresh brand on a grown animal meant one of three things: the animal was a maverick recently caught and branded, it had been sold and the new owner had slapped his own brand on it, or the brand had been altered. If a cow brute had been sold and branded twice, the old brand would still be there. The brands on these calves were no indication of anything.

Or were they?

Damn. Bill pushed his hat back and frowned. He wished he knew more about the cattle business. These brands had started to scab over. They were a couple of months old. Maybe older. If the brands on the stolen calves had been altered recently, they would look different somehow.

Turning to Mr. Chance, he asked, "Did you keep the hides?"

"The hides? Why no. I believe our cooks buried them along with the entrails and other inedible parts. We can't have them smelling and drawing flies."

"Would you show me where they are buried?"

"Why, uh . . ." The superintendent pointed to a mound of dirt a hundred yards away. Near the mound was a tall triangle of poles. Part of a beef carcass, wrapped in canvas, hung from it.

38

The thought of digging up cattle entrails brought a bitter bile to Bill's throat. He could just ride away and forget it. Digging up old guts, cut-off heads and legs was not a job a lawman was supposed to do. Bill said:

"Can I borrow a shovel?"

The mess wasn't buried deep, only about three feet, but wouldn't you know it, the hides were at the bottom. To uncover the hides, Bill had to dig up the entrails, heads and all. The smell was sickening, and Bill was glad now he'd missed dinner. Several times he had to turn away and draw a few fresh breaths before he could dig farther. Only the black flies liked the smell and they gathered in droves. Finally Bill uncovered a hide, pulled it out, and spread it on the ground. Again, he had to walk away a few steps, fight down the sickness in his stomach, and breathe deeply. Then, trying to hold his breath, he studied the brand. It was new. No scabbing. Still a pink wound. A circle J could be changed with a hot iron to an overlapping double O.

This had been one of the calves stolen from the Circle J.

The superintendent was standing far enough away that he was not bothered by the sight nor smell. When Bill had the mess buried again, he walked over. "I believe at least one of the calves butchered was stolen. I don't know about the others. The men you bought them from, have you ever seen them before?"

"Yes, they've delivered beeves here before."

"Can you describe them?"

"Well, uh . . ." The superintendent rubbed the back of his neck, squinted at the horizon, and went on, "They were cowhands. At least they looked like cowhands. You know, big hats, boots and spurs and all. One was young, about twenty-five, and the other was older, maybe forty. I don't recall anything unusual about them. No beards or anything."

"What color were their hats?"

"Let's see. Black. Or maybe brown. Or . . . I must apologize, Sheriff, I just don't remember."

"They said they were working for Hiram Jackson, did they? Have you ever seen Jackson with them?"

"No." Mr. Chance pondered the question and repeated himself. "No, don't believe I have."

"Would you know Jackson if you saw him?"

"Oh yes. I'm in charge of buying groceries, and I personally made an agreement with him to furnish beef. He told me he would have his hired men drive the cattle to the rail camps."

"How did you pay them? Cash or . . . ?"

"Oh no. I paid them with a draft on the Mountain National Bank at Rosebud. The draft was made out to the Double O Land and Cattle Company."

"Hmm. Well. If you see those two jaspers again, try to get their names, will you? Learn as much about them as you can, then send somebody to tell me. Will you do that, Mr. Chance?"

"I will. You're convinced they're cattle thieves?"

"Yeah, I'm pretty sure."

Walking back to the way car and his horse, Bill guessed the two cowhands had collected the bank draft and ridden to Rosebud, where they managed to cash the draft. Or tried to. Somehow they knew about the deal between Hiram Jackson and the railroad, and used that as a way to turn stolen beef into cash.

Mounted again, he turned the horse west toward the notch. He had rustlers on his mind, and he also was worried about four desperate men. Which way had they gone? Where were they now? Hell, Billy Walker shook his head sadly, they could be anywhere. They could have stolen some horses, robbed somebody, and were far away. Or they could be still afoot looking for a chance to rob somebody. They could be lost in the Wet Mountains, or they could be . . . aw hell.

Muffled booms came from Dynamite Ridge just north of the notch, and huge puffs of dust and rocks shot up with each boom. The railroad was blasting its own way through the ridge. Railroad engineers had found a deep narrow ravine through the ridge that could be widened with enough blasting. It was on Circle J land, and Angelina Peterson had made the railroad pay a good price for the right of way. Hiram Jackson had to be suspicious. His cowhands had to have driven some beeves to the railroad only to be told somebody else had sold some beeves ahead of them. Somebody had to be suspicious.

As he passed the stage relay station, he waved at Luke Somethingorother, and Luke waved back. He would have stopped to bat the breeze awhile, but he wanted to get back to town. He hoped to find Hiram Jackson in his office at the mercantile before the store was closed for the night.

The dun horse traveled at a steady stiff-legged trot until they were halfway up Dynamite Ridge, then Bill let it slow to a walk on the steep places. Thinking of Luke at the relay station made him long for his old job. Driving a six-up was better than sheriffing any day of the year. Grinning to himself, he recalled how Luke never failed to have a fresh team harnessed and ready to hitch to the singletrees when the stage pulled in.

"I got old Butch and Jinks in the lead," he once said to Billy Walker. "They're purty steady. You need your steadiest team in the lead. The off-wheel horse is a little green, but old Duke'll make 'im behave. He'll be quieted down by the time you get on top of the notch." Dependable and knowledgeable as he was, Luke's biggest fault was the way he treated the passengers. As far as he was concerned, they were dumb animals who had to be yelled at.

"Git back in there, damnit, this ain't no place to stretch your laigs. This rig's gonna be movin' again in a minute and if you ain't in it you're gonna git left here and I don't need your company."

Samuel Price had talked to him about that, but couldn't change him.

Chuckling, Billy Walker rode to the top of the notch, around the curve, and downhill toward Concha Lake. From the top of the notch he could see the town off in the west, across the low Quaker Ridge, across a wide valley. He could see the twenty-acre cold water lake it was named after. Snow runoff from the Wet Mountains had backed up behind a huge moraine, forming the lake, so named because from across the valley it looked like a decorative silver Mexican concha. It was a good source of water for the town, and Concha Creek was a source of irrigation water for the homesteaders. The town sat on top of layers of sandstone while the eastern edge of the valley was dotted with huge granite boulders that had rolled off Dynamite Ridge thousands of years ago, or were pushed off by glaciers at the end of the Ice Age. Stands of tall pine and spruce grew out of the hills, and a few aspen grew in the draws and on the hillsides. But most of the valley was bare of timber. Lordy, Bill wished he was back driving a stage.

Billy Walker was raised on a farm in the green hills of Tennessee, and he learned to harness and drive a team of mules as soon as he was big enough to stand on a wheelbarrow and buckle the hames around the collars. His family had no plantation and no slaves, only a small cotton farm, so when he was old enough, Billy started working for the neighbors. He pulled bolls, chopped weeds out of the long rows of growing cotton, and drove and rode horses and mules. He had a talent for handling them. His ambition was to save enough money to enlarge and better equip his folks' farm, and he was making some progress in that direction when the shooting started.

The quarrel over slavery didn't interest Billy one way or the other, but he didn't like having those braying jackasses up there in Washington telling him and his neighbors what they

43

could or couldn't do. Some of the things said up there were fighting words. Billy was too young when the shooting first started, and it wasn't until he was fifteen that he was allowed to sign up with the 37th Tennessee. By then the Confederate forces were so desperate for men they would take anyone.

It was a hopeless cause. The Union had more men, bigger and better factories to make weapons, and all the money in the world to buy whatever it needed. The Confederates had horses and mules, but animals couldn't shoot. It was at Shy's Hill that Private William Walker was hit. He was crawling, trying to find a place to hide, when Captain Koen picked him up and half carried him to a Rebel hospital wagon.

There, the overworked surgeon took a quick look at the young soldier's left leg and said, "Compound fracture as well as a bullet wound. We'll have to amputate."

When Battalion Commander Koen came to see how he was, young Walker begged him to get him away from there. But, the officer argued, a wound like that could result in gangrene, or worse yet, blood poisoning. The fifteen-year-old private said he'd rather be dead than crippled. So the officer got him out of the wagon and hid him until the Rebels, now in full retreat, moved on. Then he half carried him to a farmhouse, where he was hidden in a root cellar.

Somewhere on the battlefield Captain Koen had taken a hospital knapsack from the body of an orderly. In the root cellar, by lamplight, he opened a small apothecary jar, rubbed the white powder of morphine into the wound, and went to work with the surgical instruments he found in the knapsack. The leg wasn't broken. A splinter of bone made it appear worse than it really was. With the splinter removed and bandages applied, the wound healed.

Private William Walker spent the last six months of the war hidden in a root cellar and foraging over the South with a small band of guerrillas. Their main goal was to stay alive, but they couldn't pass up a chance to harass the Yankees either.

In late May 1865, the band got word that it was all over, and they split up and started walking home. At sixteen, Bill was a grown and hardened man. He walked more than two hundred miles to get home. Home was no longer there. The house and barn had been burned to the ground and the fields were overgrown with weeds. His mother and dad were living in a one-room shack in Memphis, and Bill went to work in a cotton gin to pay for their groceries. A year later, the senior Walker managed to sell his land to a neighbor, and that gave them enough to live on for as long as they cared to live. Like a lot of war veterans, Billy Walker drifted west.

He plowed farm fields in eastern Kansas, hauled freight behind four-mule teams to Santa Fe, prospected for gold in Colorado, and helped drive two thousand Texas longhorns to Wichita. He tried hunting buffalo but discovered he had no stomach for it. Later he rode a horse to Denver and got a job driving freight wagons to the gold fields as far away as Rosebud. At Rosebud he hired on to Samuel Price to drive four-ups to points west and south. From four-ups, he graduated to six-ups and the fancy, fast-traveling stagecoaches.

He'd stopped at the relay barn in Concha Lake and was gulping down a plate of beans and beef in the Home Café when he saw his old battalion commander. He couldn't believe it. This man was wearing a lawman's badge. It couldn't be. But it was. All Billy Walker could do was stare. Everyone else in the café was busy shoveling food into their faces and they paid no attention to what was happening.

Bertram Koen knew there was something familiar about the man staring at him, but he couldn't quite place him. The man stammered, "Cap . . . Captain Koen? Is that you?"

"I apologize, mister, but I'm afraid I can't put a name to your face."

"Billy Walker. Private Walker of the 37th Tennessee."

Then the older man's mouth dropped open. "Private Walker? Why, I'll be damned if it isn't. Private, what in the wide world are you doing here?"

Their first visit was a short one. Billy Walker had to climb up on the coach's high seat, gather the driving lines, and head south to a town named Columbine. But they vowed they would meet again when Bill made his return trip. And they promised never to again address each other by their former Army rank.

Bert Koen had been appointed sheriff in a brand new county, and he needed a deputy. Billy Walker was talked into taking the job. Bert Koen was shot to death and now Bill was sheriff.

And while he was thinking about his former boss being shot, he suddenly realized he was being shot at.

He felt the heat of the bullet as it zinged past his head and a second later he heard the shot. Without looking to see where it had come from, without thinking, he fell off his horse, keeping a tight grip on the bridle reins. Another shot, and the horse's knees buckled. It grunted and fell over. Bill hit the ground.

Crawling, scrambling, he got as close to the dead horse's body as he could, between the forelegs and the hind legs, keeping his head down. Then he began to think.

The shot had come from behind him. Not from the road. Probably from a pile of granite boulders just south of the road. Behind him and to the south. Slowly, cautiously, he raised his head to look. Yep, that was the likeliest place. A dozen men could hide there.

Bill ducked his head, expecting another shot. After a full minute, he raised his head and took another, longer look at the boulders. Nothing moved. He waited and watched, eyes wide open, afraid to blink. Still nothing. His breathing was shallow, his heart was beating a mile a minute. He swallowed a lump in his throat.

"Come on," he muttered. "Show yourself."

Was it a waiting game? Did the shooter intend to just sit still out of sight until Bill moved away from the dead horse — out where he would be a good target?

Right now, Bill thought, it would be suicide to do anything but stay put. He waited with only his hat and his eyes over the dead horse's back. The horse's forelegs twitched. It wasn't quite dead. It shuddered and was still again. Now it was dead.

Wait.

Then a volley of shots came from the rocks. Bill ducked. One shot, two, three, four, five. Bullets thudded into the dead horse, sang angry songs over Bill's head, spanged off the road. As suddenly as it had started, the shooting stopped. Bill waited a half-minute, then cautiously peered over the horse.

He saw a rider going at a gallop away from the rocks, headed toward Concha Creek. He was too far away to even try to shoot with a pistol. Bill waited another half-minute, then stood, ready to drop again if anything moved over there.

After a full minute, he started walking toward the boulders. He cussed. His horse was dead, he was afoot, and it was a good four miles to town. Let's see, there was at least one homestead between him and the town, two including the Widow Osborne's a mile from town. But Lordy, he hated to walk up to a house and ask for help. A sheriff was supposed to have more dignity than that. He walked to the pile of boulders and studied the ground behind them.

The boulders had once been a single rock as big as a barn. But hundreds of thousands of years of freezing and thawing had fractured it into a half-dozen pieces. Wind and rain had rounded the edges. Now it looked as if the rocks had been piled there by a giant hand.

And sure enough, there were boot prints behind them, and a cigarette butt and a burned wooden match. Someone had seen him coming down from the notch and waited for him to pass here. The prints were made by a narrow-heeled riding boot. A cowboy. The cigarettes had been hand-rolled, but nearly everyone who smoked rolled his own. Bill picked up a butt, mashed it between thumb and forefinger, and studied the tobacco. Flake tobacco, not the stringy kind. Did that tell him anything? Probably not.

No empty cartridge cases. The shots had to have come from a rifle, but the shooter had picked up the empties.

The sun was near the top of the Wet Mountains when Bill left the rocks and walked back to the dead horse. The animal was near the edge of the road. Bill's saddle was partially under it.

Bill unbuckled the cinch and tried to pull the saddle from under the horse. Couldn't. When he gave up and looked up, he saw a rider coming. This one was coming from the north and was too far away to recognize.

Instantly, Bill drew the Navy Colt and dropped behind the horse, ready.

Whoever the rider was he'd seen Billy Walker and was coming directly toward him. Bill stayed down, straining his eyes, trying to recognize the man. The man reined to a halt, trying to figure out who was lying behind the dead horse. He had a rifle in a boot under his right leg and a six-gun on his right hip, but he made no threatening moves. Finally, he urged his horse on again, cautiously.

Bill waited, waited until the rider came within six-gun range where he'd have a fair chance in a shootout. Then he recognized the rider. It was Eddie, the big young man who rode for the Circle J. Bill stood. He still didn't know whether the rider was friend or foe, and he kept the Navy Colt in his hand, the hammer back.

Eddie reined up again. "Howdy, Sheriff. You hurt?"

"No, Eddie. What brings you over this way?"

Urging his horse forward again, Eddie said, "Thought I heard some rifle shots. Thought I'd come over here and see what was goin' on. Somebody shot your horse, huh?"

"Yeah. Did you see anybody or anything?"

"No. Where'd the shots come from? Them rocks over there?"

"Yeah. Whoever did it is long gone, headed south on a high lope."

"There's squatters livin' over there and beyond them the Double O." Eddie dismounted. "Could of been anybody."

"It was somebody who had a reason for wanting me dead."

Bill let the hammer down on the Navy Colt and holstered it. "Somebody thinks I'm a threat to him."

"Must of been one a them cattle thieves."

"Yeah."

"Well, you need a ride to town. I don't know if this horse'll carry double, but we can try 'im." The horse was a chunky red roan, weighing about a thousand fifty.

Grinning a crooked grin, Bill allowed. "He might put us both afoot."

"I'm game if you are."

"All right. Think he can pull this dead horse off the road?"

"We'll see." The big young man took his catch rope off his saddle and tied one end around the dead horse's forelegs. He mounted and wrapped the other end of the rope around his saddle horn. The roan horse strained and pulled the dead animal half off the road. The rider slacked up and Bill took the rope off the forelegs and tied it around the hind legs. The horse pulled again, and the dead one was off the road and into the tall wheat grass. When the dead horse was moved, it was moved off Bill's saddle. He took the bridle off, then looked around for a place to hide his saddle and bridle. The nearest place was the pile of boulders, and that was too far to carry a heavy stock saddle.

"I'll pack it over there for you, Sheriff. Hand 'er up to me." Bill did, and waited while the big young man carried the saddle to the boulders. When he came back, he took his left foot out of the stirrup and said, "Want to try 'im?"

With a wry grin, Bill said, "I'll try anything before I'll walk to town, but it'll be dark when we get there. Won't they miss you over at Circle J headquarters?"

"Yeah, but they won't worry about it."

"Are you single, Eddie?"

"Yep. Nobody's gonna worry about me."

Bill took hold of the saddle horn and put his left foot in the stirrup. Awkwardly, he swung up behind Eddie. The roan humped its back, but stood still. Eddie touched it with his spurs. The horse kicked up its heels, bouncing Bill above its rump. Eddie touched it with his spurs again. "Behave, Roanie. Behave now." Roanie laid his ears back, took a few steps, kicked up again, then walked on peacefully.

In front of the sheriff's office and jail, Bill slid off the horse's rump. The few men on the street stared at him, wondering why the sheriff was having to ride double. "You'll probably be too late for supper at the Circle J, Eddie. Come on in the café and I'll buy you a meal."

They sat at a table in the corner farthest from the door, the same table Bill and Bert Koen had once occupied. The coffee was strong and good and the bread was tolerable, but the potatoes had been sliced and fried in too much bacon fat and the steak would have made good boot soles. The waitress was a young woman, kind of pretty, with wide cheekbones, a dainty mouth, and short brown hair, neatly combed. Her shoulders slumped with weariness, but when she saw Eddie, she straightened up taller and smiled a weak smile.

With his hat off, Eddie was a different man. He had thick curly dark hair and clear blue eyes. Bill guessed he would be attractive to young women. Guessed. He never could figure out what women were attracted to.

"This is Old Lady Witter's heartburn special," Bill commented. "Bet they feed better at the Circle J."

Eddie, too, was having trouble chewing the steak. He swallowed a lump and allowed, "They feed purty good sometimes. Depends on how old Limpy feels and whether Mrs. Peterson'll let him butcher a fresh beef."

"Does she eat with the help?"

"Naw. She's got her own cook, an old lady that cooks and cleans house for her. Ever been to the headquarters?"

"Only once, and then I didn't get off my horse. Looks like a big place."

"Yeah. I worked for a bigger outfit in New Mexico Territory, but there wasn't any women down there and the houses was nothin' but mesquite poles stood on end with more poles for roofs. Mrs. Peterson, now, she's got a fine house. Must be four or five rooms."

"The foreman, Jeff Overton, does he eat with the help?"

"Yeah. He eats what the rest of us eat."

Bill hadn't had a chance to bat the breeze with anyone since Sheriff Koen's death, and he was enjoying himself in spite of the tough, greasy food. But not for long.

The woman who came in was middle-aged in a dirty ragged dress so long it dragged on the floor. She peered from behind her straggly gray hair, which hung down in her face, until her squinty eyes settled on Billy Walker. "Sheriff, I been lookin' for you, where you been anyhow."

Standing, Bill chewed fast and swallowed before he could speak. "I, uh, is something wrong, ma'am?"

"There dern sure is somethin' wrong. Somebody stole my pig and I want 'im back."

"Stole your pig? Do you know who?"

"I dern sure do and I want 'im in jail and I want my pig back."

"Uh, excuse me, ma'am, my name is Walker, would you mind telling me your name and where you live?"

"I know who you are. I'm Amanda Jones. I own and operate Amanda's Boardin' House over by the sawmill. I got four boarders, all bachelors, and I feed 'em good. Better feed than you'll get in here."

"Oh, I see." Bill had heard about the boardinghouse, a log house at the foot of a canyon that came out of the Wet Mountains, but he'd never been in it. He remembered seeing some chickenwire pens behind the house and some red chickens. "Well, about this pig, who stole it?"

"Pete Green. He admits it too."

"Well, uh, I'll come over as soon as I finish my supper."

"I want you to come right now. That's what we're payin' you for."

Billy Walker wanted to tell her to go jump in the lake, but she had the attention of everyone in the room now, and she was obviously ready to make a shouting match of it. Reluctantly, Bill fished some coins out of his pants pocket, dropped them on the table, put on his hat, and said, "Thanks for the ride, Eddie. This'll pay for everything."

Somberly, the big young cowboy said, "See you again sometime, Sheriff."

It took an hour and a half to settle the dispute. That and all the patience Billy Walker could muster. Pete was a grizzled old ex-logger who lived alone in a one-room shack a quarter mile from the boardinghouse, and he had been taking some of his meals from Amanda Jones. Handy with a saw and hammer, Pete had done some carpentry work for Mrs. Jones, fixing up her three-room house, and also her chicken pens so the chickens couldn't get out and the coyotes and red foxes couldn't get in. He thought Mrs. Jones was going to pay him cash money. She thought he was working for his meals and nothing more. To get even, he stole her pig. She wanted him tossed in jail and the key thrown in Concha Lake. He maintained he wouldn't give the pig back until she paid him.

Bill had known lawmen who would have locked them both in jail just to get them to shut up. He was tired, hungry, discouraged. And he was tempted. But he didn't do it. Speaking softly, placatingly, he eventually got them to quit yelling and talk in a civil manner. He even got them inside Mrs. Jones's kitchen, sitting at the table, drinking coffee. The two of them compromised. She would feed him his supper for a week instead of paying him cash, which she had little of.

"But I ain't gonna fix your breakfast unless you pay me."

"All right, make that suppers for two weeks."

"Ten days."

Pete slurped his coffee, put the cup down. "All right. But if you want some more carpenter work done, you'll have to pay me or fix my breakfast too."

"Well." Mrs. Jones had to think about that. "Well, I do need a man to do some of the things a poor old widder woman like me can't do."

Pete grinned a wide toothless grin and ran a callused hand over his nearly bald head. "Tell you what you can do, Mandy, you shore can cook."

The sheriff was forgotten. He cleared his throat, stood, and put on his hat. "If you folks don't mind, I think I'll go on about my business."

Walking back to the sheriff's office and jail, Bill was glad he was wearing flat-heeled boots instead of the high-heeled boots the cattlemen wore. He'd had very little to eat since breakfast, but instead of going back to the Home Café he decided he'd try to find something to eat in his room. Then he'd take a bath out of a bucket heated on the stove and go to bed. Tomorrow he'd ride his bay horse bareback to get his saddle, and while he was out that way, he'd question everybody he saw, find out if they'd seen or heard anything that would give him a clue to the identities of the cattle thieves, find out if they'd seen the four ex-railroaders. And try to find out who the sonofabitch was who'd tried to dry-gulch him. He wished he could communicate with the sheriff at Rosebud, find out how the cattle thieves had cashed a bank draft made out to the Double O Land and Cattle Co. Reckoned he'd have to go to Rosebud himself. Take the stage. Wished he had a deputy.

He had reached the plank walk and was two doors past the Pink Lady when a gunshot blasted the night. It had come from the saloon. The sheriff of Concha County spun on his heels and loosened the Colt in its holster.

8

The shooter was drunk. He stood in jack boots and baggy wool pants held up by suspenders. A floppy wide-brim hat was tilted back on his head. He had the look of a gold prospector, a breed of men that was familiar to Billy Walker. He was weaving on his feet and waving a long-barreled pistol in the general direction of a man Bill knew as Silver Adams. "Ain't nobody gonna steal my stake and live ta brag 'bout it," he said through tight jaws. "You goddamn double-dealin' . . ." A long burp came out of him. "You goddamn double-dealin' shit-eatin' gut-robbin' sonsofbitches're gonna give me my gold back or I'm gonna put the next ball in your goddamn soft asses and let your . . . *burp* . . . let your sneaky brains leak out."

Billy Walker knew what had happened. It had happened before and it would happen again.

The bleary eyes saw him coming. "What're you? Some kinda law?"

"Yessir, I am. I'm the sheriff of Concha County. Did you shoot anybody?" Bill stepped up to the man.

"Not yet, I' ain't, but I'm a-goin' to if that shit-eatin' slick-haired sonofabitch don't give me back my gold."

Glancing at Silver Adams then back to the prospector, Bill said, "Beat you at cards, huh?"

"*Burp.* Naw, he didn't beat me. He cheated me. He think's he's so—*burp*—goddamn smart, thinks I didn't see 'im pull that king of diamonds out of his—*burp*—sleeve."

Bill took another look at Silver Adams. He suspected, but

55

couldn't prove, that the well-dressed dandy cheated at cards. The only time the dandy lost money in a card game was when he wanted to appear to be an easy mark. He always more than made up his loss in the next game. "Did you cheat this man?" Bill's eyes were hard.

"Of course not. It's not my fault he can't read the cards." The gambler always wore a loose-fitting white shirt that could have hidden a whole deck of cards, and Bill suspected it concealed a hideout gun. The gambler never had a gun in sight.

Bill considered it all. There was nothing he'd like better than to lock up Silver Adams. He'd never known the man to do a day's work. All he did was wait for someone to come out of the hills with money or gold in his pockets and entice him into a game. It was easy money. After a few drinks, the prospectors, cowboys, sawmill workers, loggers were eager to gamble. Silver Adams was a professional. They couldn't beat him.

But there was no way on God's earth to prove he cheated — if he did.

"You know," Bill said, his voice hard now, "I've heard too many complaints about you, Mr. Adams. There has to be some truth to them. If I ever catch you doing anything illegal, I'll throw your ass in the hoosegow and keep you there till the judge comes around. And he doesn't come around very often." He started to turn away, then stopped, "Get it, Mr. Adams?"

Men in the Pink Lady knew Billy Walker to be a soft-spoken, mild-mannered man. But when his jaw was set and his voice sounded like clanking steel, they knew he meant business. No one spoke. No one wanted to argue. Not even Silver Adams, who stood dead still, looking at the floor.

"Now then," Bill turned to the prospector, "I'll have to ask you to give me that gun and accompany me to the county jail."

"What? *Burp*. Me?"

"Yeah you. It's not illegal to fire a gun, but in here with so many men around it's a breach of the peace. You do that again and you'll kill somebody. Maybe get killed. Hand it over."

"*Burp*. No, by God, no goddamn law is gonna—"

Bill hit him. He didn't draw the Colt, he doubled his right fist and smacked the man in the left temple. When the prospector's eyes crossed, Bill grabbed the long-barreled sixgun out of his hand. The prospector's knees sagged, but before he could fall, Bill had stuck the pistol inside his belt and grabbed him by the shirtfront. "Come on. Walk. Move those feet."

It was only a half-block to the sheriff's office and jail, and Billy Walker managed to get the drunk there right side up. Before he shut the jail door, he went through the man's pockets to be sure he had no other weapon. A worn leather wallet contained some old letters addressed to Mr. Arnold Tobias. Bill clanged the door shut and locked it. "I'll let you out in the morning when you're sober," he said. Then he went out through the office, around the building, and into his own room behind the jail.

He was too tired now to eat or take a bath. All he wanted to do was flop down on the bed and sleep. After pulling his boots off and hanging the Colt in its holster over the back of a chair, he flopped down on the bed. But he didn't sleep.

The drunk prospector started yelling. Yelling and cursing. "Let me out of here. Goddamn it to hell, you goddamn badge-toting pile of law shit, open this goddamn door and let me the hell out."

Bill muttered, "Aw-w-w, no." He rolled over on his stomach and put the pillow over his head.

"Goddamn it, I said to open this goddamn door and let me the hell out of here. Do you hear me, Mr. Shurff? Unlock this goddamn door."

Fifteen minutes of that and Bill sat up. He ran his hands over his face and through his hair. Some lawmen he knew, maybe even most of them, would go in there with a club and knock the man senseless. But Billy Walker had never been an admirer of most lawmen and he wasn't going to be like them. Listening to that kind of racket was part of the job, and anyone who couldn't stand it ought to turn in his badge. Bill fell back on the bed, rolled onto his stomach, and put the pillow over his head.

Two hours later the drunk shut up and went to sleep. Ten minutes later Bill was asleep.

A beautiful high-country summer dawn greeted Bill when he stepped outside his room next morning. The stars were still out and a half-moon hung overhead, but a pale light was creeping over the top of Dynamite Ridge. Long shadows stretched westward. Bill inhaled deeply, enjoying the clean cool air, and reached through his unbuttoned shirt to scratch his bare stomach. He tried to pump a bucket of water from a long-handled pump, then remembered that the pump always had to be primed. He ducked back inside and returned with a pitcher of water, which he poured into the top of the pump, down the well, while he worked the handle furiously. Finally, the sucker leathers at the bottom of the rods began bringing up water, and then water was gushing out of the spout and into Bill's bucket.

Back inside, he put a pan of water over an open fire box on the cast iron stove, and sliced some bacon while it heated. Before he ate, he stropped his straight razor and shaved out of the pan. A lawman was a public employee and was supposed to keep himself presentable. By the time breakfast was over and he'd washed the skillet, his tin plate, and knife and fork, the sun was showing itself on top of the Dynamite Mountains. Billy Walker put his hat on and reached for the door handle. There was a knock on the door.

Hand on his gun butt, Bill opened it. Hiram Jackson, chairman of the board of county commissioners, stood there. "Mornin', Sheriff," he said pleasantly. "Got a couple of things I want to talk to you about."

Bill stepped back. "Come on in. I think there's still some coffee in the pot." He was glad he'd made the bed and put the dishes away.

"I've had all the coffee my bladder can hold for a while," the portly Jackson said. He plopped into one of the two chairs at the table and scooted the chair half around. He pushed his cattleman's hat back, pulled a short-stemmed pipe out of a vest pocket, a can of tobacco out of another, squinted at Bill, and said, "Need you to do some tax collecting."

"What? Tax collecting?"

The rancher-businessman packed his pipe, struck a wooden match on the sole of his right boot. "Yeah, some a these stock growers and squatters ain't paying their full share. We got a nickel a head tax on livestock, you know. Have to have. The county's got to raise some money someway to build a courthouse and things like that." He puffed smoke out of a corner of his mouth. "Pay your wages. Somebody's got to go out and put the fear of the law in these folks."

"Well, uh . . ." Bill sat in the other chair. "I didn't know . . . I mean, isn't there somebody else to do the tax collecting?"

"Nope. That's the sheriff's job. That's one of the most important parts of your job."

Bill's heart dropped into his stomach. He looked at his boots and shook his head. Finally, he looked up. "Listen, there's been two murders, a stage robbery, cattle stolen, I was shot at yesterday, my horse—the county's horse—was shot from under me. I've got more than one man can do. I haven't got time to go collecting taxes."

The portly man was sympathetic as he puffed on his pipe. "I know. You're trying to be in six places at once. Shot at, you say? Shot your horse? Well, I'll get you another horse. You're authorized to hire a deputy if you can find a good man. But we got to collect some tax revenue to pay him and all the other county government expenses. The board is considering charging a penny tax on every drink of whiskey poured in the saloons, and that'll help. But we got to make these folks take this tax business seriously. They want a government but they don't want to pay for it."

"Well, if all the government does is collect taxes, they . . ." Bill suddenly clamped his mouth shut. Saying what he'd started to say would accomplish nothing. Of course taxes had to be levied and collected. Someone had to do it.

Hiram Jackson was studying his face, squinting at him, waiting for him to continue speaking.

"Well," Bill drawled, "I'll be horseback, talking to some of the ranchers and farmers, and I'll remind them that taxes have to be paid."

"Don't just remind them, tell them. We have authority to confiscate their property if they don't pay taxes. Tell them that."

A lump was stuck in Bill's throat. He decided right then and there he wasn't going to bully honest, hard-working people. If he refused, he'd have to hand over his badge, but maybe that was what he ought to do. He didn't want to be sheriff anyway. Only . . . when he thought of it, he wasn't ready to resign just yet. There was a killer out in the county somewhere. He'd killed Bert Koen and tried to kill Bill. Bill wanted to identify him and arrest him. Or shoot him. With a sheriff's badge he could ask questions and get answers. Without it, he couldn't. He didn't know what to say or do. As it turned out, he didn't have to say anything at the time.

"And speaking of cattle stealing, I lost fifteen head of prime beeves and some calves over the last few weeks. This cattle rustling has got to stop. If it doesn't, us ranchers are going to be out of business."

"Yeah," Bill said, glad the subject was changed. "I'm riding all the time, asking questions. Tell me something, Mr. Jackson, I understand you've got a contract to sell beef to the railroad, is that right?"

"That's right."

"How often do you drive cattle to the work camp?"

"About every ten days to two weeks. They don't want to feed them, and meat won't keep long."

"I was up to their camp yesterday, and the superintendent, a Mr. Chance, showed me some calves that were driven up there a few days ago. They were branded with a Double O. Did you send five calves up there?"

"What?" The county commissioner sat up straighter, teeth clamped on the pipe stem. "Not me. Branded with a Double O? That must be some of the calves that was stolen."

"I was told the men were paid with a draft on a bank in Rosebud. Do you have an account there?"

"Of course. There's no bank here, but we expect some of the entrepreneurs to establish one soon."

"Any idea how two cowboys could cash a draft made out to the Double O Land and Cattle Company?"

Running a hand over his smooth-shaven jaw, Hiram Jackson shook his head. "No. No idea at all."

"Well, that's something else I ought to do. Go over there and . . . say, maybe you could do that. Next time you go to Rosebud, why don't you go to the bank and ask about that?"

"I will. I surely will." Jackson stood and tugged down the bottom of his gray vest. "Matter of fact, I'm going over there on the stage today. I damned sure will ask about that." He stomped to the door and opened it. "Who knows, maybe they'll even know who cashed that check. Somebody had to have signed it."

"Yeah, but . . ." Bill shrugged. "They wouldn't use their own names. See if you can get a description of them, will you. The railroad superintendent thinks all cowboys look alike."

"I will. I surely will." The county commissioner was gone. Bill heaved a sigh of relief. Tax collecting was forgotten for the moment.

He walked around to the sheriff's office, unlocked the big padlock, stepped inside, and unlocked the jail. The prospector had been asleep, but now he rose up on one elbow, squinted through red eyeballs at the sheriff, and sat up. Bill swung the cell door wide open. "I hope you've got the price of breakfast. The county can't afford to feed you. You're gun's over there on the desk. Don't play any more cards with Silver Adams."

As a kid, Billy Walker rode horses bareback often, but as a grown man, riding bareback was something he tried to avoid. He kept his bay horse at a walk. "Go easy on my poor tired ass," he said to the horse. "Let's go find my saddle."

"And hope I don't get shot out of it."

He rode past the Osborne place, but didn't stop. He could barely see the house back in the cottonwood trees along Boulder Creek. None of the farms were near the road. They lay south near the creek. The farmers needed the creek for irrigation water. At the pile of boulders, Bill found his saddle. Horseback comfortably now, he rode on east, his mind working.

Stealing cattle was a way to make an easy dollar for men who knew their business. In a territory where there were few fences, where cattle ranged in rocky canyons, on high ridges and peaks, along brushy creeks and among the tall timber, there were mavericks that had been missed in the roundups. Every cattleman knew where his range ended and another's began, and the mavericks belonged to whoever's grass they were grazing on. But they could be driven off one man's range and onto another. Many small herds in the West had grown into big ones with the addition of mavericks.

Still — Bill's mind was heavy as he puzzled it over — the cattle reported stolen were not mavericks. They were branded cattle, prime beeves and calves. And the cattle themselves were worth nothing more than food to whoever stole them unless — and here was the puzzle — they could be converted to cash.

All right, some were driven to the railroad work camp and sold as Double O beef. The thieves were paid with a bank draft which they had found a way to cash. But that accounted for only a few. What happened to the rest?

The Circle J had reported at least twenty head of grown

63

steers and heifers stolen in the past six months, and Hiram Jackson's Double O had lost—how many? Just a day ago, one of the Double O cowboys said eight or ten were gone. Hiram Jackson himself said this morning that fifteen had been stolen. Were they talking about the same cattle? Must have been. Why different figures? Maybe they didn't know how many were stolen. The Double O was a big outfit with more cattle ranging over more land than they could keep track of. The Circle J was even bigger. A homesteader scratching for a living could shoot a steer, butcher it, feed it to his family, and get away with it. No doubt that was being done. It was easy. Unless the thief was seen. Then his life wasn't worth a dime. He'd be shot on the spot or hung. The thieves knew that so sometimes they shot first.

But it wasn't the farmers who were doing the rustling in Concha County. They wouldn't need that much beef. It was someone who had a market for ten or fifteen head at a time.

Sheriff Billy Walker rode at a walk up the Notch Road, trying to figure it out. Who would buy that many stolen cattle?

It was possible that someone had a ranch in some hidden valley where cattle with worked-over brands could be kept until the brands aged. It was possible, but not likely. A hidden valley would be discovered sooner or later. No, it had to be a slaughter operation. Someone was slaughtering stolen cattle, selling the beef, and burying the hides. And whoever was doing that had to have a market for his beef. He had to be selling his meat on the open market.

Let's see, Bill mused, there was a slaughterhouse in Rosebud. That was out of his jurisdiction but he was sure the sheriff over there would cooperate with him. The two of them could pay a surprise visit to the slaughterhouse, look over the cattle, check the brands, and . . .

"Aw hell," Bill muttered to himself. The owner wouldn't be so dumb as to keep stolen livestock in his pens more than a few hours, and he damned sure wouldn't keep the branded hides around.

Still, it might be a good use of time to go over there, look around, ask questions. The owner, whoever he was, could lie, but how about his employees? Surely, they'd notice brands. If the two sheriffs asked enough questions of enough people, they might uncover a ring of rustlers and buyers of stolen cattle. It was worth a try. But not today.

It was an all-day ride to Rosebud on horseback, but only seven hours on a stage. There were four stage stops between Concha Lake and Rosebud, where fresh horses were ready. The stage teams could be kept at a trot on the hills and at a gallop on the level places. That was the fastest way to get there and back. Still, if he went to Rosebud, he'd be gone at least two days and probably three. Today wasn't the time for it. But soon. If nothing else happened. Meanwhile . . . Bill reined up.

What could he do today? He'd seen no one on the road this morning, and he'd already questioned the homesteaders. Come to think of it, there was the Double O's Concha Creek camp. That's what the cowboy he'd passed yesterday morning called it. Bill didn't know where it was, but it had to be on the creek. The cowboy said he'd seen nothing suspicious, but that was before Bill was shot at. The shooter was headed for the creek on a high lope. Maybe the Double O cowboy saw him. Anyway, Bill couldn't go back to his office and sit. He had to be doing something. He turned his horse south to Double O country.

Riding along the creek, Bill figured he'd see the cow camp eventually. In places he had to push through buckbrush high and thick enough to hide a small army, and in other places the creek wound between hills so steep he had to walk his horse in the water. He rode around huge boulders, bucked through bogs, and climbed rocky hills. It was past noon when he saw the camp, nothing more than a log cabin with a three-sided stock shelter and a few corrals. A wagon road led from it to the creek. The road had to be a better route than the one Bill had traveled. The camp sat under the west side of the Dynamite Mountains, at a point where the mountains reached higher. As he rode up, he saw no cattle. Three horses stood in one of the pens. At first he saw nothing human, then he noticed the cowboy, a thin wiry man, digging a posthole on the other side of the stock shelter, repairing a log fence. The man was so busy he didn't see Bill coming until Bill reined up and hollered:

"Hello."

He expected the man to jump in surprise and grab for the six-gun on his hip. Instead, the man put the shovel down and yelled back, "Hello, Sheriff."

Bill rode over. "See you're earning your keep," he said by way of conversation.

"Yup. There's more to holdin' down a camp than settin' on a horse."

"Looks like tough digging."

"You have to fight for ever' inch. What brings you over this way, Sheriff?"

Bill expected an invitation to "Get down," and when none came, he dismounted anyway. "Just looking to see what I can see. Your boss came around this morning and said fifteen head of beeves were stolen."

"Yeah, that's what I told you yestiddy mornin'."

"Where were they stolen from?"

The cowboy pointed south. "Yonder about five-six miles the country flattens out onto a prairie. Cold windy sonofabitchin' place in the winter but good grass in the summer. Old Jackson was keepin' a hunnerd head or so over there to drive to market this fall."

Looking in that direction, Bill said, "I guess you could drive a herd from there to Rosebud easy enough. If you were moving cattle from here to Rosebud, which way would you go, over the Notch Road or around it?"

"Around it." The man pointed east by southeast. "There's a good trail yonder. A lot of cattle've been over that trail."

"Uh-huh. And I guess that would be the best way to get to the railroad camp too."

"I dunno. Never been there. But you're prob'ly right."

Bill's stomach reminded him he'd missed the noon meal, and he wished the hired hand would invite him inside the cabin for a cup of coffee. Or something. Squinting, he said, "Can't see a trail from here. Can you see cattle going over it from here?"

"Naw. Not from right here. Get over there on the other side of them rocks and you can. If you can see fur enough."

"Then somebody could move some cattle over the trail without being seen from here."

"Yeah. Prob'ly could. Say"—the man's leathery face brightened—"you don't think some a them rustlers're movin' stole cattle over that trail?"

Shaking his head, Bill answered, "I don't know. Could be. If they crossed Dynamite Ridge anywhere near the Notch Road, they'd be seen. Over there is as good a place as any."

The man nodded. "Yup, yup. Could be. I better keep my eyes peeled."

"Don't go getting yourself shot."

"Nope, nope. I avoid gunfire ever' chance I get."

"That brings up another question. Some jasper took a shot at me on the road late yesterday. Killed my horse and high-tailed it over this way. Don't suppose you saw anybody?"

"No." The man appeared to ponder the question. "Nope, I sure didn't."

They were quiet a moment, then Bill said, "You know my name, Billy Walker, but I don't know yours."

"Hudson. Walt Hudson."

Another pause. Bill decided Walt Hudson wasn't going to offer him a cup of coffee or anything else, and he got on his horse. "Well, Mr. Hudson, like I said, don't get yourself shot, but if you see any cattle being driven over the ridge, come and tell me about it."

"I'll do 'er, Sheriff."

As he rode past the corrals, Bill again noticed the three horses standing in one of them. He turned his horse onto the wagon road instead of retracing his route. Hell, he thought, there are no doubt a lot of cattle trails over Dynamite Ridge. He hadn't learned a thing except that . . .

Well, two of the horses in the corral had sweat marks on their back. They had been off-saddled recently. Walt Hudson couldn't have ridden both of them.

Riding down the Notch Road, Bill kept a wary eye on every boulder, tree, or clump of brush where a bushwhacker could be hidden. It reminded him of the war, after the disaster at Shy's Hill, after his leg had healed. The guerrillas were always looking behind them, fearful that an army of Yankees was on their trail. Always fearful.

It was a relief to get back to town. But he didn't even get unsaddled when a rider came up on a lathered horse.

"Sheriff, you'd better git up there, they're fixin' to hang 'im."

"What? Hang who?"

"That kid. They caught 'im in the act. They're fixin' to hang 'im."

Bill retightened the cinch he'd just loosened. "All right now, tell me who's doing the hanging and where."

"The Circle J. Up there on Quaker Ridge. Just south of the road."

Bill was mounted, reining the bay horse east, kicking it in the sides with spurless bootheels. He rode out of town on a dead run.

10

Billy Walker kept the bay horse going on a good gallop for a couple of miles then turned north onto Circle J territory. The horse had to slow to a trot going up the ridge, and by the time it had carried its rider that far, it was so winded it had to slow to a walk or drop from exhaustion. Bill let it walk. Off to his left he saw a small knot of men and a wagon under a half-dozen ponderosas. He didn't see a body dangling from one of the trees, but guessed that that was the hanging party. With his spurless bootheels he got the horse into a trot again, but he was afraid of being too late. Drawing the Navy Colt, he fired a shot in the air to get the attention of the hanging party.

It wasn't necessary. They had seen him coming.

Riding up at a trot, Bill saw a boy standing in the back of the wagon. A light team of horses was hitched to the wagon. The boy's hands were tied behind his back, and a rope was looped around his neck.

"Hold up there," Bill yelled, holstering the Colt. "Hold on to them horses."

One man was in the driver's seat of the wagon, the driving lines in one hand and a whip in the other.

"Don't anybody move," Bill barked, reining up. His eyes went over the men. There were two he'd seen in town, but didn't know. The man in the wagon was Jeff Overton, foreman of the Circle J. Another, the man holding the saddle horses, was a cowboy Bill didn't remember ever seeing before. The outfit's boss, Angelina Peterson, was not among them.

"Now just what the humped-up hell do youall think you're doing?"

"We caught him in the act, Sheriff." It was Jeff Overton talking. "He's the one's been shooting cows and stealing calves."

Glancing around, Bill saw no cattle, dead or alive. "What're you talking about? What did he steal?" Now that he had a closer look, he recognized the boy as one of the Widow Osborne's boys, the oldest one. The boy's round face under a sunbleached cowlick was screwed up in fear. Dry streaks on his face showed he had been crying.

"We caught him before he got a chance," the foreman said. "Look." He picked up an old weather-bleached Henry rifle from the wagon. "He's got the gun and the wagon, and he's in our country."

Reining his horse next to the wagon, Bill said, "What's your name, son?"

"D-Daniel, Mr. Sheriff."

"What were you doing here?"

"Hunting, sir."

"Hunting what?"

"Deer, antelope, turkeys, anything." He added quickly, "Sir."

To the foreman, Bill said, "Take that rope off his neck. Do it right now, before something boogers that team."

"Now look here, Sheriff . . ."

Bill barked, "Now, by god. If that boy gets hurt, you get jailed. Understand?"

"Now listen, we've had enough cattle stealing, and if the law can't do anything about it, we're going to."

Jaws clamped shut, Bill climbed from his saddle into the wagon, loosened the hangman's knot in the rope, and lifted it off the boy's head. Then he untied the boy's hands. Relief flooded the boy's face. He rubbed his wrists, wiped his nose with a shirtsleeve, and stuttered, "M-many thanks, sir."

"All right now, son, tell me the truth, did you shoot any cattle?"

"N-no, sir."

"Did you ever shoot any cattle that didn't belong to you?"

"No-no, sir." The boy's voice was still shaky.

"Why were you driving a team and wagon?"

"Well, sir, I need a wagon 'case I shoot some meat."

"Haw," snorted one of the cowboys. "Shoot some meat. That's just what he's done. Somebody else's meat."

"Got any proof of that?" Bill asked.

"Haw. What kinda proof do you need?"

"Like maybe a carcass."

"We caught 'im before he had a chance to kill anything."

"Where did you catch him?"

"Over north a mile. There ain't no trees over there to hang 'im from."

"Well then," Bill said, rubbing the back of his neck, "he traveled several miles onto Circle J land, and he probably saw some Circle J cattle before he got there."

Jeff Overton spoke next. "That ain't necessarily so. It takes a hell of a lot of country to graze a few thousand cows, and we've got cattle scattered over more than three hundred sections. If you don't know where to look, you can ride all day without seeing a cowbrute."

"Besides," another man put in, "what's he doin' over here?"

"Son," Bill said to the boy, "how much land have you and your family got?"

"A hundred and sixty acres, sir."

"Well," Bill said, "he can't find wild meat on a hundred and sixty acres, unless he can live on rabbits. If he's going to hunt, he has to hunt on somebody else's land."

"It's plain to see," Jeff Overton said, "that you're going to turn this kid loose. What if he's the one's been shooting our cows?"

"Then I'll have made a mistake. I've been known to be less than perfect. Besides, I know what happened to at least two of your calves. They were stolen, all right, but not by this boy."

"Who? Who stole them?"

"That I don't know, but it was grown men. They sold them at the railroad work camp."

"Yeah? You found that out?"

"I found that out. Now I have to find out who."

The foreman climbed out of the wagon. "Well, it sounds like you're working on it, Sheriff. Eddie told us how your horse was shot down." Glancing at the other men, Jeff Overton added, "If you vouch for this kid, I'm willing to let him go and not even charge him with trespassing."

Bill climbed out of the wagon too, and reached for his horse. "You almost hung him."

"We-el now, you think about that, Sheriff. I know who fetched you. It was one of my boys. He didn't want no part of a hanging. Think about how long it took him to fetch you."

"I get your point. But this is a hell of a way to treat a boy who's only hunting wild meat."

"We still aint' sure he's innocent. Don't be feeling sorry for him. We all know these squatters steal beef."

To the boy, Bill said, "Go on home, son. These gents won't bother you again. And if you see a buckskin on the way, go ahead and shoot it."

"Just make sure it ain't beef," the foreman said.

"Y-yes, sir." The boy picked up the driving lines and clucked to the team. The wagon rattled and bounced over the rocks, heading downhill.

Jeff Overton stood spraddle-legged, hands on hips, facing Bill. "I'll tell you, Sheriff, you're the law and we're just a bunch of nobody citizens, but if we catch anybody stealing cattle, we'll hang him."

Bill stood the same way, facing the foreman. His jaw was set. "Don't do it, Jeff. Don't do it. Understand?"

The two men faced each other for a long moment, then the foreman reached for the bridle reins of his horse and mounted. The others followed. They rode away without another word and without looking back. Shaking his head, Billy Walker watched them leave, and muttered to himself:

"There's trouble about to boil over." He mounted the bay. "More trouble. Nothing but goddamn trouble."

There was another horse in the pen when Bill rode up, a horse with a Double O brand on the right shoulder. Bill guessed Hiram Jackson had had one of his hired hands bring the horse for him to use. It was a short-backed brown horse, about a thousand pounds. Bill walked up to it and scratched its neck. "You seem to be gentle," he murmured. "But I won't know for sure 'till I get on your back."

Instead of going to the Home Café, Bill went to the Longhorn Saloon. A beer before supper would taste good. Only two men stood at the bar and only two gaming tables were occupied. Payday at the sawmill wasn't for a few days. Payday always brought business to the saloons. The two at the bar appeared to be carpenters.

"Howdy, Sheriff," the bartender said genially. "Care for a drink?"

"Beer," Bill said. The two carpenters were eyeing him and the badge on his shirt. The beer was served, and Bill dropped a silver dime on the bar.

"It's on the house, Sheriff."

"Thanks, but I'll pay."

One of the carpenters asked, "You're the sheriff?"

"That I am. Are you gentlemen building the hotel?"

"Yeah, Sheriff. Say, it ain't agin' the law to gamble in this town, is it?"

Draining his beer mug, Bill said, "Naw. But take some advice and be careful who you gamble with. There are one or two gents in Concha Lake who almost never lose, and there's others who hate like hell to lose."

"We'll be careful." Neither man was carrying a gun.

The bartender folded his arms on top of the bar. "This

town sure needs a hotel. These gentlemen are living in a tent and eating at Old Lady Witter's."

"Is Samuel Price's barn filled up?"

"That's what they say. He put some more cots in 'er, but they're taken already."

"There's gonna be more builders comin'," one of the men said. "They're gonna start buildin' a bank in a few days."

"Is that right?" This was something Bill hadn't heard before. He'd been out of town so much he was behind the times. He wanted to ask who was financing it, but he didn't want to show his ignorance. "Another beer," he said.

As bad as the grub was at Old Lady Witter's Home Café, she had all the business she wanted. Customers lined the counter and filled the tables. Bill stood just inside the door, looking for a place to sit. There was none. He envied men who had wives to cook for them. Now he'd have to go to his room behind the jail and cook something himself.

Bacon and flapjacks for supper. Well hell, it was probably as good as anything he'd get from Old Lady Witter anyway. Stomach filled, dishes washed, Bill sat at the table, turned the lamp wick up, and tried to read a week-old newspaper from Denver. It held nothing interesting. He considered taking a bath and going to bed, but as tired as he was, he felt restless. Finally, he clamped his hat on his head and went outside. The sky was clear and the stars seemed so close he could reach up and touch them. Inhaling deeply, enjoying the cool night air, Bill let out a long sigh. Then he walked over to the Longhorn Saloon.

The first man he saw when he went inside was the big young cowboy named Eddie. Eddie stood at the bar towering over everyone else. When he saw Bill, his face split into a wide grin. "Hey, Sheriff, let me buy you one. You can drink when you're off duty, can't you?"

Grinning with him, Bill allowed, "Seems like I'm never off

duty, but I'm entitled to drink in the evening if I want to. Make it a beer."

He was introduced to another Circle J cowboy whom he'd seen before but was not acquainted with. The three men stood at the bar and drank cool beer. Cool but not cold. Eddie remarked, "Seems like with all the ice they cut out at that lake in the winter they'd be able to keep beer cold."

"Beer's beer," the other cowboy said. "Looks and tastes like hoss piss anyway." He grinned. "If ol' Eddie here hadn't tole me—I mean ordered me—to drink it, I wouldn't touch the stuff." Draining his mug, he said, "Tell me again, Eddie."

"Seen your foreman today?" Bill asked.

"Not since this mornin'. Me and Tubb here decided we needed to associate with somebody once in a while besides cows and cowboys."

"All we ever see is cows, cowboys, cow horses, and cow shit," Tubbs said.

"Yeah, but we rode Circle J horses to town and we'll have to get back pretty soon," Eddie allowed.

"Well, let me buy youall one," Bill said.

He was lifting his third mug of beer to his mouth when he was bumped from behind so hard he spilled it. Turning, he found himself face to face with a short husky man in a plaid shirt and pants held up with red suspenders. His face was square and ugly, with a week's growth of black whiskers. He glared at Bill. Bill looked him over, from the high, laced logging boots to the round cap on his blocky head. Finally Bill shrugged and turned back to the bar.

"Say what are you, some kinda law?" The logger said "law" with a sneer.

Bill tried to ignore him. It didn't work. A rough hand grabbed him by the shoulder and spun him around. Another hand grabbed the front of his shirt. "I eat laws for breakfast, and that's before I take my morning crap."

11

Hissing through his teeth, Sheriff Billy Walker said, "Let go of my shirt and stand back away from me."

"What're you gonna do, shoot me with that purty little pistol?" The logger had no gun in sight.

"I will if I have to."

"Huh. You goddamn laws can't do nothin' without a pistol. Why don't you put that gun on the bar and show us what you can do without it?"

"I'm not paid to fight everybody who comes along," Bill said. "If you don't let go of my shirt right now, you're not going to make it back to your logging camp tonight."

"All right," the logger said, letting go his hold and backing up two steps. "Come on, put up your dukes. Let's see how tough you are." He doubled his fists and held them face high. "Come on, law dog. Let's see you fight."

"You hit me and I'll shoot."

"You're a coward. You can't fight. Without that pistol you ain't nothin' but a pissant with a badge."

"I'm not paid to take insults either. Get away from me and keep quiet."

"Nossir, I'm gonna make you admit you're a coward. Put up your dukes."

Bill put his hand on his gun butt, ready. But he didn't have to draw it. Another man moved between them. A big man. The logger had to look up to him.

"Seems to me," Eddie drawled, "the sheriff gave you ever'

76

chance to behave yourself. Now if it's a fistfight you want, try me."

"Wha . . . listen, this is 'twixt me and him."

"I just dealt myself a hand, mister. I'll be more'n happy to put my gun on the bar and fight you anyway you wanta fight. Whatta you say?"

The logger looked up at Eddie and didn't like what he saw. Eddie towered over him and he was scowling.

Bill started to object and tell Eddie he was plenty able to fight his own battles. But this was interesting. Eddie's right hand shot out and a big fist grabbed the logger's shirtfront. "Say somethin'."

A squawk came out of the logger. "I didn't start no fight with you. This ain't none of your business."

"I'm makin' it my business. Sheriff Walker here is a fine man, and if he needs any help, I'll damn sure help."

Again, Bill started to object, but he had to step around Eddie to do it. Another squawk, and the logger's hands fell to his sides. "I ain't got nothin' agin' you cowboys."

Twisting the logger's shirtfront, Eddie lifted him up onto his toes, then gave him a hard shove. "You gonna be quiet or do I have to wring your neck like a chicken?"

"I . . . I . . ." With that, the logger backed away until he was near the door. Then he ducked outside.

"A-hum," Bill said, "I, uh, don't want to sound ungrateful, Eddie, but I wasn't in any danger or anything." He, too, had to look up to the big young man.

"I know it, Sheriff. I apologize for buttin' in."

"It's, uh, a-hum, it's all right."

"You want another beer?"

"No, uh, it's been a long day. I think I'll hit the blankets."

"Time we was goin' too, ain't it, Tubb? We'll see you later, Sheriff."

The narrow bed on springs felt mighty good to Bill, and he was soon asleep. Before he dozed off, he decided he'd take the stage to Rosebud in the morning, get together with the sheriff there, and visit the Rosebud slaughterhouse. Yeah, he muttered, shifting onto his side, that was probably the thing to do.

A telegram changed his mind.

He had shaved and was throwing out the pan of soapy water the next morning when his former boss came around the corner of the building. "Wups. Goddamn, Sam, didn't mean to do that."

"Reckon I'd better holler afore I come back here," Samuel Price said, hitching his pants up higher on his skinny hips. "I already had my summer bath. Hell, it ain't been more'n a month ago." His grin was wide under a bushy gray mustache.

"Or I'd better look before I throw out my wash water. What brings you over? Want a cup of coffee?"

"Naw, too much coffee goes through me like a dose of salts. Got a telegraph for you." He unbuttoned his shirt pocket and took out a folded sheet of yellow paper. "Come in the telegraph station at Rosebud yestidy, but missed the mornin' stage. The telegraph feller sent it down on one a them lumber wagons. Got here last night. When I come over to give it to you, you wasn't to home."

Bill took the paper and read it. "Aw hell," he said. "I was planning to go to Rosebud today and try to learn something about cattle rustlers, but now I have to go to Ford and bring back a prisoner."

"Is that the feller that shot the sawmill worker the other night?"

"It's him. Him and his pals must have walked. The Ford County sheriff says he won't give his name, but his pals identified him. John Wicher is his name."

"Glad they caught 'im. Westbound is fixin' to pull out in about ten minutes, but I'll hold 'er for you."

"I'll be there in five minutes."

It took most of the day to get to the incorporated town of Ford in the state of Colorado. The teamster changed horses twice going up the Wet Mountains, and twice on the way down. Bill shared the coach with two well-dressed men who he took to be drummers, and two men who looked like miners. In fact, one of the miners said he was going to Ford to look for work. "Too many damn rock drillers in Black Hawk," he said. "Damn mine owners c'n git all the help they need and they treat us like we was horse shit on their boots. Maybe it'll be better over at Ford."

"If it ain't," said the other miner, "I'm goin' on to Utah. A man's gotta eat."

One of the drummers, a well-fed gent in a dark business suit, was puffing on a cigar. With the coach windows wide open, the smoke was blown outside. "I heard," he said, "that some cowpoke found gold over on the west side of Pikes Peak. That might be where the next boom town is built."

"Pikes Peak ain't got no gold," a miner said. "They gave up on 'er years ago."

A plate of beans with stale bread to sop it with cost two bits at the relay station on top of the Wet Mountains. Bill knew the stage line owner, his former boss, made little profit on the grub, and he paid cheerfully. The station man recognized Bill immediately, and greeted him with a smile. "Billy Walker, you old dog, I heered you was sheriff now."

Bill grinned. "Sort of fell into it. Who you married to now, Biff?"

"Nobody today, but tomorrow who knows?"

Biff, past middle age with a weathered but smooth-shaven face, often bragged about how many wives he'd had. He said he was divorced legally, but no one believed him. "Lots of women stop here on the stage, and some a them ain't bad lookin'."

"Well, with all your charm," Bill said, "I'm surprised you don't talk them into coming back with mattresses."

Winking, Biff said, "You'd be surprised how many of 'em do that."

The trip down into a narrow valley rimmed on two sides by sandstone ledges was faster than the trip over the top of the mountains. The stage pulled up with a loud "Whoa," and a rattling of trace chains before a log house with a high, false front. "This here's the Ford stage stop," the teamster bellowed. "Hotel's across the street." Ford was the end of Samuel Price's stage line, but another transportation company took over here and went on west.

The town was older and bigger than Concha Lake. It had started as a silver mining camp and grown as a supply town for cattle and sheep ranchers as well as for the miners. A telegraph line had been strung from Denver a year earlier, and everyone was told a railroad was coming in another year or two. There were two hotels, at least three restaurants, a dozen saloons, three mercantiles, a stamp mill, and a two-story stone courthouse.

When Billy Walker stepped inside the Ford County sheriff's office on the first floor, he was envious. There was a big desk, four chairs, a card table, wanted flyers on the wall, and a gunrack holding four lever-action rifles and a pump-action shotgun. A heavy iron door connected the office with the jail. But what interested Bill the most was the two deputies loafing in the office. Boy, could he use them.

"Heard you're havin' some rustler trouble over in Concha County," a deputy said. He had a hard face with narrow eyes under a broad-brimmed hat. "Glad we could help you with this gent."

As soon as he stepped into the jail section, Bill recognized the railroader. "He's the one. Did he give you any trouble?"

"Naw. We had 'im covered like a blanket. Three guns pointed at 'im. He threw up his hands so fast he almost jerked his arms out of their sockets. He played innocent at first, but his pals snitched on 'im."

Three of the railroaders were jammed inside a cell at the back end of the jail block, and the one named John Wicher was alone in the first cell behind the connecting door. He stood when the lawmen came through the door, but said nothing.

"I ought to take the bunch of them back," Bill allowed, "but that would be near impossible. I'll settle for this one. He did the shooting."

"He ain't gave us no shit, but he's got a sneaky look about 'im. I wouldn't trust 'im."

"I brought some handcuffs with me. I'll take him back on the stage tomorrow."

"Well, we'll have to turn them others out, then, but we'll keep 'em a few days so they'll be glad to git out of town and not come back."

One of the things Billy Walker liked about the town of Ford was a good restaurant in a good hotel. He finished off a steak, medium rare, with mashed potatoes and brown gravy, peach pie, and two cups of coffee. Then he took a bath in a tin tub big enough to soak in, and went to sleep in a clean bed in a clean room on the hotel's second floor. Then came the morning.

"Better get your bowels moved and your bladder emptied before we start," Bill warned his prisoner, "because you won't get another chance for a while." When they left, the prisoner was handcuffed to his belt, and the belt turned so the buckle was in the back where the prisoner couldn't reach it. Bill was disappointed when he saw a woman waiting for the stage. She was middle-aged, and she eyed the prisoner with a worry wrinkle on her face. Two men got inside the Concord just as the team was being hitched to the singletrees. One was a laboring man, either a sawmill worker or a carpenter. The other worried Bill. Not the man but the gun he was carrying. He wore a long gray coat and a dark wool vest, and he carried a small-caliber pistol inside his belt on the left side. Bill could see a leather loop around the belt, and figured the gun rested in a holster out of sight in the waistband of the pants. Only the butt of the pistol showed, but it was positioned so it could be drawn fast.

Bill got John Wicher seated on the far left, and he sat on the right so the prisoner would have to reach across him to get at his gun. He warned the other passengers, "Don't let him touch you. Keep as far away from him as you can." He noticed with some satisfaction that the man in the long coat sat on his right, leaving the opposite seat for the working man and the woman.

"What's he done, Sheriff?" the woman asked.

"He's under arrest on suspicion of murder, ma'am."

"Oh my. Sakes alive. Don't let him touch me."

The prisoner was sullen but quiet.

"Is he gonna hang?" one of the men asked.

"He's entitled to a trial, and if he's found guilty, it will be up to the judge."

"Think he'll be found guilty?"

"I believe he'll be found guilty of something. There were at least a half-dozen witnesses to the shooting."

"That's the thing to do with 'im, then. Hang 'im."

At the summit relay station, Biff, the station tender, put his hand on the big pistol in its holster when he saw the man in handcuffs. "Gonna feed 'im, Billy?"

"Yeah. Can't let him starve." Bill unbuckled the prisoner's belt so he could use his hands, and marched him to one of the houses out back. At the dinner table, Bill sat on the man's right, and kept an eye on his hands. John Wicher had said nothing, only nodded his head when he was asked if he needed to relieve himself.

The meal was beans again, with some bacon rind cooked in for flavor, and a slice of roast beef. Meal over, everyone stood. The man in the long coat walked around the table toward the door.

That was when John Wicher took his gamble for freedom.

He had been so quiet and peaceful his sudden move caught everyone by surprise, even the sheriff. And he moved unbelievably fast.

In what seemed like one motion, he bumped the man in the long coat, got the man's pistol in his hands and was behind the woman, holding her by the back of her dress.

The woman screamed, and Billy Walker's Navy Colt jumped into his hand. But he couldn't shoot. John Wicher held the woman in front of him, his lips skinned back in a cruel grin. "Well now, lookee here," he said, "I've got a gun and I've got a shield. Drop your gun, Sheriff, or this female woman gets a bullet in the back."

12

Desperately, Billy Walker looked around for a way to disarm John Wicher. Old Biff was on the same end of the room he was, with the woman between him and Wicher. The teamster and shotgun messenger were outside and could come in any second. When they did, they might be in a position to shoot without hitting the woman. Or they might distract Wicher long enough for Bill to take careful aim and shoot. But Wicher thought of that too.

"Drop that gun, Sheriff. If I go down, I'm taking this woman with me. You, too, over there. Take that hogleg out of its cradle and drop it on the floor. Do it right now. Or else, by God."

The woman was screaming. The teamster and guard might hear her scream and come running. They would run right smack into a bullet from Wicher's stolen gun.

"All right." Bill tried to keep his voice calm. "No sense anybody getting shot. Biff, put your gun on the floor." Bending at the knees, he placed the Navy Colt on the floor. He left it cocked. Biff did the same.

"Now, I can cover the door too," Wicher said. "When them two come in, I'm goin' out and I'm takin' her with me."

"You won't get far," Bill said. "We'll be after you."

"Maybe. Maybe not. I can shoot all of you. Then you won't come after me. Got any saddle horses here?"

Biff answered with a growl, "Not for you."

"That means you got one. At least one. When I leave here,

I'll be ridin' the only horse. The rest of 'em are gonna be scattered."

The only hope that Bill could see was the handcuffs. With his hands shackled, Wicher had to move both hands together. That wouldn't spoil his aim with a pistol, but it ought to be a handicap some way. Again, Wicher was matching his thoughts.

"Now, Mr. Sheriff, take the handcuff key out of your shirt pocket where you put it and hand it to this woman. Do it right now."

Aw hell, Bill muttered to himself. He did as he was told.

"Now, lady, if you don't do exactly as I say, you're gonna die right here, get it? Take that key, turn around slow-like, and unlock these here bracelets."

"Please," the woman begged, "don't shoot me. I never did you any harm. Please, sir."

"Shut your trap and do like I told you."

With tears running down her face and hands shaking, the woman unlocked the handcuffs. Bill eyed the Colt on the floor, wondering if he could scoop it up fast enough while Wicher was rubbing his wrists. But the woman was still between them.

Any second now, the door was going to open and two men were going to come in. Somebody would be shot. Bill's prisoner was loose with a gun, and he was ready to kill everybody at the relay station rather than be taken prisoner again. Somebody was going to be killed. He was my responsibility, Bill thought. If anyone gets killed, it ought to be me. Again, he calculated his chances of grabbing the Colt off the floor. If he tried, he'd attract immediate fire from Wicher—and maybe that would give the teamster and guard time to draw their guns. Maybe.

Bill waited, muscles tense.

The pistol in Wicher's hand was a small caliber, the kind that could be carried in a man's waistband. No bigger than a .32. A bullet from it might not be fatal. Breathing in shallow breaths, Bill waited for the right moment. Any second the door was going to open.

Men's voices came from outside. Heavy footsteps approached the door.

Bill yelled, yelled as loud as he could, *"Look out!"* Wicher's head jerked toward the door. The woman fell, just dropped to the floor. In the same instant Bill hit the floor on his belly, grabbing for the Colt.

A shot, and a bullet splintered the floor near Bill's face. Another shot. The Colt in his hand, he rolled. His left hip went numb. He fired from the floor, thumbed the hammer back and fired again.

Lying on his stomach, Billy Walker fired a third time. Saw Wicher double up and grab his stomach with both hands. Saw him fall forward onto his face. Saw the door slam open and two men jump inside, six-guns ready.

The woman sat on the floor and screamed.

No one moved. The two men just inside the door stood with wild faces, wondering who to shoot at. Biff had picked up his gun and was ready to shoot then realized the shooting was over. Finally the woman's screams subsided, and Biff spoke:

"Billy, you hit?"

"I, uh, don't know." Bill picked himself up. His left hip still was numb. "Think maybe I took one but it's a long way from my heart."

"What happened?" the teamster asked.

"Him," Biff nodded at the prone man, "got hisself a gun and was fixin' to shoot ever' one of us. Billy here shot straighter."

Limping, Bill went over and picked up the pistol dropped by Wicher. Painfully, he knelt beside the man. Wicher's eyes were squinched tight. Blood was pouring out of a hole in his stomach and spreading across his shirt. He moaned through clenched teeth and seemed to be trying to hold the blood back with his hands.

86

Standing straight, Bill looked down at himself. He saw no wound. He wanted to take his pants down and examine himself, but the woman was looking at him. "Ma'am, would you mind turning around."

She stood and turned around. Bill unbuckled his cartridge belt first and let it drop, then he unbuttoned his pants. With a glance at the woman, he pulled them down. The numbness was still there, but there was no blood. "See anything, Biff? Something doesn't feel right."

Biff walked around him, bending low, looking carefully. "Red spot. Big one. But it ain't bleedin'. Slug musta hit somethin' and bounced off."

By twisting his hips and straining his neck, Bill could see the red spot at waist level just behind the hip socket. "Damn, Biff know what happened? I think the slug hit my belt. Let's see." He picked up the cartridge belt and examined it. "Yep, look here." Men gathered around to see. "Hit a cartridge. Two of them. Knocked them plumb off. Dug a furrow through the leather. See here."

"Well, I'll be gone to hell. Excuse me, lady."

"Little gun, but a bullet from any gun packs a wallop. Bet it hurt."

"Still feels a little numb, but it's getting better." Pulling his pants up, Bill rebuckled the cartridge belt.

"That pistol you're carryin' ain't much bigger, Billy. What kinda gun is it?"

"A Navy Colt, .36 caliber. It doesn't hit as hard as that hunk of iron you're packing, but it's lighter and faster."

"It shorely is 'cuz you sure as hell shot fast."

"Well," Bill said, "I've got a wounded prisoner here. Got to get him to Concha Lake. There's a man there who claims to be a doctor."

"I don't think he'll last that long, sheriff."

"We have to try."

"The team's ready."

They no sooner had got on board when the Concord was

rolling again, going downhill, the horses on a gallop. The wounded prisoner was bent at the waist, groaning. His wound was still bleeding and his face was white.

"Don't you know something about medicine?" asked the man in the long coat.

"No. I could make a bandage out of something, but it wouldn't stop the bleeding. It's going to take a surgeon to tie the blood vessels."

"How about yourself, Sheriff?"

"I'm fine." The numbness had turned to a steady ache, but Bill figured that was a good sign.

"Sheriff." The prisoner was trying to sit up and talk through pain-clenched teeth. "I got a sister. She's a good woman. Not like me. If I tell you her name and where she lives, will you write her a letter or somethin'?"

"I will." Bill reached into his shirt pocket for a stub of a lead pencil and a small pad of paper, some of the tools of his trade.

"Mrs. Helen Gotswald." Pain forced another groan from the prisoner's lips. "One hundred and twelve Elm Street. Saint Louis, Missoura."

"I've got it. I'll send her a telegram."

"Thanks, Sheriff. I done wrong. Good-bye ever'body." John Wicher slumped forward, his face on his knees, and died.

No one spoke for a moment, then the woman said, "He was a dangerous man but God rest his soul."

At Concha Lake, Bill got the shotgun messenger to help carry the body to the shack, then he went to the Longhorn Saloon. There he asked for witnesses to the shooting of the sawmill worker, and when two men stepped forward, he asked them to go look at the body. He wanted to be doubly certain he had the right man. Next, he went to his office and composed a telegram to Mrs. Helen Gotswald, St. Louis, Missouri. "Dear Madam . . . It is my sad duty to inform you . . ." It would go out on the morning stage to Rosebud and the rest of the way by telegraph wire. While he was in Samuel Price's stage barn, he saw that one end of the building was lined with canvas cots. Price himself explained:

"More builders. They're comin' by the dozens. Whoever is fixin' to build a bank ain't wastin' no time. Most of 'em come from Denver, and one of 'em said they was gonna build a courthouse too. They're puttin' up another big tent back of my place."

"Who in hell is going to feed them?" Bill asked.

"Way I heard it, Old Lady Witter's hired another cook and some more kitchen help and is gonna make a mint feedin' these gents."

"Damn, the things that happen when I'm out of town," Bill muttered. "Seems like everybody knows more about what's going on than I do." His curiosity still not satisfied, he went to the mercantile and hunted up Chairman Hiram Jackson. The businessman-rancher was a proud man.

"My hotel's going to be finished ahead of schedule, and the bank will open for business before winter. This town, Sheriff, is going to boom. We'll have lumber to ship east, silver and gold ore to ship to the mills, cattle, sheep, you name it, we've got it."

"How are you financing a courthouse?"

"Five cents tax on every bottle of liquor sold in the saloons and two cents on every meal sold at the café. With all the new workers in town, that should add up to a tidy sum. And we're raising the livestock tax to ten cents a head per year. And if that doesn't bring in enough, we have authority to add more."

"What's the city council doing, anything?"

"Yessir. Mayor Hutchins said they are considering taxing all real estate in town and adding a cent to every dollar spent. They want a city hall and they need to improve the water system so it don't freeze up in the winter. This is going to be a lively town in the very near future."

"Yeah," Billy Walker muttered, "if anybody can afford to live here."

He found a place at the counter in the Home Café and had a supper of fried potatoes and boiled beef. The pie was stale, but the coffee was good. Old Lady Witter herself came out of the kitchen to speak to him. Her gray hair was pulled behind her head and tied in a knot, and a gray apron covered her dress from throat to shoes. She spoke with a nasal whine.

"Gonna get me some fresh baked goods in a few days, sheriff. Mary Osborne, you know, the Widow Osborne, is gonna do the bakin' at her place and send it over with one of the kids ever' day."

"That will be appreciated, Mrs. Witter. Your customers will appreciate it and Mrs. Osborne will be happy to get the income."

Old Lady Witter went back to the kitchen and the pretty young waitress approached. "Evening, Sheriff Walker. How are you this fine evening?"

"Good, Miss, uh . . ."

"Ringley. Irene Ringley. Say, uh, who was that cowboy you were with the other evening, you know, the tall one?"

Billy Walker had to grin. "I'll tell you for another cup of coffee."

The coffee was poured out of a big galvanized pot.

"His name is Eddie. Come to think of it, I've never heard his last name. He works for the Circle J."

"Does he come to town very often?"

"I don't know. I don't remember seeing him until a few days ago, and he's the kind of man you'd remember seeing."

"Yes. Ain't he, though."

Still grinning, Bill said, "Tell you what, the next time I see him, I'll tell him to stop here and say hello."

"Oh no." The girl was mortified. "Don't say that. Don't, uh . . ." But now she was having second thoughts. "Well, you might say something like, uh . . . tell him we've got another cook and we're gonna have some fresh-baked stuff, and, uh, you might mention that, uh . . ."

Chuckling, Bill said, "All right, I'll tell him all that and I'll tell him there's a right pretty young lady working at the café."

Mortified again, she said, "You won't tell him I asked about him, will you."

"Naw. Naw, I wouldn't do that. I'll think of some way to get him in here, though."

She smiled. She really was pretty. "You're a nice man, Sheriff Walker."

When he turned in that night, Billy Walker again decided he'd go to Rosebud the next morning and try to find out whether anyone was selling stolen beef to the packing house there, and while he was at it, he'd nose around and try to pick up a clue as to who robbed the stagecoach about ten days ago.

He had a hunch that the rustlers and road agents hung out in Rosebud. If they hung out in a small town like Concha Lake, someone would sooner or later get suspicious of them.

With that plan in mind, Bill dozed off. He didn't get to sleep long.

A loud hammering on his door brought him awake with the Colt in his hand. He pulled on his pants and went to the door. "Who's there?"

An excited man answered through the door. "You got to come quick, Sheriff. They robbed the sawmill. They killed Old Josh and stole the sawmill's payroll."

13

News of the murder-robbery had spread through the saloons before it got to the sheriff, and when Billy Walker ran up to the sawmill office, he found the room full of curious men. They were all looking down at another man on the floor near a big desk. Two lamps put out enough light that Bill could see the downed man was either dead or near death. Squatting, he saw the wound in the middle of the chest. It had been bleeding heavily, but the bleeding had stopped. This told Bill the heart had stopped pumping.

"All right," he said, looking up at the curious faces, "who found him?"

"I did." The gent who stepped up was one Bill had seen before.

"You're the owner here, aren't you? Your name is Jeremiah Hardin?"

"I'm the manager and part owner. I found 'im just like this."

"Did anybody touch anything?"

No one spoke.

"All right, clear out of here, all of you, except you, Mr. Hardin." Bill waited until the room was cleared before he said, "Tell me everything you know."

"Wal, tomorrow's payday for about twenty-five men that work for me, and we ain't got no bank so we have to pay in cash. Old Josh was figgerin' how much each man was to get and puttin' it in envelopes with their names on 'em."

Bill saw a half-dozen envelopes on the desk and a list of

92

names. The envelopes were empty. So was an iron safe sitting in a corner with its door open. "You say you hire twenty-five men?"

"Yessir, I b'lieve that's the exact number."

"Then some of the envelopes are missing."

"Yep. And all the money."

"How much money?"

"We had over fifteen hundred here."

"Was Josh alone?"

"Part of the time. I was here with 'im till about an hour ago, then I went to have my usual shot of whiskey. When I come back, this is what I found."

"How long ago did you get back?"

"No more'n twenty minutes ago."

"Wait here." Bill went outside, where a small crowd of men were still gathered, and asked, "Did anybody see anything?" It was too dark to study their faces. No one spoke. "Well, did you see anyone riding through town?" Still no answer. "Did you hear anything?"

Finally someone spoke. "I was in bed over there." A bearded man pointed to a one-room shack a hundred yards east of the office. A pale light illuminated a curtained window. "I was wide awake. My missus was coughin' and keepin' me awake. I heered horses goin' thataway." He pointed west toward the Wet Mountains. "They was runnin'."

"Could you tell how many horses?"

"More'n one. Maybe two or three."

"Thanks. Did anyone else see or hear anything?"

When he got no further information, Bill went back inside the office. "Was the safe open when you went for your usual shot of whiskey, Mr. Hardin?"

"Yep. Old Josh was fixin' to put the money in it when he got it sorted out."

"All right. Josh is dead. I'm sure of that. Looks like a knife wound near the heart. Will you do something for me? Will you hunt up Dr. Hadley and have Josh officially pronounced dead, and will you try to find out who his next of kin is?"

"Yessir, I'll do 'er. What're you gonna do, Sheriff?"

Pondering that, Bill remembered another killer who'd gone west—recently—and he remembered how the killer would have gotten away if the Ford County sheriff's department hadn't caught him. He couldn't let that happen again. He said, "I'm going west and hope to cut their sign."

"You can't find 'em in the dark."

"Probably not. I can't just sit and wait either." Bill went outside and started walking toward the corral behind the mercantile. A big dark form loomed up.

"Want some help, Sheriff?"

"Eddie. What are you doing in town?"

"I quit the Circle J."

"The hell you did."

"Yeah. I was sleepin' in Price's barn when I heard the ruckus. Are you ridin' out tonight?"

"Yeah."

"I heard somebody say the killers headed west on a high lope."

"That's the only clue I've got."

"Do you know that country, Sheriff?"

"Naw. I've been over the road a few times, is all."

"I've chased cows all over up there."

"Is that right? Tell me something, if they went west what would they do, stay on the road all the way to Ford?"

"They prob'ly would. There's a lot of hills and canyons between here and the divide where Samuel Price's stage stop is. Anybody goin' anywhere would stay on the road."

"Have you got a horse?"

"Over in Price's barn."

"I shouldn't do this, Eddie, but your knowing the country might be a big help. If you want to, get your horse and meet me here."

"I'll do 'er." Eddie left on the run.

A quarter moon put out enough light that the two men could see each other, the road, the black mass of woods, and that was all. "We're probably wasting time, Eddie, but maybe we'll get lucky." Their horses walked side by side, climbing steadily.

"I was thinking, Sheriff, if them fellers stay on the road, they're headin' for Ford. But what if they're tryin' to fool somebody and figure on circling back around the lake and headin' east?"

"That's possible. Can they get around the other side of the lake in the dark?"

"I wouldn't try it. That's rough country. There's cliffs up there that drop a hundred feet. There's a way around 'em, but it'd be hard to find in the dark."

Bill reined up. Eddie stopped his horse too. "Eddie, I got a hunch you're right. Do you think maybe they're planning to camp somewhere tonight and make their way around the lake in the morning?"

"It's just a guess, Sheriff."

"Everything is a guess. Do you know of a camping spot on the west end of the lake?"

"Yep, I do. And it ain't too hard to find in the dark. There's a grassy park where horses can graze and men can unroll their beds. I camped there once myself."

The night made Eddie barely visible. Bill appreciated the young cowboy's help and he appreciated not having to go on a manhunt alone. "Let's think about this, Eddie. No matter what we do, it'll be a gamble, but let's think it over and do what seems like the best thing to do."

"All right, Sheriff."

"Now, if they continue west, they're heading for Ford. Ford is a fair-sized town, but not big enough for two or three robbers to spend a pile of loot without somebody getting suspicious. What do you think?"

"Makes sense. And to the east is Rosebud. That's a bigger town. There's enough saloons and whorehouses in Rosebud that a feller could spend considerable money without anybody wonderin' where it came from."

"Right. And if they got tired of Rosebud, they could take a train to Denver. In Denver there are all kinds of ways to blow money."

"So, Sheriff, you think they're plannin' to circle back east and head for Rosebud?"

"What do you think?"

"Like you said, no matter what we do, it's a guess and a gamble. But I think our best bet is to try to head 'em off before they can get around that water."

"If they scouted the country—and I'm betting they did—then they know about that park on the west end of Boulder Lake. If they can find it in the dark, they just might be there. How far is it?"

"Four-five miles. There's an easier way to it but we passed that. We can go back and pick up that trail or go from here. If we go from here, we'll have to ride through tall timber where it's darker'n a stack of black cats. A man can get dragged off his horse by the tree limbs. But when we get to the water, that little ol' moon will show us the way around it."

"All right, Eddie, you lead the way." With a dry chuckle, Bill added, "If I hear you get knocked off your horse, I'll know when to duck."

Chuckling with him, Eddie said, "If I can get through the timber, as big as I am, you can't lose."

They turned their horses into the black woods and downhill. Bill followed the sound of Eddie's horse. Tree limbs dragged at his shirt and hat, and he rode with his hand in front of his face. The horses, glad to be going downhill, walked faster than Bill wanted them to. At one place, they had to ride around a pile of granite boulders, and at another the horses dipped into a shallow ravine and climbed up the other side. At still another, Bill's hat was knocked off his head. Whispering, he asked Eddie to wait a minute while he

96

dismounted, groped in the blackness, and found his hat. From there on he kept his hat pulled down and his chin tucked into his shirt collar. He couldn't see where they were going anyway. And when he thought about it, he had to admit to himself that he was lost. If he'd been alone, he'd have had to stop right here and wait for daylight.

It took two hours to get to the edge of Concha Lake. There, the dim moonlight reflected off the water and their side of the lake was clearly visible. Eddie reined to a halt, and Bill reined up beside him. Their horses were standing on a rocky hill about ten feet above the edge of the water.

Whispering, Eddie said, "That park's about half a mile west, Sheriff. If they're there and if they had a fire, we could see it from here."

"They wouldn't be dumb enough to have a fire."

"No. And I'll bet they ain't asleep either."

"Which means we'll have to walk from here. Horses make too much noise. What's the ground like?"

"There's places where the edge of the water is sandy and there's places where it's rocky."

"Well at least it has to be level."

"Except for one spot where some big rocks raise straight up out of the water. We'll have to climb around them."

"All right, let's find a place to tie these horses and start tiptoeing."

"This could be all for nothin', Sheriff. I hope I'm not leadin' you around in the dark for nothin'."

"However this turns out, I'll be grateful for your help. But Eddie, I don't want you hurt. I'm getting paid for this and you're not."

With a low chuckle, Eddie said, "I always avoid injuries ever' chance I get."

They tied their horses to some low tree limbs, and again Eddie started leading the way. Then Bill said, "Let me go first, Eddie. We don't know what we're walking into."

"If you say so. Just keep the water in sight."

They walked, stumbling at times over rocks. With a grunt, Bill fell to his knees in a shallow draw, then groped his way out of it. Where there was sand, it pulled at his boots and made walking hard work. He could hear Eddie breathing behind him.

Eddie whispered, "Them rocks is right ahead, Sheriff. We can go to the south a little and get over 'em."

Turning south by southwest, Bill walked on, stumbling, trying to be quiet. His feet were going uphill now, and the ground was as hard as concrete. Stepping carefully, he climbed to the top of a granite slab. There he stopped. The big young cowboy was right behind him.

"How far, Eddie?"

"Not far."

"Let's be quiet a minute and listen."

Ears straining they listened. For a full minute they heard nothing but the breeze sighing through the pine tops. Bill started to speak, then suddenly clamped his mouth shut. He heard something.

It was a low, quiet thump. Something ahead of them thumped the ground. The two men stood stock still and listened. Another low thump. Standing close to Eddie, Bill whispered, "That's a horse, isn't it?"

"Yeah. It's a horse shiftin' his weight from one hind foot to another. They're right over there, Sheriff."

"My guess is they aren't on the edge of the water, but back in the dark woods."

"Right."

"You wait here, Eddie. If you hear shooting, go back to town and get help."

"I'll come with you, Sheriff."

"No. I don't want you hurt." With that, Bill started groping his way with his feet. At the bottom of the granite slab, he stopped. "Damnit, Eddie, wait here."

"Right."

Bill went on, measuring each step. What, he asked himself,

was he going to do when he found them? Shoot it out? Naw, they'd probably get away in the dark. What? All right, he decided, the thing to do was to find their horses. Cut the horses loose. Leave the killers afoot. Afoot, they wouldn't go far. Yeah, the horses would be easier to find anyway.

That's what Billy Walker was thinking when an angry hornet whined past his ear. At the same instant he heard the ear-splitting POP of a gun and saw the flash of gunfire.

He hit the ground, rolling, the Colt in his hand.

14

Lying on his belly, Sheriff Walker fired in the direction of the gunflash. Another shot came from ahead of him, and he heard the bullet spang off a rock. He fired at that gunflash. More lead sang over his head and ricocheted off the rocks. Two guns ahead of him were blazing away. Bill fired back, aiming at the gunflashes. Then another gun boomed off to his left.

"Damnit, Eddie, I said —"

"Right."

The gunfire ceased. Footsteps. Running.

"Uh-oh, they're going for their horses. Wait here, Eddie."

Jumping up, bending low, Bill ran in the direction of the footsteps. He knew his boots were clatterintg on the rocks and thumping in the pine needles, but he stayed low and ran on.

The woods were black. Nothing was visible. But there was the sound of footsteps and a horse moving. The horse snorted. It was right ahead.

Bill slowed to a walk, moving cautiously now, listening. A big dark shape loomed ahead and Bill ran into it. A horse. The animal shied away from him. And then a gun fired. The gun was so close the racket numbed Bill's left ear. Bill fired the Colt. Fired again.

Quiet. Except for the horses moving nervously. Groping with his left hand, Bill found one horse. It was shuffling its feet, but not trying to break loose. Bill's feet stumbled over something on the ground. Something soft. Reaching down, he discovered it was a man. The man wasn't moving.

The night was quiet, then gunfire opened up again. Two shots. Over near the lake. Two more. Another. Then quiet.

Deathly quiet. Nothing moved. Not even the horses. Not even the tree tops in the breeze. Sheriff Billy Walker wondered where Eddie was. Was he hit? He wanted to call his name, but didn't dare. Couldn't even whisper his name. That would give away his position. And his position was a good one, here with the horses. If anybody came for the horses, Bill would hear him and stop him with a bullet. But what if it was Eddie, trying to find him? No, Eddie was smart enough to stay put. Anything moving would be shot at. Stay put and wait for daylight. Bill found the tree the horses were tied to and sat on the ground under it.

Eyes straining in the dark, he waited. Come on, daylight.

He tried to remember how many shots he'd fired. The Colt couldn't have more than one live round in it. Groping with his fingers he punched out the shells in the cylinder and re-filled it with cartridges from his belt. He tried to muffle the sound the cylinder made when he snapped it back into place, but in the still of the night the "click" could be heard from a hundred feet away. "Damn," he muttered under his breath.

The horses were shuffling their feet now, and that worried him. The sound would cover the footsteps of a man approaching. Ears straining, Bill listened, hoping he could hear a man breathing—if a man was near.

Tense at first, Bill began to relax as the night wore on. If a man was coming for a horse, he would have come by now. He worried about Eddie. Eddie could be hurt or dead. He'd hate himself if Eddie was hit. Going after killers was his job, not Eddie's. He shouldn't have allowed the young cowboy to come along. On the other hand, he'd never have found the killers without Eddie's help.

Come on, daylight.

It seemed like the night would never end, but eventually he

101

could make out the tree tops. These were tall trees, ponderosas and some spruce. With the dawn came the sweet, pleasant smell of the trees. Now he could make out the horses. It was still too dark to see what color they were, but he could see their shapes. His legs were cramped, but he stayed still. The killers could be waiting for dawn to make a run for it. They could be afraid to move in the dark the same as he was. This might be the most dangerous time of the night. With his fingers curled around the butt and trigger guard of the Colt, Billy Walker waited.

Then he could see the saddles on the horses. Next he could see their colors. One was a blaze-faced bay and the other was a zebra dun. There were only two. That meant there were only two killers. One was on the ground not ten feet from where Bill sat. He was still. Still and dead. Bill had been keeping company with a dead man. Where was the other? And where was Eddie?

There was enough light now that he could see clearly. No use sitting here any longer. Slowly, stiffly, Bill stood, keeping the tree between him and the lake. He waited a minute, then called, "Eddie." Called louder, "Eddie."

"Sheriff? Where you at?"

Was that Eddie's voice? Bill couldn't be sure. It could be somebody else trying to locate him. "Eddie," he called again. "You hurt?"

"Naw, Sheriff. I'm as sound as a dollar."

It was Eddie. Bill asked, "Do you see anybody else?"

"Yeah. One man down over here. How about you?"

"One down here too. I think there were only two."

"I'm comin' out in the open, Sheriff."

"Come on out." Bill left the shelter of the tree and walked toward the edge of Concha Lake. He hadn't walked more than fifteen feet when he saw Eddie, walking toward him. Limping. "Aw, no," Bill muttered. When he was closer, he asked, "You're hit, Eddie. Where?"

The big young man stood still and waited for the sheriff.

He touched the outside of his right thigh, a spot where blood had seeped through the denim of his pants. "Right here."

"How bad?"

"Don't think it's bad. Now that it's daylight, I'll have a look."

"First, let's have a look at these two gents. Don't want them playing dead." He went to the one on the ground near the water, squatted, and rolled him over on his back. The face was familiar, but Bill couldn't put a name to it. Then he went back to the horses and examined the other man. This one he didn't recognize. Eddie was behind him.

"Recognize either one, Eddie?"

"I've seen 'em before. That 'un over there rode for the Circle J for a while early last spring. His name is—was—Joe. Never heard his last name. He quit a couple of months ago. This 'un I've seen in town, but I don't know nothin' about 'im. I see a gunny sack over yonder by the lake. I'll bet that's the stolen money."

"Yeah, well, we'll see, but first let's have a look at that wound."

Eddie unbuckled his gunbelt then unbuttoned his pants and pulled them down. Standing in his shorts with his pants around his knees, he studied a raw red streak across the outside of his right thigh, between his knee and crotch. "No bullet in there," he said. "Looks like it went on by and took a bite out of me on its way."

Squatting, examining the wound, Bill agreed. "But it needs some care. Could get infected. The dye in those denim britches could cause infection." Standing, he pulled his shirt tail out and tore off a wide strip. "Here, maybe this'll help." He wrapped the strip around the wound and tied it in place. "Let's get back to town and let that doctor do his job on it."

"All right, but I'm itchin' to take a peek inside that gunny sack, Sheriff. It's gotta have money in it."

"Go ahead."

Eddie was right. There was loose money and money in envelopes with names written on them. It was the sawmill pay-roll. Eddie grinned a wide grin. "We got it, Sheriff. How much do you reckon is here?"

"Supposed to be over fifteen hundred. Do you want to count it or just take it back and let old Whatsisname at the sawmill office count it?"

"Can I just touch it? I never seen this much money before."

Grinning with him, Bill said, "Go ahead."

There were also two blankets and a loaf of bread near the edge of the lake. The two killer-robbers had obviously planned to wait here for daylight, eat the bread, then be on their way around the lake and around the town. They hadn't even unsaddled their horses. Bill and Eddie wrapped the two bodies in the blankets, got them tied across the saddles. Eddie moved sorely, stiff-legged. Bill tried to get him to wait here while he went after their own horses, but the young cowboy insisted on hobbling along, even though he winced with pain at times. They led the two horses to where they'd left their mounts and started back to town. Eddie pointed out the way over a dim trail that was little used but easier to follow than riding through the timber. "Yup, this's the way they came," he allowed. "Clear as day."

In town, a crowd gathered and walked behind them. By the time they got to the shack, a dozen men and a few women and kids were following, curious. "Is that them robbers, Shurff?"

Grim-faced, Bill said, "Yeah, it's them. Let's get these bodies inside and laid out, then I want youall to look at them and tell me if you've ever seen them before."

The shack already held the bodies of John Wicher and Old Josh, the sawmill bookkeeper, and the two new bodies had to be laid on the wooden floor. Curious men came in and studied the faces.

"Yup. I rec'lect seein' both of 'em in the Longhorn one night recent. Don't know their names, howsomeever. They looked like cowhands."

"That 'un there rode for the Circle J. Least that's what he said. Played cards with him and some others once."

Sheriff Walker went through the pockets of the dead men, hoping to find some identification. One carried a long-bladed folding knife. There was a trace of dried blood on the blade. It had to be the murder weapon. The other carried a smaller folding knife. They both carried small cloth bags of crumbled-leaf tobacco, cigarette papers, matches, and nothing else. "Tell everybody you see to come and look at them. I want to learn as much about them as I can."

"Did they shoot at you, Shurff?"

"We all fired a few rounds. Go hunt up Dr. Hadley, will you? Eddie's got a flesh wound that ought to be doctored."

"Yup, yup, I'll do 'er."

"We'll be in my room at the back of the jail. Send the doctor over there."

The news had spread, and when Bill went to the mercantile to buy some fresh bacon and bread, he had to answer questions from a half-dozen customers. Chairman Jackson was one of the questioners. "By God, Sheriff Walker, if you keep killing off the hardcases, we're going to have to start a cemetery for them." He was smiling when he said it. "Like to have some trials and do things the right way, but as it is, we don't have to feed jail prisoners. Tell me, Sheriff Walker, did they say anything at all or just start blasting away?"

"Nobody said a word."

"Do you think maybe those two were responsible for the other crimes in Concha County?"

"I don't know. They could be. That's why I want everybody to look at them and see if they recognize them. If you see Sam Price, ask him to get his teamsters to take a look, will you?"

"I certainly will."

Dr. Hadley was there when Bill got back to his room. He'd bandaged the wound and was closing his satchel. "Not critical, but he's got to stay off that leg awhile. Thank heavens it

105

doesn't need surgery, but we've got to keep it from bleeding. The limb is going to be sore for a few days. I'll come back tomorrow."

"Thanks, doctor. What do we owe you?"

"Ten bucks. I suppose I'll have to wait for the county to pay me."

"No. I'll pay you. Eddie doesn't work for the county." Bill handed the doctor two five-dollar bills. Then he cooked a breakfast of flappjacks, bacon, and coffee. Eddie was sitting up on the one bed. His boots stood on the floor and his pants were draped over a chair. He was covered to his waist with a blanket. "Just stay where you are, Eddie, till that wound gets better. I'll do the cooking, and I can sleep on the floor. I've slept on a lot of floors."

"Don't want to put you out, Sheriff. I can walk. Hell, I got back here, didn't I?"

"Rest easy, Eddie. And how about calling me Bill? Or Billy?"

"Right."

Breakfast over, Bill went out on the street. Nearly everyone he passed had questions.

"Heard you had a hell of a gunfight, Sheriff. Heard that cowboy that went with you got shot."

"Hell, Sheriff, mebbe that'll put a stop to some of the robberies and stuff that's been goin' on."

"One thing's for sure, Shurff, ever'body'll know you mean business now."

Bill was surprised at how fast the hotel was going up. Workmen were putting on the roof and siding. Others were hammering and sawing inside, separating the structure into rooms. On down the street, a stone foundation for a bank was nearly completed. A sign nailed to a tall post proclaimed: *Future Rocky Mountain State Bank. Watch Concha Lake Grow.*

At his office, Bill was about to unlock the door when he heard a feminine voice calling his name. Turning he saw Miss

Irene Ringeley bearing down on him with a worried look on her face.

"Sheriff Walker," she said, a little breathless from hurrying, "is it true what they say that the cowboy named Eddie was with you and was shot?"

"It's true, Miss Ringeley."

"Is he. . . ?"

Bill had to grin. "Don't worry. He'll live. A bullet stung his leg, is all."

"Oh. Thank goodness."

Still grinning, Bill said, "Tell you, though, he won't feel much like walking for a while, and I don't cook too good. He could use some good woman-cooked grub."

"Oh, well, I'll take him something. Do you think he'd mind?"

"Naw." Bill's grin widened. "Naw, he wouldn't mind at all."

Inside his office, Bill leaned back in his chair and put his boots on the desk. Remembering that he hadn't slept for two days, he let his eyes close. Could he hope that the deaths of the two killer-robbers would put a stop to the crime that had been going on? Could those two be guilty of it all? Naw, that was too much to expect. However, it was possible.

He started to doze when the door opened. His eyes popped wide and his boots came down with a thud. Angelina Peterson stood in the door. Stood in her men's khaki britches, plaid shirt, and big hat. Spurs on her boots. A stern expression fixed on her sun-tanned face.

"Sheriff Walker," she said, "it happened again."

"Huh," Bill snorted, "what happened?"

"One of my cowboys came up on two men driving some of my cattle north. They shot at him."

"When? Where?"

"This morning. Just this side of Dynamite Ridge. Get on your horse, Sheriff. You've got work to do."

15

It was another bone jarring ride at a fast trot. Billy Walker was riding the Double O horse he'd found in his corral and was pleased to discover that it was easy-gaited. But how in hell could anybody ride at a fast trot for an hour or more without having to replace every bone in his body? He sat, he posted, he stood in his stirrups. Mrs. Peterson didn't seem to mind. Her foreman Jeff Overton didn't seem to mind. The cowboy named Tubb didn't seem to mind.

Finally, near noon, they reined up at the foot of Dynamite Ridge. Bill estimated they were six miles north of the Notch Road. "Right over there is where I seen 'em," Tubb said, pointing straight ahead. "Them's the cattle they was drivin'."

There were fourteen steers and heifers, two- and three-year-olds, grazing near a shallow draw. Bill was happy to stop. He dismounted, hoped nobody noticed the way he staggered a step, and walked studying the ground. He walked in the direction Tubb had pointed, and soon found a metal cartridge case gleaming in the sun. Picking it up, he said, "Rim fire. Looks like a .44-40. Which doesn't mean a heck of a lot. Most rifles in this part of the country shoot this cartridge." Squinting up at Tubb, he asked, "How many shots did they fire?"

"Three or four. After the first one, I seen they had long guns whilst I had only this six-shooter, and I hightailed it for them rocks over there." He nodded toward a low ridge of small granite boulders pushed there by a sliding glacier a million years ago. "When I looked back, they was hightailin' it south. I watched 'em till they turned east again and headed up the mountain."

"Two of them, you say?"

"Yeah."

Bill soon found two more of the metal cartridge cases. "Lever-action rifles, but that's no clue to anything either." He squinted up at Tubb again. "You already said you didn't get a good look at their faces, but can you tell me what color clothes they wore and what size men they were? Can you describe their horses for me?"

Tubb cleared his throat and did his best. "Both of 'em wore big hats like ours. They was dark-colored, either black or brown. One of 'em had on a brown shirt and the other'n a blue shirt. Didn't notice their britches. They wasn't tall and they wasn't short. They wasn't fat and they wasn't skinny. And, uh, oh yeah, one of 'em had a beard. I b'lieve. Don't know about the other'n. Their hosses was a bay and a brown. That don't help you much, does it, Shurff?"

Grinning a wry grin, Bill shook his head. "That description could fit me. Except for the beard. Or Jeff there. How many hours ago did this happen?"

" 'Bout an hour after sunup. Maybe an hour and a half."

On his horse again, Bill said, "Tubb, would you point out exactly where you saw them last."

Tubb said, "I'll show you, Sheriff."

"We'll all go," Angelina Peterson said.

Again, they rode at a bone-jarring trot, but this time for only a half-mile. There Tubb reined to a stop and pointed to a dim trail that traversed a steep rocky hill, covered in places with scrub oak. "That's where they went. A blind man could find their tracks."

"Over Dynamite Ridge," Jeff Overton mused.

"Can you drive cattle up that trail?" Bill asked.

"Yup," Overton said. "We've done it."

"That was their plan, then, to cut out a handful of cattle and drive them over the mountain."

109

"The question is," Angelina Peterson said, "where did they plan to go from there?"

"I've never been far off the Notch Road up there," Bill said, "and all I ever saw for five-six miles is a wide prairie with a few arroyos, some cattle, and nothing else. What's the country like beyond the prairie?"

Overton answered, "Hilly, rocky, some tall timber, but not too rough. We drive cattle to market at Rosebud in that direction." He pointed almost due east.

Angelina Peterson took her hat off, allowing her dark hair to fall to her shoulders. She was a darned attractive woman. Running her fingers through her hair, she bunched it up on top of her head and put her hat back on. "It's obvious, then, that they were planning to sell the cattle at Rosebud. Do you agree, Sheriff?"

"It appears that way. Tell you what, I'll follow their trail over the top and see which way they went from there. If they kept going east, they'll be in Rosebud and part of a crowd before I can get there." Bill looked up at the sun. "What I've had in mind to do, when I get a chance, is go to Rosebud and make some medicine talk with the sheriff there and see if we can find out where stolen cattle might be turned into cash. I'll do that tomorrow. I'll take the stage. If," he added, "nothing else happens."

"That sounds like a good idea." Angelina Peterson turned her horse around. "You do that." She started to ride away, but Bill called to her.

"Oh, Mrs. Peterson, I'd like to ask you something." When she stopped and looked back, he said, "Don't know whether you heard, but one of your former cowboys, Eddie, and I shot it out with a pair of robber-killers last night and killed both of them. Eddie said one was another of your ex-employees named Joe. What can you tell me about him?"

Angelina Peterson turned to her foreman. "Tell the sheriff everything you know, Jeff."

"Well," Jeff Overton began, "I don't know much about

110

him. He's dead, you say? His last name was Wells. He drifted up here from somewhere south and asked for a job. That was early this spring. Not a bad hand and not a 'specially good one either. Like a lot of cowboys, he got tired of working and decided one day to roll up his bed and draw his pay."

"That's all you know about him? You don't know where he went from here?"

"No. Never saw him again."

"Hmm." Bill pondered that, then asked, "How about Eddie? What do you know about him?"

"Eddie is a good hand. But he's like most cowboys, he's got the wonderlust. I was the same way when I was his age. Never stayed in one place more'n six months."

"Yeah," Bill mused, "I know the feeling. What's Eddie's last name?"

"Wilhoit. Eddie Wilhoit. You say he helped you catch up with two killers?"

"He sure did. He knows the country over west and went right to them."

With a chuckle, Jeff Overton shook his head. "Eddie's an easygoing kind of feller, which is a good thing as big as he is, but I always had a hunch he'd fight like a cornered wolf if he had to."

"Your hunch was right."

Angelina Peterson was looking from one man to the other as they talked. She said, "Tell Eddie he's got his job back if he wants it. And you, Sheriff, stop at the ranch headquarters anytime. We'll find a bed for you and we'll feed you and your horse. Anytime."

"I appreciate that, Mrs. Peterson."

She rode north and her two employees followed.

The narrow trail that wound its way to the top of Dynamite Ridge was easy to follow, though it was steep and slow-going. Relieved at being able to set his own pace, Bill allowed the Double O horse to take its time and stop twice to blow. "No use killing a horse," Bill said to himself. "Wherever those two were headed, they're a long ways from here by now, far enough that I can't catch them." It took most of an hour to get to the top. Bill reined up to let the horse blow and to study the terrain. Off to the southeast he could see a railroad crew hacking a route through the ridge. Several miles farther east was the other crew, building a road bed and laying rails. A big steam locomotive stood idle behind them with a short string of railcars behind it. "They're making progress," Bill mused. "Bet it'll take two of those big engines to pull a string of cars over this hill. They can't do enough blasting to level a mountain."

He followed horse tracks until he lost them in the tall prairie grass. There were no cattle or horses in sight. Then he turned his horse toward the closest work crew, hoping they would do no blasting before he got there. About a dozen men saw him and stopped to watch him approach. "Howdy," Bill said when he was within speaking distance.

"Howdy," said a youngish man in corduroy pants and a flat brim campaign hat. His pants legs were stuffed inside high, laced boots. Bill figured he was a boss, not a laboring man.

"I'm Sheriff Walker from Concha Lake," Bill said, staying on his horse. "Two men tried to drive some stolen cattle across the prairie up there. I wonder if you saw anybody today."

"Well, yes, I saw two men on horseback about the middle of the morning. I figured they were from one of the ranches around here."

"Did you get a good look at them?"

"No, they were too far away."

"Which way were they going?"

"East. Due east. I didn't see any cattle."

"Thanks." As Bill rode away, he heard the boss yell, "All right, get hot on those picks and shovels. They ain't made to lean on."

On the way east Bill came to a deep arroyo, one of the few land breaks on the high plain. The bottom of the arroyo was

112

sandy, the result of rain running down it at some time or other. Horse tracks were easy to see in the sand. They stayed in the arroyo, going south. Since he was only a mile or so from the railroad camp, Bill rode out of the arroyo and stayed on an easterly course. His horse didn't like the looks of the steam engine and refused to go near it. Again, workmen leaned on their tools and watched him approach. Bill got the horse close to a boss he'd talked to before. "Howdy."

"Howdy, Sheriff. Who are you looking for now?"

"None of your men. I'm hoping you saw two riders this morning."

"Nope. I didn't." Half-turning, he yelled, "Anybody see two riders today?" There was no answer. "Seems like someone would have seen them, Sheriff. Some of these men would rather look around than work."

"Well, thanks anyway."

"We heard you shot John Wicher. Killed him."

"Yeah. Had to. I wanted to bring him to trial, but he took a desperate chance at getting away."

"Don't matter to me. John Wicher was one mean sonofabitch."

"Yeah. Well, thanks again." Sheriff Walker turned his horse back toward the arroyo.

It was easy to figure now. The rustlers were going to Rosebud and they were taking the Notch Road, where they couldn't be tracked. And sure enough, after following the east side of the arroyo and watching for tracks coming out of it, Bill picked up the trail about a half mile from the road where the arroyo shallowed out. The road was covered with tracks and there was no way to distinguish one horse's tracks from most of the others. But while he was over that way, Bill rode on east to Samuel Price's relay station.

Luke saw him coming and waited, leaning against a corral post. "Say, Billy, you look like you been ridin' some. Howsomeever, that horse looks better'n you."

113

"He ain't the first horse I've been on today. Luke, how in hell are you?"

"Finer'n the fur on a cat's ass, Billy. How's sheriffin'?"

"I wish I was drivin' a six-up."

"Well, git down and come in. When'd you eat last? I got some spud and bacon soup on the stove and it won't take more'n a minute to heat it up."

Luke was a better cook than Old Lady Witter and a hell of a lot better than Billy Walker. Bill cleaned the bowl and drank a cup of black coffee. Leaning back in his chair, he sighed. "Luke, if you weren't so damned ugly you'd make some woman a good husband. Where'd you learn to cook like that?"

"My mammy didn't raise no helpless kids. We 'uns had to learn or go hungry." Luke picked up the dirty dishes and stacked them in a pan of water near a tin sink. "What're you doin' over this way?"

"Lookin' for rustlers. Two of 'em fired some shots at a Circle J cowboy this mornin' and took off on a lope. I tracked them to the road out there. I'll bet they came by here."

"Well, no." Luke scratched a two-day growth of whiskers. "Two of 'em you say? I didn't see no horsebackers all day."

"Well now." Bill was puzzled. "Could you have missed seeing them?"

"Could have. But I gen'ly don't miss much."

"That beats all. I would have bet they came by here."

Horseback again, Bill turned west, rode over the notch, and headed down into the wide Concha Creek valley. Concha Lake shimmered like a gem away down there beyond Quaker Ridge. Sitting his horse, Bill let his gaze wander to the far end of the lake, probably ten miles away. It was hard to believe he'd come from there early this morning, carrying two dead killers. He and Eddie. Eddie Wilhoit. Two killers dead. Now he was hunting two more men. These two must have doubled back to Concha Lake on the Notch Road. A lot of men drifted in

114

and out of the town, and according to Tubb's description of them, they would be hard to identify. They were probably as safe in Concha Lake as anywhere else. Just the same, Bill would keep an eye out for them and he'd ask at Sam Price's barn about two men who rode up on two horses, a bay and a brown.

But before he got there, he'd have to pass the pile of boulders where a bushwhacker had shot at him only a few days ago. Thinking of that, Bill reined off the road and headed for the north side of those rocks, planning to come up on them from a different direction.

Some jasper had tried to kill him, and whoever it was would probably try again.

16

The country was dry, Billy Walker noticed. The summer had been drier than usual. Most summers an afternoon shower drummed down at least twice a week. With the showers came thunder and lightning. And hail. The lightning was what cowboys feared most. Men had been killed by the Colorado lightning.

Men had been killed by bullets, too, and Bill rode wide around the north side of the granite boulders. It was a relief to get on the other side of them and back on the road. It was an even bigger relief to get back to town, off-saddle the horse, and walk stiff-legged to his office. No one was waiting to see him, so he left the office and walked around back to his room. Eddie was dressed and sitting at the table with a small pile of dirty dishes in front of him.

"See you're up," Bill said pleasantly. "You're not supposed to be."

"Aw," Eddie said, and grinned sheepishly, "I can't lay there all the time. Besides, I had to go to the toilet."

"See you've been fed. Was it good?"

The sheepish grin turned into a wide one. "Yeah. You'd never guess who brought it."

"I don't have to guess. She asked about you."

"She did? She asked about me?"

"Twice."

"I wondered how she knew my name. Ain't she nice?"

"Yeah. Pretty too." Bill sat in a chair on the other side of the table, smiling. "Wish I was a few years younger."

116

"Aw, Sheriff, I mean Bill, I ain't got nothin' to offer a smart girl like her. All I got is a horse, a saddle, and a bedroll. And maybe two changes of socks."

Bill's face turned serious. "Where'd you come from, Eddie?"

"Wyoming. But that's not where I'm from. I was fetched up in West Texas. Knocked around on my own since I was fifteen. Worked here and there. Worked for Old Man Goodnight down in the Pecos Valley and helped drive twenty-five hundred beefs to northern Wyoming. Spent the rest of the summer and all the next winter on a cow outfit up there, then drifted down here."

"Charlie Goodnight?"

"Yeah. Never saw 'im, though. His outfit is so big I worked for 'im almost a year and never saw his headquarters. They said his health wasn't too good."

"Where do you think you'll go from here?"

"I don't know. I like New Mexico, but . . ." Eddie shrugged.

"How would you like a permanent job? Right here."

"Here? Doin' what?"

"I need a deputy, and I'm authorized to hire one. It pays fifty a month and. horses. This room's big enough for two beds and you can stay here."

"Huh? Me? A deputy sheriff?"

"Yeah. You're past twenty-one, ain't you? I know what you're thinking. I always tried to stay away from lawmen myself. Never trusted them much. But there are some good lawmen, Eddie, and I'm betting you'd make a good one."

"Me? How come me?"

"You've got a good head on your shoulders and you're not afraid to dodge bullets. I saw you ready to fight a feller once, but you weren't even a little bit excited. Hell . . ." Bill grinned again. "As far as anyone could tell, you weren't even mad." The grin vanished. "That's what it takes, Eddie."

"Well, I don't know, Sheriff, I mean Bill. Sure, I'll fight

117

when I have to, but I never killed a man before last night I've been thinkin' about that and I don't like it."

"I wouldn't want you to like it. Me, I was in the war and fired a lot of rounds. Some of the Yankees I shot at wen down. I wish to God it had never happened. I've though about it a lot. Some men can kill and play a game of card right after. I won't have that kind of man for a deputy."

They were silent, each with his own thoughts, then, "Don' decide right now, Eddie. think it over. Then when you make a decision, stick to it."

"I'll think about it, Bill. Meantime, I've got a good bedrol over at Price's barn and a cot saved for me. And it's gonna be suppertime pretty soon, and I'm goin' over to that caf and speak to Irene again. We had a good talk today, and can't wait for another chance."

Standing, Bill said, "I've got to go over to the barn too I've got to look for a couple of horses and a couple of mer with quick trigger fingers."

There were plenty of bay horses in the pens around Price' barn but no brown horse. And nobody had seen two mer ride up. Bill went back to his office, sat in his desk chair tilted it back, and tried to figure it out. Either the two would-be rustlers had a camp somewhere west of Dynamite Ridge or Old Luke just didn't see them when they went eas on the Notch Road. Luke said he usually sees everything, bu hell he had to go to the toilet. Suppose they came here? I they did, they were keeping their horses in somebody's corral and there weren't so many corrals that Bill couldn't find them.

Wearily, feeling the need for sleep, Sheriff Billy Walke went to the pen behind the mercantile and caught his third horse for the day. If he rode at a trot, he should be able to see every horse in Concha Lake by sundown.

Supper for Bill was late that day. And, he knew when h stepped inside the Home Café, it was just as well. Though i was dark outside and men had quit working an hour ago there was no vacant stool at the counter and only one vacant table. Eddie Wilhoit was there, a dirty plate in front of him at the counter, a coffee mug in his hand. Bill dropped into a chair at the table for two. He nodded across the crowded room at Eddie. Eddie brought his coffee mug over, dragging his right foot as he walked.

"That leg ain't getting any better, is it, Eddie."

"Not yet, but it will," the big young man said, sitting.

"You had your knee bent sitting at the counter. Does it hurt?"

"I can bend it, but it pulls a muscle right where I don't want a muscle pulled."

"You ought to stay off of it."

"I ain't doin' no more walkin' than I have to."

"What's for supper tonight?"

"The roast beef ain't bad, but I heard somebody say the steak tastes like a boiled owl. The spuds needed more cookin'."

While he ate roast beef and mashed potatoes that needed more boiling, Bill noticed Eddie's eyes following Irene Ringeley as she hurried from counter to kitchen and from table to table. He noticed, too, that she glanced at Eddie every chance she got. He would have envied the young cowboy if he hadn't been so tired.

"Feller was lookin' for you just before dark," Eddie said.

"Do you know who he was?"

"Naw. Never saw him before. He drove up in a buggy. Looked like a businessman."

"Well, I guess if it's an emergency, he'll show up again." Bill finished his meal silently, hoping to hell nobody showed up. Draining his coffee mug, he said, "You're welcome to bunk in my room tonight, Eddie."

"Naw. I can't take your bed. I'll bunk at Price's barn."

"Whatever you say. Take care of that leg." Bill left.

As tired as he was, he dropped off to sleep within minutes of crawling between the blankets. His plan for the next day was to go to Rosebud. He hadn't found any horses that fit the description of the ones the rustlers rode. They had to be in Rosebud.

Again, he was forced to change his plan.

Breakfast over, dishes washed, shaved, Bill opened his office and sat at his desk. In a few minutes, he'd catch the eastbound stage. A man came to the door, stepped inside, a well-dressed man in gray wool pants, a black finger-length coat and a necktie.

"Are you Sheriff Walker?"

"That I am." Bill stood.

The man stepped closer and handed Bill a small card. "I am Thomas J. Trundle, attorney at law. I am here on behalf of two clients in the city of Rosebud." He didn't offer to shake hands.

Bill read the name on the card and put the card on his desk. "Who are your clients, Mr. Trundle, and what can I do for you?"

The lawyer reached into a pocket inside his coat and produced two folded papers. "These, sir, are eviction notices signed by His Honor Judge William Portman of the U.S. District Court."

Bill unfolded one of the papers and tried to read it. "NOTICE OF EVICTION. To all who may now be occupying the property described as lot 13, section 21, township 14, range . . ." Skipping on down the paper, Bill read, "You are hereby ordered to vacate said property . . ."

Frowning, Bill said, "Not being a land surveyor, Mr. Trundle, I have no idea where this property is or who is to be evicted."

"I can show you, and if you will read further, you will find the names of the present occupants."

Bill read further. The occupant named on the first paper was Tobias Worster. Where had Bill heard that name before? Then he remembered. "Isn't he one of the homesteaders on Concha Creek?"

"Yes sir, both the properties are on Concha Creek. Judge Portman has concluded that Mr. and Mrs. Worster and Mr. and Mrs. Boswell James have no legal claim to the properties, and my clients have."

"I don't understand." Bill's frown deepened. "If these are the folks I'm thinking of, they've been there a few years. Both families. The Jameses have two or three youngsters. As I understand it, some of the land along Concha Creek has been claimed under the U.S. homestead laws and the rest of it — for ten miles at least — was bought by Hiram Jackson and is part of his Double O ranch."

"Correct. Except that the law has not been properly adhered to. Mr. and Mrs. Worster and Mr. and Mrs. James have failed to comply with the law."

Pondering that, still frowning, Bill said, "I think I see what you mean. They didn't do everything according to law, and now somebody else wants their property. And they want it bad enough to hire a lawyer to get it for them."

"That is my client's right."

"Who are these clients?"

"Their names, as you can read for yourself, are Mr. Theodore Magill and Mr. Shelby Swasso."

The sheriff's eyes were drilling into the lawyer's face now, and his voice was turning hard. "And they want me to go over there and order those folks off their land."

With an exasperated sigh, the lawyer said, "In the first place the land is not legally theirs, and in the second place carrying out the orders of the court is one of the sheriff's duties. Do you know where the properties are?"

Billy Walker could feel his face getting hot. He was on the verge of exploding. He wanted to tell this pompous sonofabitch to take himself and his goddamned clients and go take a flying jump into Concha Lake. Tell the sonofabitch to get out and kick his ass on the way out. "Yeah," Bill said through clenched teeth, "I know where they are, but I'll be damned if . . ." No. His mind took over.

Don't say it. Calm yourself. Think before you say another word.

Bill dropped into his chair. He sat with his head down, trying to think. If he didn't serve the eviction notices, somebody else would. Maybe a U.S. Marshal. Not only that, he could be charged with nonfeasance in office or some such damned thing. The notices would be served, and there was nothing the sheriff could do about it. Unless . . .

"Well," Bill said finally, looking up at the lawyer, "I'll go see the Worsters and the Jameses."

"Good day, sir." The lawyer was gone.

Unless, Bill thought, he could delay things. Fail to serve the notices. It would take time for the lawyer to realize they hadn't been served and do something about it. Meanwhile, maybe the homesteaders could do something. Hire a lawyer if they could afford it. Which they probably couldn't. Reading the first notice again, Bill came to the section that gave the occupant thirty days. Something could happen in thirty days. What? Well, Bill was going to Rosebud to see the sheriff there, and while he was at it, he would see Judge Portman. Find out how somebody had managed to claim the properties. Then what? Well, at least he'd know more than he knew now. Yeah, he'd do that and figure out where to go from there.

Let's see. The first thing to do was go over to the Worster homestead and warn them about what was happening. Then over to the Jameses. One thing was certain:

Law or no law, Billy Walker was not going to force honest folks off their land.

17

The eastbound stage left town while Bill was saddling his bay horse. It would get to the Notch relay station, change horses, and be on its way again before the westbound got there. Well, he'd go to Rosebud tomorrow.

The first homestead he passed was the Widow Osborne's. The house was back in the cottonwoods along the creek where it was barely visible from the road. All Bill knew about the homestead laws was what he'd heard, and he wasn't sure that was correct. If he understood it right, each family was entitled to one hundred and sixty acres if they built a place to live on it and farmed it. The land had to be surveyed, and that cost something. Not much, but something. And the homesteaders had to record something or other at the U.S. Land Office. There was a land office in Rosebud. Bill had also heard about the preemption law which gave the first man to settle on the land the first chance at homesteading it or buying it. The cattlemen were the first to use the land and they figured it was theirs. The farmers came later and homesteaded along the creeks. That started quarrels between the cattlemen and the homesteaders. Trying to settle those disputes without gunfire was another chore for the county sheriffs. That was one problem they hadn't had in Concha County. Not yet, anyway.

Bill rode on past the Osborne place. Maybe he'd stop there on his way back and warn Mrs. Osborne that somebody was trying to grab up the properties along the creek. He remembered, though, that Mrs. Osborne's late husband had once told him he was the first to homestead on Concha Creek and had done everything according to law.

It was another mile to the Worster farm. When Bill rode into the yard he saw no one. He went around to the back of the house where Mr. and Mrs. Worster were hoeing weeds out of a row crop of some kind. Their milk cow was grazing near the house. Not wanting to startle them, he yelled, "Hello."

They straightened their backs, leaned on their hoes, and watched him come. When he got closer, he could see suspicion on their faces. Bill understood. Working folks had plenty of reason to be suspicious of the law. The news he had for them was one of the reasons.

"Morning," Bill said, forcing a smile. "How are you folks this morning?"

Worster's greeting was not enthusiastic. "Mornin', Sheriff." Mrs. Worster was a plump woman, big in the bosom, with a plain, work-worn face. She said nothing.

Riding up, Bill said, "Mind if I get down?"

"All right."

Trying to be pleasant, Bill said, "Pretty piece of land. What kind of crop have you got there?"

"Lettuce."

"Oh. I'd guess there's a market for lettuce."

"Yup."

"I remember you telling me your name is Worster. Is that right?"

"That's right."

"Well, folks," Bill said, looking down at the ends of the bridle reins he held in his hands, "I've got bad news for you."

The Worsters didn't speak. Bill figured they'd probably never heard anything but bad news from a lawman.

"Let me ask you something, Mr. Worster, when you settled on this land, did you record your claim in the U.S. Land Office?"

"Yup."

"Are you sure?" Bill squinted from under his hat brim.

124

"Yup."

"Did you go to the land office and sign some papers? Was this piece of land surveyed?"

"Well . . ."

Mrs. Worster spoke for the first time, "Why are you askin', Sheriff?"

"Folks, somebody has claimed this land. Somebody says you didn't sign the papers or didn't do something right and you're not entitled to it."

"I did so," Worster said. "I went to the land office and showed some gover'ment feller on a map where we was livin'."

"Was the man a U.S. Land Agent?"

"He was in the office."

"And you signed some papers?"

"Well . . ."

Shifting his weight from one foot to the other, Bill said, "Mr. Worster, can you read and write?"

"Shore I can. I can sign my name."

"Did you sign your name with an X?"

"Well . . ."

"I don't know everything about the law, but I believe an X is a legal signature. Are you sure you signed the right paper?"

"I signed what that feller gave me to sign."

"Have you got anything to prove it?"

"Nope. Nary a thing."

Bill stood with his head down, thinking. Mrs. Worster said, "Sheriff, did you say somebody wants us off this land?"

"Yes, Mrs. Worster. He's hired a lawyer and the lawyer got an eviction order from a U.S. judge."

"We ain't goin'." The farmer's jaw was set. "Ain't nobody gonna run us off our land."

Shaking his head sadly, Bill said, "They can get an army to force you off if they have to. There are lawmen who would shoot their own mothers if they were told to."

"We ain't goin'."

"I know how you feel. I'd fight too. But—"

125

"Sheriff," Mrs. Worster said, "are you gonna order us off?"

"No, ma'am. I'm supposed to, and I've got an eviction notice here in my pocket." He patted his shirt pocket. "But I'm not even going to show it to you. You didn't see it, understand? That will give you a little more time."

"And then what're we s'posed to do?"

"I'd hire a lawyer. Maybe a lawyer can find something in the law that will save your properties. I've got another eviction notice for the Jameses, and maybe between the two of you, you can scrape up money to pay a lawyer."

Forty-five minutes later Bill was saying the same thing to Boswell James. He'd found the farmer working with a shovel, turning water from Concha Creek onto an acre of growing potatoes. He heard the same story. Yes, Boswell James had signed papers in the U.S. Land office in Rosebud, signed with an X, and no, he had no survey. Yes, some fellers came around last spring with a spy glass on sticks and said they was gov'ment surveyors. Yes, they drove some stakes in the ground. James made the same vow. He'd take the missus and the young'uns to town where they'd be safe and he'd fight to the death to keep his land and his home.

"They'll kill you, Mr. James. I'm on your side, but I don't know what I can do. I'll try." And he gave the farmer the same advice: hire a lawyer. The judge will listen to a lawyer. Only a lawyer can argue the law.

It was mid-morning when Bill got back onto the Notch Road. Glancing at the sun, he wondered if the westbound stage had gone by. If it hadn't, it was due any minute now. He wished he didn't have to wait until morning to get on the eastbound. Now, more than ever, he wanted to go to Rosebud.

While he was standing his horse in the road, he saw a string of freight wagons coming. They were carrying lumber, no doubt. He waited the fifteen minutes it took them to get to him, recognized the teamster on the lead wagon, and held up his hand as a signal to stop.

"Hey, Billy," the teamster said, rolling a chew of tobacco

from one cheek to the other, "when're you gonna turn in that there badge and go to work?"

"Work?" Bill said, going along with the joke, "I wouldn't want to get into a bad habit like that. Hell, all you do yourself is sit up there on that spring seat and cuss the horses."

"It do beat sheriffin', don't it? Heered you shot a couple of fellers."

"There are a few more who need shooting. That's why I stopped you. Have you seen anybody on the road this morning? Or anywhere near the road?"

"Only the stage to Rosebud. Who you lookin' for?"

"Two gents who shot at a Circle J cowboy yesterday morning. One was riding a bay and the other was on a brown horse. Know anybody like that?"

"No-o." The teamster spat on the opposite side of the wagon. "Can't say I do."

"Know of any place around here where they could hole up?"

"Wal, there's the farmers' shacks and the relay station, and the railroad work camp, and, uh, that's about all."

"I've got a hunch they're holed up somewhere around here. Wish I knew the country better. Well, you've got lumber to deliver. The stage to Concha Lake ought to be coming along any minute."

"When we see 'er, we'll stop till she gets by. We all work for the same boss and that's what he said to do." The teamster yelled at the four horses and the wagons went on down the road.

There was one more homestead between Concha Lake and Dynamite Ridge. Concha Creek turned south this side of the mountain, and Hiram Jackson's Double O claimed all the country there. Bill decided he'd go to that homestead and nose around.

He was just under the mountain when he looked up the road and saw people walking. Reining up, he wondered if his eyes were playing tricks on him. People walking? One of them was a woman. Three of them were carrying suitcases. They were walking down off the notch.

Bill kicked the bay horse with his spurless boot heels and rode toward them at a gallop. When he pulled up, he recognized a stage teamster and a shotgun messenger. Their gun holsters were empty.

"What in heck is going on here?" he asked.

The bearded shotgun messenger stood spraddle-legged, his thumbs hooked inside the waistband of his pants. He squinted up at the sheriff. "We was robbed, Billy. They took all our money and run off all the horses."

18

Sheriff Billy Walker asked, "Was anybody hurt?"

"Naw," the shotgun messenger said. "They was hidin' in the house, and when we went in to see why Luke didn't have a team ready, they got the drop on us. Luke was inside tied like a calf for brandin'."

"How many were there?"

"Two. They went through our pockets, took a bank bag from the boot of the coach, then unhitched the team. They opened the gates and stampeded all the horses."

"Where's Luke?"

"He's tryin' to catch a horse on foot. I don't think he can. We started walkin', hoping some a them freight wagons would come along."

"They're ahead of you."

"Well, folks," the messenger said to the four passengers, "I reckon we walk."

"How much farther to Concha Lake, mister?" the woman asked. She was young and well dressed, but overweight.

"About five miles. Maybe you can get one of those farmers to hitch up a wagon and carry you. I'll go on up to the relay station and see if I can wrangle in the horses."

He rode at a fast trot until he came to the steepest part of the Notch Road, then he let the horse walk. At the top, at the man-made notch, he let the horse blow a minute, then booted it into a lope. By the time he got to the relay station, the horse was badly winded. Luke wasn't in sight.

The Concord stood empty, and the corral gates were open.

Looking to the south, he saw a scattering of horses about a mile away on the high prairie. A man was walking toward him. Bill booted his horse into a lope again and went to meet Luke.

"I guess you ain't hurt," he said, reining up. "You look kinda pooped, though."

Pushing his hat back, wiping his face with a dark blue bandanna, Luke grinned a weak grin. "Pooped is what I am, Billy. I was a fool tryin' to catch them animals on foot. I'm headin' for the house."

"Well," Bill said, "I ain't much of a horse wrangler, but at least I'm horseback. This pony has already earned his pay this morning, but I think he can run a little farther."

"I've wrangled aplenty. Them old ponies know where they're s'posed to go, and if you get behind 'em and pop 'em on the ass, they'll come on in. Bring 'em in on the run and maybe they won't scatter on you."

"All right. I'll let this horse walk and get his wind till I get on the other side of them. Then I'll try to play cowboy."

"You'll have to do some ridin'. I'll try to get over on the east side of the pens and help haze 'em in."

Bill walked his horse the mile to the other side of the free horses. They were all bays and blacks, averaging about thirteen hundred pounds, the kind of horses Samuel Price liked. There were sixteen of them, all with collar marks on their necks and shoulders. They moved away from him, not wanting to give up their freedom.

"All right, fellers," Bill said, "just go on home and don't give me any horse races." Now that he was behind them, with them between him and the corrals, he hollered and waved his right arm. The horses trotted away. Two bays took off on a gallop to the north. Bill booted his mount into a run to turn them back. For a while it was a horse race. But the free horses finally turned and went back to the rest of the bunch. Now that he had them together, Bill whooped, hollered, and

130

waved his arm, trying to get them moving toward the corrals. They all broke into a run heading west.

"Damnit. You're supposed to know where to go. Go there, you dumb brutes." Bill's horse raced them, running over sagebrush, dodging small boulders, jumping narrow gulleys. The wind whipped Bill's shirt collar and pushed at his hat. He ducked his head, held on to the saddle horn, and kicked the horse in the sides with his spurless bootheels.

Then the free horses tired of the race and turned south. Bring them in on a run, Bill had been advised, and that's what he tried to do. Hollering, whistling through his teeth, waving his arm, he kept them on a gallop. Looking ahead, he saw Luke running, trying to get into a position where he could help.

A black mare in the lead suddenly switched directions and galloped west, and the horse race was on again. Yelling, cursing, Bill booted his horse after her. "Turn, godamnit, turn." Finally, the black mare realized she was alone and turned back to the bunch. Bill heaved a sigh of relief, but he couldn't let the horses rest. He had to keep the pressure on. Keep them running, he reminded himself, and he whooped and whistled.

The corrals were coming closer. Luke was to the east where he could help keep the bunch from going in that direction. All the horses were running now, with Bill behind them, whooping and waving his arm.

Now Luke was waving his hat at them, cursing, jumping, and waving. The horses turned toward the biggest of the corrals. But they went past it and headed toward Dynamite Ridge. Bill pleaded with his mount. "Do your best, feller. Get after them." The horse did its best. The bunch turned again. And then finally they were inside the corral, milling. Luke ran up stiff-legged and shut the gate.

Bill's horse was blowing hard, and he dismounted and loosened the cinches. Luke was so winded he had to hang on to a corral pole to keep from collapsing.

Bill waited until Luke's breathing slowed a little, then said, "When you feel like it, tell me everything that happened."

"Just a . . . minute, Billy . . ."

Inside the cabin, Luke half fell into a chair and slumped there with his legs stiff in front of him. "Whoo," he said. "this runnin' ain't what my mammy raised me for. If the Almighty meant for me to run like that, he'd of gave me four legs."

Impatient, eager to get started after the robbers, Bill said, "Tell me everything, Luke."

"All right, all right. There was two. Wearin' flour sacks with eye holes over their heads. They had a double-barreled scatter gun that looked to be as big as a canon."

"Did you see their faces at all?"

" 'Fraid not. They had hats on top of them flour sacks and they was the big, wide kind. They wore ridin' boots with spurs. I didn't see their horses myself 'cause I was tied up in here till they were out of sight, but somebody said they was ridin' a bay and a black."

"Damn," Bill said, "I should have questioned the teamster and guard. I don't suppose you know, then, which way they went?"

"Somebody said they run the horses north till they was almost out of sight, then turned east."

"Headed for Rosebud, no doubt," Bill mused. "What size men were they? What color shirts did they wear?"

"About your size. Not fat nor skinny not tall nor short. Their shirts was, uh, blue and, uh, I don't know, nothing that would stick in my mind. They looked like cowboys, you know, they had poker asses and that way of walkin', like somebody that lives on horses."

"I've heard of them," Bill said. "They got enough of a head start that they'll get to Rosebud way ahead of me, but maybe when I get there I can find them. I have to try." He went to the door, looked back. "You all right, Luke? How's your ticker?"

132

"Still tickin'. I'll live. Just need a minute, that's all."

"If anybody comes by going to Concha Lake, tell them where I am, will you?"

"Shore. Git after 'em, Billy. Bring 'em back alive if you can. I'd like to have a hand in hangin' 'em. But look out for that goddamn scatter gun."

"I'll try."

On the road, riding at a trot, Bill guessed what had happened. The two gunsels were foiled in their attempt at stealing beef yesterday, and rather than go back to Rosebud empty-handed, they camped somewhere near and robbed the stage this morning. They were lucky. The guard said they took a bank bag. That meant cash.

Standing in his stirrups, posting, Sheriff Billy Walker rode on, knowing he had little chance of finding the pair in the city of Rosebud. But knowing, too, that he couldn't just go back to Concha Lake and do nothing. It would be a long ride.

It was past noon and his stomach was growling when the bay horse went lame. It started favoring the right fore. Every time the right fore hit the ground, the horse's head went down. The farther they went, the worse it got. Bill dismounted and picked up the hoof. The horse was shod and the iron shoe had plenty of wear left on it. But when Bill pushed on the sole of the hoof with both thumbs, the horse jerked.

"Must be a rock bruise," Bill said aloud. "Well hell, this just ain't one of my lucky days." He got back on the horse and turned it around. "If it gets worse, feller, I'll get off and walk. Let's see if you can make it back to Luke's corrals. Take your time. We're in no hurry now."

Bill didn't realize how far he'd traveled until he had to turn around and go back. His bay horse was getting worse by the minute. He got down and walked, leading the horse. After two more miles, he decided the horse couldn't walk the rest of the way, and he pulled the saddle off and turned the horse

133

loose. "When you get better, you'll get lonesome and you'll find the relay corrals. I'll come back for you." Bill hid his saddle out of sight of the road in some sagebrush and started walking.

It was late afternoon and Bill was tired when he dropped into a chair in Luke's cabin. "I agree with you, Luke, if the Almighty had intended for man to walk, He'd have given us four legs. I wish He'd given that bay horse of mine better feet."

"It could happen to any horse," Luke said, stoking the cook stove. "They step on a sharp rock the wrong way and next thing you know you're afoot."

"With all the horses you keep here, you ought to have something to ride. Something I can borrow."

"No, Billy. I keep tellin' Samuel we ought to keep at least one saddle horse here, but we ain't got a one. I doubt if any of these animals have ever had a saddle on 'em."

"Damn. There won't be another stage or wagon come by here today, will there?"

"Not unless there's somebody travelin' in a buggy. You can try one of these horses if you want to. There's a big black gelding that's so old and gentle he's a pest. We only use 'im when we have to. He might carry you."

"Anything's better than walking."

After a meal of Luke's stew, they went to the corrals and caught the black gelding. The horse was used as a wheel horse and weighed about fourteen hundred pounds. With a wry grin, Bill said, "I'm gonna have to have a ladder to get on him. If he throws me, it's a long ways down."

"I'll lead 'im up to the back end of that freight wagon there and you can climb on 'im. I don't think he'll throw you."

The horse was bridled with a workhouse bridle, snaffle bit, blinders and all. Luke had found some short reins. Bill climbed from the wagon onto the horse's bare back and took the reins. Grinning, Luke allowed, "At least he's fat. He won't split you up the middle."

134

"If you see half a man between here and Concha Lake, the other half of me will be around someplace." He kicked the horse in the sides. It didn't move.

"He don't savvy bein' kicked, Billy. You got to talk to 'im."

Bill clucked, and the horse started walking, dancing sideways at first at the feel of a man on its back. Bill turned the animal by pulling on one rein at a time.

Riding bareback wasn't bad going uphill, but when the horse tipped downhill, Bill had to hang on to the mane to keep from sliding up onto its neck. "I'm not so sure this is better than walking," he mused. "But keep going, feller."

A mile and a half from the bottom of Dynamite Ridge was the pile of boulders that had once hidden a bushwhacker. Bill kept a wary eye on it, but as tired as he was and as slow as the big horse was, he decided not to go around them. On fairly level ground now, he got the horse into a trot and bounced on its back like a sack of grain. Once, when the horse shied sideways at a piece of trash in the road, he almost lost his seat.

He didn't hear the crack of the rifle. He was only vaguely aware of falling off the horse and hitting the road. He felt no pain at all, only the blackness closing in on him.

19

Sheriff Billy Walker's spirit was hovering nearby, hearing and seeing but not feeling. A man came up on a horse. Then another man on another horse. They were looking down at him.

"We won't have to worry about that sumbitch no more," one of them said. "Prob'ly broke his neck."

"Better make sure. Put a slug in his head."

"Somebody's comin'. A wagon's comin' up the road. Don't shoot now. Let's lope."

It was unreal. What the spirit saw were dark shadows for faces, blue mountains, wavering valleys, sparkling water. Everything was a strange dark blue color. Even the next figure that appeared from somewhere. Dark blue, fading and reappearing. The spirit was above it all, looking down. Everything moved slowly. It was a man. No, a boy. A wagon. Two horses. The boy was tugging at something on the ground, something that refused to move. Tugging, straining, lifting, the boy got the strange object halfway into the wagon, paused to get his breath, then pushed and strained. The mountains and valleys shimmered like heat waves, shimmered and changed colors—from dark blue to black and green. The wagon turned around and started back down the road. It took hours to turn around. The object in the back didn't move. There was no sound now. The horses were trotting above the ground, their legs moving without effort. The wagon was above the ground, floating. Everything was so slow.

The spirit was impatient, keeping ahead of the wagon, beckoning. The horses broke into a gallop. The boy was yelling at them, yelling silently, flicking the ends of the driving lines at them.

The wagon went on down the road. The object in the back still didn't move.

Then the spirit, believing everything that could be done was being done, floated away and disappeared into the dark blue sky.

Another face was above him now, a different face. It was round and attractive in a plain sort of way with long hair pulled behind and tied where it hung down the back. The hair was dark, with a few gray strands. The face was worried. Its mouth moved but no sound came out. It faded.

There it was again. Still worried. The mouth moved again. "Sheriff? Mr. Walker?"

Billy Walker was feeling no pain. He wished the face would go away and let him rest in peace. But the voice persisted: "Sheriff Walker? Are you awake?" His eyes tried to focus, but that hurt. He squinched his eyes closed and tried to speak but could only groan.

"The doctor will be here soon, Mr. Walker. Daniel went on his saddle horse to fetch him. Don't try to talk. Don't move."

He tried again. "Wha . . . ?"

"You were shot. Daniel brought you here in a wagon. Don't move."

"Where . . . ?"

"I'm Mary Osborne. Daniel owes you and he'll do anything for you. So will the rest of us here. My late husband considered you a friend."

"Oh-o-o." Everything dissolved.

The next face was a man's, a long sad face. It studied him through wire-framed glasses. "Rest," the face said. "You're in good hands here."

Now there was nothing above him. Well, yes, there were some pole rafters and a board ceiling. Bill could move his eyes now without pain, but not his head. When he tried to move his head, something stung the side of his neck. His eyes took in part of the room, the plain hand-made dresser, the window with a curtain, the foot of the bed with polished wooden posts. His ears heard footsteps, then the man's long sad face was above him again.

"I see you're awake. Good. I believe we've got the wound sterilized. The fact that you survived this long is definitely a good sign."

Bill mumbled, "What? . . . Where?"

"You're at the Osborne farm. I'm told you were found lying on the road and brought here in a wagon. Thank God you were found early."

"What . . . ?"

"The bullet entered the left side of the neck, three-quarters of an inch from the carotid and one-half inch above the left clavicle. It exited through the left shoulder. Thank God it missed the carotid. You would have bled to death. And if it hadn't exited, I'd have to probe for it."

All Bill could do was grunt.

"You'll be weak for a few days, and you'll have a sore shoulder for a time. Don't move your left arm. When you have to get up, let Mrs. Osborne make you a sling for it."

With an effort he managed to say, "Yeah." His eyes took in Mrs. Osborne standing near the bed and the boy, Daniel. "Thanks. Thanks, everybody." Bill's eyes were heavy. He let them close.

Another face. This one was small, framed with golden curls. It had wide bright blue eyes. "Uh," Bill said, "are you an angel?"

It smiled, showing gapped, immature teeth. It disappeared and footsteps ran away. A child's voice yelled, "Mama, mama, he's awake."

"Sh-h-h, Joanna. Be quiet. Let Mr. Walker sleep."

Billy Walker smiled. And dozed.

He had to get up. But when he tried, his head swam. He couldn't move his head without bringing a sharp, tearing pain to the left side of his neck. But he had to get up. He grunted, trying.

"Lay still, Mr. Walker. Let me put a sling around that arm."

"How . . . how long have I been here?"

"A day. You had a visitor this morning, but you were sleeping so good he didn't bother you."

"Who?"

"His name is Eddie."

"Oh. I have to get up, Mrs. Osborne."

"I understand. I'll get Daniel to help you." She finished tying a clean white towel around his neck for a sling. His left arm was held against his side. Then the boy came in, a tall, slender boy with sandy hair and pale blue eyes.

"Yes sir, Sheriff. Let me help you. The doctor said you ought not to move any more than you have to." Strong young hands helped him pull on his boots, helped him outside to the little house in back.

Now he was sitting up in bed, propped up with fat feather pillows. A delicious smell was coming from the kitchen. Another child, a girl twelve or thirteen with dark hair and serious brown eyes, brought him a bowl of soup. "Aunt Mary said it's bad manners to blow on your soup, Mr. Walker, but you can if you want to."

"Thank you kindly, young lady. What's your name?"

"Cissy. Least, that's what ever'body calls me. My real name is Cressanda."

"Pleased to meet you, Cissy. Tell your Aunt Mary this is the best soup I ever tasted."

Dr. Hadley came the next morning and Eddie Wilhoit came with him. Eddie stayed out of the way and kept quiet while the doctor changed the dressings, then he stepped forward, limping only a little. "I'll do it, Sheriff."

139

"Do what, Eddie?"

"I'll be your deputy if you still want me."

Grinning a lopsided grin, Bill said, "I need a deputy. I need a keeper. Sheriffing seems to be a dangerous job around here."

"I'm not scared. I'm ready anytime. Matter of fact, I found a deputy badge in your room and brought it with me."

"How's that leg?"

"Still a little sore, but gettin' better. I always did heal fast."

"You're sure you want to be a deputy sheriff?"

"Yep. I've thought about it a lot."

"All right." Bill managed to sit up straighter. "I'll swear you in right now. Dr. Hadley can be a witness. Will you do that, doctor?"

"Yes. I'll witness a swearing-in."

"All right. I don't remember the exact words, but I'll do the best I can. Hold up your right hand, Eddie. Now, here goes: I, Billy Walker . . . no, I got it backwards. Do you, Eddie Wilhoit, swear to uphold and enforce the laws of the state of Colorado, and abide by the constitution of the United States?"

"Yessir."

"Then I, Billy Walker, sheriff of Concha County, Colorado, do hereby declare that one Eddie Wilhoit is my deputy, and as such has authority under the law to enforce the law. There, Eddie, you are now a deputy sheriff. First thing you have to do is hunt up Hiram Jackson, the county board chairman, and tell him. The doctor can back you up."

"Fine. Can I pin on this badge now?"

"Yep. Don't do anything, Eddie, 'till I get back on my feet. I mean don't do any more than you have to to keep the peace. That's enough work for any man. And you can stay in my room."

In two more days Bill Walker was restless. He was up and walking, holding his head steady, afraid to look anywhere but straight ahead. His arm was out of the sling, but he didn't move it any more than he had to. He was getting stronger. The Widow Osborne didn't want him to leave.

"I've been a heavy load on you and your family, Mrs. Osborne. I'm in your debt. But I know you've all been sleeping in one room so I can have a room to myself and you can't be comfortable. I can't impose on you any longer."

"Stay, Mr. Walker. You're not strong enough to leave. If you're worried about us bein' too crowded, you can sleep in Daniel's room in the barn. He's got a good room fixed up in there and he'll be more'n happy to sleep on the floor and give you his bed."

"Oh no, I can't do that."

"Besides, he's leavin' tomorrow. He's goin' to work on the Circle J, and he won't need the room."

"He is? He's going to work for the people who almost hung him?"

"Mrs. Peterson came over one day and apologized for what her hired men done, and she offered Daniel a job. Daniel always wanted to be a cowboy."

"She did? Angelina Peterson did that?"

"She's a nice lady, Mr. Walker."

Billy Walker silently agreed. Apologizing in person and offering the boy a job was a good gesture. That took class. It seemed Angelina Peterson wasn't the tough hard woman she appeared to be. Another nice lady was Mary Osborne. Not as colorful as Mrs. Peterson, but a damned fine woman. Raising three kids of her own and two of her dead sister's. Doing it by herself. And the kids were clean and well mannered. Mary Osborne would never turn men's heads, but she was neat, pleasantly plump, pleasant all around.

During the wagon ride to town, Bill could look nowhere but straight ahead. Sitting on the spring seat, holding his left arm in his lap, he thanked Daniel for picking him up and taking him home.

"You saved my life once, Sheriff."

"They weren't going to hang you, Daniel. They only wanted to scare you."

"That's what Mrs. Peterson said. They sure scared me, all right."

"If Jeff Overton and his crew don't treat you right, you don't have to work there. There are other places to work."

"I can't blame 'em too much. Somebody'd been shootin their calves. Somebody in a wagon." He grinned a shy grin. "I must've looked awful guilty."

When Bill went into his office, he found nobody there, and when he walked around back to his room, he found a narrow cot on the side of the room opposite his bed. A canvas bed tarp, blankets, and a pillow were unrolled on the cot. A shirt and a pair of denim pants hung on the wall over it and a scarred leather suitcase was stashed under it. Eddie had moved in.

Restless, Bill went back onto the street, wondering where Eddie was. Women nodded at him, and two men came up and spoke: "Mighty close one there, Sheriff. Any idee who done it?"

"Naw. I didn't see them."

"Glad to see you still akickin', Sheriff. Hope you find out who done it. I'll help hang 'em."

"We berried them dead men you had in the shed. They was beginnin' to stink. We got a graveyard staked out over west a ways."

"See you got a depitty. It's a good thing he's got a cool head as big as he is. Seen 'im in the Longhorn last night when two a them carpenters was afixin' to duke it out. All Ol' Eddie had to do was show up. He never said a word, just stood there and looked down on 'em. They right quick got fightin' notions out of their heads."

"Have you seen Eddie today?"

"Naw, but I heered. There was some more cattle stole over on the Double O, and Eddie went out there."

"Aw for crying out loud," Bill said. "I was hoping, after

142

the stage was robbed, the rustling would stop for a while."

"It ain't never gonna stop, Sheriff, till you track 'em down and kill 'em."

"Yeah," Bill muttered. "It's never going to stop."

20

On down the street, a small group of men were watching
the frame of the new bank going up. One of the men stepped
out of the group and came forward. "We're all mighty pleased
you survived, Sheriff Walker. This county needs you."

"I'm kind of tickled about it myself, Commissioner Jackson. Did you meet my deputy?"

"Yes. He came into the store and brought Doc Hadley with
him. He seems to be a level-headed young man. I told our
county clerk to put him on the payroll. Just in time too.
More of my cattle were stolen, and with you laid up, your
deputy took out after the thieves. I hope he catches up, but I
hope he doesn't get shot. Say, there's a gentleman here I'd like
you to meet." Hiram Jackson called, "Oh, Mr. Rutledge,
would you step over here a minute?"

A well-dressed, well-fed, middle-aged man came out of the
crowd. He wore a dark suit and a narrow-brim hat. His mut-
ton chop sideburns were turning gray.

"Mr. Rutledge I'd like you to meet our sheriff, Bill Walker.
Sheriff, this is Vincent Rutledge, chairman of the board of
the Mountain National Bank of Rosebud and president of the
future Rocky Mountain State Bank."

The banker looked Bill over carefully before he put out his
hand to shake. Bill shook with him. It was a weak hand-
shake. "I heard you had a fracas out on the road, Sheriff
Walker. Have you any clues as to who robbed the stage?"

"None, I'm afraid. I was told they took a bank bag. Did it
hold much money?"

"Quite a sum. It was to pay the carpenters for their labor

and Samuel Price for hauling materials. We managed to secure more funds, but from now on, I'm going to insist that Mr. Price keep more guards on the stage from Rosebud. It seems there's a lot of lawlessness in Concha County."

"Sure. Uh, Mr. Jackson, where on your ranch were the cattle stolen?"

"On the south end. No telling when they were driven off. My riders can't keep an eye on the whole territory."

"Are they beeves or cows and calves or what?"

"Young stuff. About twenty head. Some heifers I was planning to keep for breeding stock, and some steers too."

"Who reported the theft?"

"One of my cowboys. I had three men riding all day looking and counting. There's about twenty head missing."

"Did they pick up a trail or anything?"

"They think they did. They tracked them about ten miles south."

"Well, I hope Eddie doesn't get bushwhacked. The rustlers might be watching their back trail."

"We can only hope, Sheriff." The rancher-businessman looked at the sky. "We can only hope for rain, too. Clouds are gathering. Well, I must get back to the store, Sheriff."

Yeah, Bill muttered under his breath, you're more interested in the weather than the safety of my deputy.

After a noon meal of beans and biscuits at the Home Café, Bill walked over to Samuel Price's barn and was pleased to find his former boss going over papers in his cubbyhole office. "Seems that's what a businessman does a lot of," Bill commented. "Paperwork."

Looking up, Price grinned. "Glad to see you back on your feet, Billy. Yep, you're right, got to keep records of ever'thing."

"I'd like to talk to the teamster and shotgun man who were robbed. Maybe they can tell me something I don't know." With a small smile, he added, "I sure as hell don't know much."

"Think the jaspers that robbed the stage are the ones that shot you?"

"I just don't know, Samuel. I thought—and Luke thought—they went east from the relay pens. I got shot west of there."

"Don't make no sense, does it?"

"No sense at all."

"Well, I'll tell you, from now on ever'time we're carryin' a bank bag or anything valuable, I'm sendin' a rider ahead to scout the country."

"Got to protect your business."

"Yep. Right now I'm the biggest businessman in the territory, but not for long. When the railroad gets here, I'll lose some business, and I'll have to let some men go and sell some horses and wagons."

"And I reckon that'll leave Hiram Jackson the biggest businessman."

"Yep, what with his hotel, store, and ranch. All I can say is his business'd better be good. I'd hate to pay off his mortgages."

"What do you know about his mortgages?"

"Nothin'. I'm only guessin'. Ever'body that goes into business in a big way borrows money. If I can get a fair price for the horses and wagons I won't need, I can pay off my papers. He's gotta be goin' deeper in hock."

"Maybe I shouldn't ask, Samuel, but who did you borrow from?"

"The Mountain National over at Rosebud. I was late with a payment once, and Old Rutledge let me know the bank board wasn't gonna put up with that."

"That would be Vincent Rutledge?"

"That's him. I'll be tickled to get him paid and off my ass."

By dark, Bill began to worry. Eddie was out there somewhere trying to track stolen cattle, and there were killers out there who liked to shoot lawmen. Irene Ringeley was worried too. While Bill sat stiffly at the counter in the Home Café, trying not to move his head, waiting for his supper of canned ham and fried potatoes, she said, "I wish he'd get back, Sheriff. He went all alone. I wish he'd get back."

"Oh," Bill said, trying to ease her worries, "he'll be back. He probably trailed cattle till near dark. A horse can find its way in the dark."

"He's still awful sore from that bullet wound. I wish he'd get back."

Around ten o'clock it rained. The storm was brief, but severe. Lightning lit up the sky and thunder cracked like canon fire. The squall started as hail, then turned to a hard rain which drummed on the roof over the sheriff's room. Lying in bed, Bill figured the cattlemen and farmers would be glad to get the moisture.

But where was Eddie?

At daylight he decided to get horseback and look. He'd need some help from a Double O cowboy to pick up the trail and he'd have to go to the ranch headquarters to get help. He walked, neck stiff, to the home of Hiram Jackson, the biggest house in town. It was a sprawling one-story house, made of good lumber, painted white with a white picket fence around it. Jackson was a bachelor, Bill knew, and the house had no curtains in the windows or flowers in the yard.

A woman housekeeper about sixty answered Bill's knock on the carved wooden door. Mr. Jackson was taking coffee, she said. Would he care to wait? Bill removed his hat and stepped inside a big room with two upholstered couches and three stuffed armchairs. Moving stiffly, keeping his head straight, he sat in one of the chairs. Within a few minutes, Jackson came into the room, followed by Vincent Rutledge. Bill stood.

"I apologize for bothering you so early, Mr. Jackson, but I'm worried about my deputy and I'm going to go look for him. I need, first of all, to know where your ranch headquarters is. I've never been there. And I need one of your cowboys to show me where Eddie was last seen."

"Of course, Sheriff. Would you care for some coffee?"

"Thanks just the same, but I would like to get started."

"Very well. You go south a mile on the road to Columbine and you'll see my road heading west. You follow it about five miles and you'll see the ranch house and barns. Tell anyone there that I said you are to get all the help you need. I'll write a note, if you want, but it won't be necessary. My employees will cooperate with the sheriff."

"Thanks. If anybody asks, that's where I'll be."

When Bill left the house the sun was shining, but clouds were gathering over the Wet Mountains. Walking to the pen behind the mercantile, he wondered what Vincent Rutledge was doing at Hiram Jackson's house. But thinking about it, Bill easily came up with the answer. There was no place for a traveler to stay in Concha Lake except for Price's barn and a big tent. Rutledge was probably bankrolling Jackson, and naturally Jackson was making him comfortable. Bill had saddled a horse with a spare saddle the county supplied, tied a blanket roll containing two tins of dried beef behind the cantle, and was leading the horse out of the pen when he saw a man on horseback coming. Eddie.

The horse was leg-weary, and the rider was slumped in the saddle. When Eddie was close, Bill said, "Been out for a morning canter, Eddie?"

"Yup." Eddie's grin was weak. "Had to have my morning constitutional."

"When did you eat last?"

"My stomach thinks it was over a week ago."

"Well, get down and rest your saddle and we'll find you some chuck."

Inside the Home Café, the pretty waitress put down an armload of dirty dishes and met them at the door. "Eddie, I, uh, wondered why you didn't come in last night. Someone said you went after some rustlers." She kept a respectable distance between them.

"Yeah, I reckon I'm not much of a lawman. I didn't catch 'em."

"Are you . . . ?"

"I'm fine, Miss Ringeley. Hungry, but fine."

"Well." She was suddenly all business. "Won't you gentlemen have a seat?"

It was between the breakfast rush and the noon meal, and they found a vacant table and sat. Miss Ringeley brought coffee and took their orders. She was continuously glancing at Eddie. Bill waited for his deputy to speak.

Sipping his coffee, Eddie said, "It's a puzzle, Bill. They figure the cattle were run off sometime in the past ten days. They figure three horses was run off too. That ought to make 'em easy to track. But I tracked 'em through where a bunch of cows and calves were grazin' and lost 'em. There's a creek they call Kettle Creek down on the south end of the Double O and I rode that creek for at least five miles in each direction. I rode it up to where about a hundred acres of scrub oak was so thick on each side of it a rabbit'd have to turn back. Nobody drove cattle through there. I never did see where they crossed the creek."

"They went south?"

"Sure looked like it. In fact, there was plenty of horse tracks mixed with the cattle tracks and they all went south. I was plannin' on tryin' to pick up their sign over east under the Dynamite Mountains, but it got dark on me."

"So you spent the night over there."

"Yeah. I let the horse graze on the end of my catch rope and I waited for daylight. Only it rained like a cow peein' on a rock, and when daylight came, ever'thing was washed out. I just flat lost 'em."

Without moving his head or bending his neck, Sheriff Walker took a sip of his coffee. "Well, you did everything that could be done, Eddie. I lost them a couple of times myself."

"I'm not the best tracker in the world, Bill, but I've located a lot of cattle that way. I should of been able to catch up with 'em."

149

Bill pondered that, sipped coffee, started to shake his head, and winced, "You know what puzzles me? I could have sworn the cattle being rustled in this county were going two places: to the railroad work camp and to a packing house somewhere near Rosebud. But they went south?"

"As far as I could track 'em, they went south."

Not being able to move his head much, Sheriff Billy Walker had to tip the coffee mug high to empty it. The last drop ran down his chin. He wiped it off with the back of his hand, and frowned. "That's a puzzler, all right."

21

The stage from Rosebud brought another lawyer to Concha Lake. This one, however, worked for the state government. Eddie was getting some rest in the room behind the jail, and Sheriff Billy Walker was going over the mail that had finally been sorted at the mercantile and brought to him. A dapper young man in a Prince Albert coat and homburg hat came through the door.

"Are you Sheriff Walker?"

Moving only his eyes, Bill looked up from his chair. "That I am."

"Permit me to introduce myself." The man was smooth-shaven and soft-looking. "I am Geoffrey Rodeman, the new chief deputy district attorney of the sixth judicial district."

"Well," Bill said, standing, "I'm happy to meet you, finally. I've been trying to get over to Rosebud, but something always comes up."

"Yes, I understand you have quite a crime wave going here. I also understand that you and your deputy shot and killed two men suspected of murder and robbery, and also that earlier you shot and killed a man suspected of murder."

"That we did." Bill didn't bother to explain that Eddie wasn't a deputy then. "However, the bodies have been buried. We have no undertaker here. The first man was identified by several witnesses to the murder, and the stolen money was found with the second pair." •

"I assume they fired first and you and your deputy fired in self-defense."

151

"That's correct."

"Well, I see no legal problems with that. I merely want to confirm what I'd heard and put it in the public records. Were you able to identify them?"

"John Wicher was the one who did the saloon shooting. He gave me the name of a sister before he died and I sent her a telegram. One of the other two had once worked for the Circle J Ranch. The other has not been identified."

"I see. Hmm. Well, I'll list that one as a John Doe. Tell me, is there still no hotel here?"

"No sir, there is not. A hotel is being built, but it won't open for business till sometime this fall."

"Oh my." The young lawyer dropped into a chair, took his hat off and wiped his brow with a white handkerchief. "That's why the judge and I don't like coming here. Sleeping in a barn is rather undignified, especially for public officials."

"Can't say I blame you."

"They should never have designated this burg a county seat when it doesn't even have a hotel, much less a courthouse."

"Tell you what, I've got some clean bed sheets, and you can spend the night in my room. I don't mind sleeping in Price's barn."

"I wish there were a stage back to Rosebud today. I'll be so happy when the railroad gets here."

"Yeah. This time next year Concha Lake will look a whole lot different."

Bill showed Geoffrey Rodeman to his room, put clean linens on the bed, and tried to make him comfortable. Law officers and prosecuting attorneys had to work together, and Bill intended to do what he could to build a friendship. That done, he went to Price's barn and arranged to sleep there that night, then went back to his office. There were three Wanted flyers in the mail, and a letter. The letter was addressed merely to the county sheriff in Concha Lake, Colorado. It came from Mrs. Helen Gotswald, St. Louis, Missouri, who wanted to know more about her brother's death.

152

After thinking it over, Bill took a sheet of paper and a lead pencil from his desk drawer and wrote. John Wicher died in a shootout with two stage coach robbers. He died bravely, trying to defend himself and fellow passengers. His body is buried in the Concha Lake cemetery. The Concha County sheriff's department sends its deepest regrets.

Instead of waiting for the doctor to come to him, Bill went to the doctor, had his bandage changed, and listened to the doctor's advice about doing nothing more physical than he had to. All right, he promised, he'd try.

But at first light next morning he was saddling a county horse with a county saddle, tying a saddle bag behind the cantle, with a change of clothes. Eddie would keep the peace in town—or try to—while he went to Rosebud. He would ride to the relay station on the other side of the notch and get there ahead of the stage. He would leave the horse there, ride the stage to Rosebud, then on the way back he'd pick up his own saddle and his own bay horse and lead him back to town on the county horse.

He left town early enough that he could ride at a slow trot, which caused his sore neck only a little discomfort. Luke was glad to see him, and showed him the bay horse standing in a pen munching on good high country hay. Bill was unsaddling the county horse when Luke exclaimed:

"Lookee yonder."

Looking east, far to the east, Bill saw what Luke was pointing at. There were a handful of cattle and one—two—three—no, two men, crossing the road. "Godamnit," he said, "I've got to go have a look. With all the rustling going on around here, I'd better see who they are and where they're going. Tell Charlie not to wait for me." He pulled the cinch tight on the county saddle and mounted. "I'll have to go to Rosebud another day."

The cattle and men were so far away that Bill couldn't tell at first how many men there were. When he got closer, he could see there were only two. Two men had tried to steal cattle from the Circle J, and two men had robbed the stage. Bill rode toward them at a lope, keeping his head straight, and slowed to a walk when he was within pistol range. They saw him coming, stopped, and watched him, letting the cattle wander. Bill reined up.

He wanted the pair ahead of him where he could keep an eye on both, and at the same time he wanted to be close enough to look them over. They watched him. He studied them.

Neither was short nor tall, skinny nor fat. One wore a brown hat and the other a black hat. But their horses were a sorrel and a gray, not a bay and a brown. And from where he sat his saddle, Bill could see the Double O brand on the left shoulder of the one horse that was standing broadside. The cattle were grown beeves, eight of them, and they were branded with a Double O.

The brands were fresh.

All right, Bill mused to himself, they fit the descriptions of two wanted men. Some Double O horses had been stolen. The cattle wore fresh brands. But the men looked no different than most men, and all hats were either black or brown or gray. They could be Double O cowboys driving cattle to the railroad camp.

But the fresh brands on the cattle had to be explained.

Damn, Bill muttered under his breath, wish Eddie were here. With his deputy to help him, they could approach the men from different angles. As it was, all Bill could do was ride right up to them. He touched the county horse's side with his boot heels and rode slowly forward. The pair made no threatening moves. He was close enough that they could see the sheriff's badge on his shirt.

Then the man on the gray horse moved, reining his horse away from the other, moving off to Bill's left. Bill pulled up. "Hey," Bill yelled. "Stay where you are. I'm the sheriff of Concha County. Stay together. I want to talk to you." Both men and horses stood still. Pointing to the man who had

154

moved, Bill yelled, "I need to talk to you. I'd appreciate it if you'd stand together."

The pair looked at each other. Both carried pistols in holsters on their right hips, but Bill could see no rifles. He was still far enough away that a man with a pistol would have to take careful aim to hit him. He kept his eyes on their gun-hands, and yelled again, "Stand together, will you."

Finally, the man on the gray horse reined back to stand beside the other. Bill moved his horse forward, eyes wary. As he rode, Bill worked out a plan. If either man grabbed for a gun, he'd get off his horse and try to keep the horse between him and them. Hopefully, their horses would get nervous, fidget and spoil their aim, while he would be on the ground in a better position to shoot.

Stopping about thirty feet away, Bill said, "Morning." The two men glanced at each other but said nothing. "I'm Sheriff Bill Walker of Concha County. Mind if I ask your names?"

After a pause, the man on the sorrel said, "Uh, my name is Jenkins, Walter Jenkins. I ride for the Double O outfit." The other finally spoke. "Jones. Jack Jones."

"I see these cattle branded with a Double O," Bill said, still watching their gun hands. "Would you mind telling me why they were branded recently?"

"They're, uh, mavericks," Jenkins said. "We just popped 'em out of the oak brush on Kettle Creek."

"They've been missed in the roundups," Jones added. "Mr. Jackson is afraid they'll go right back to the brush and we'll never seen 'em again, and he told us to take 'em to the railroad work camp and sell 'em while we got 'em."

"Yeah," Jenkins said, "we had to use dogs to get 'em out of there."

Bill mulled that over. It was believable. They could be telling the truth. He asked, "How long have you been working for the Double O?"

"Couple months," Jenkins said.

"Are you working out of the outfit's Boulder Creek camp?"

They glanced at each other before they answered, "Not now. We was, but now we're stayin' at headquarters."

"Isn't that a long way from here?"

"Well, uh," Jones gave that some thought, then said, "Yeah it is, but we camped last night just t'other side of that mountain back yonder. There was four of us, and when we got 'em over the mountain the other two went back."

Bill did some thinking too, then said, "Are you sure you didn't camp on this side of the mountain? That's a long way to drive cattle this early in the morning."

"No, we, uh, we started 'em movin' as soon as it was light enough to see."

While they were talking, Bill saw the stage to Rosebud go up the road behind him. An idea popped into his mind. "Do you happen to know Theodore Magill and Shelby Swasso?"

Jenkins' jaw dropped open and he swallowed a lump in his throat. "Who?"

Bill repeated the names.

"Naw. I don't. Do you, uh, Jack?"

Shaking his head, Jones said, "Naw. Don't re'clect ever meetin' anybody with them names."

All were silent for a long moment. Horses stamped their feet to shake flies off their legs. Saddle leather creaked. Bill tried to think of a way to trip them up if they were lying. "What did you say the name of that creek is, where the oak brush is thick?"

"Kettle Creek."

That, Bill thought, is what Eddie called it. These two know something about the Double O country. They were nervous, their eyes shifting. But he could think of no more questions. Finally, Jenkins said, "Them beefs are scattered some. We'll have to lope to gather 'em again." His partner nodded. "Yep."

"Well," Bill said, finally, "since it's my fault, I'll help you gather them." But before he moved, he fixed each man's face in his mind. He wanted to be able to describe them and to recognize them if he ever saw them again. He touched boot heels to the county horse and went after the cattle.

It took only ten minutes to round up the handful of steers and get them lined out in the right direction. Ahead was a deep ravine, one of the few that cut across the high prairie on the east side of Dynamite Ridge. Bill decided he'd help get the cattle across the ravine, then go back to the relay station. Too bad he'd missed the stage. Whooping and whistling, he followed steers down an old buffalo trail. He was at the bottom, trying to urge steers to climb up the other side when he noticed he was alone.

A sense of danger exploded through him, and he dropped off his horse so fast he fell onto his knees. Glancing up he saw a man on a gray horse on the rim of the ravine, aiming a pistol at him. A bullet screamed off a rock behind him. A gun popped. Drawing the Navy Colt, Bill jumped behind his horse and looked for a chance to shoot back.

22

The gunshots spooked the cattle and they wanted to stampede, but the steep slopes of the ravine kept them from doing that. Instead, they milled, wild-eyed. That saved Sheriff Billy Walker's life.

Bill was among them, keeping down and looking up. He snapped a shot at the man on the gray horse, but a steer bumped him and spoiled his aim. Two shots came from the top of the ravine, and a steer went down, kicking. Bill got on the other side of another steer and fired again. Two of the steers tried to climb up the banks, but slipped down and fell onto their backs. Then the cattle were running down the bottom of the ravine, running wildly, leaving Bill exposed. He squatted under a steep bank and watched the top of the opposite bank, the Navy Colt cocked and ready. Nobody showed.

The county horse was dancing nervously at the gunfire, but hadn't moved far. Bill waited, ready. His greatest fear was that one of the two gunsels would be above and behind him. He backed as far as the bank allowed, and pushed against it. Still nobody showed.

He should have known. He should have been more suspicious. An experienced lawman wouldn't have turned his back on this pair. Maybe Billy Walker wasn't cut out to be a lawman. But what could he have done? He couldn't arrest them on mere suspicion. Well, he could have, and some lawmen would have, but it would have been a hell of a way to treat men who might be innocent.

Away off in the distance a gun boomed. Boomed again. It sounded like a double-barreled shotgun. Luke? What could he do at that distance besides make a racket? Well, he could let the two hooligans know the sheriff had a friend. And damned if it didn't work. Hoofbeats drummed the prairie ground, going away.

"Goddamn," Billy Walker muttered, running to his horse. The county horse didn't like the sight of a man running at him, and shied away, then stepped on the reins and stopped. Wincing at the pain in his neck, Bill climbed into the saddle, got the horse scrambling up the buffalo trail to the top of the ravine. The two were riding hard, going northwest, away from the Double O's territory.

"Get after them," Bill said to the county horse. The horse jumped into a dead run. Its top speed wasn't more than thirty miles an hour, but it was hitting top speed in three seconds.

For a mile or more, the two stayed ahead, too far for a shot from a six-gun. Up there the easiest place to get over Dynamite Ridge was the narrow canyon where the railroad's powder monkeys were blasting out a railroad grade. That was where the pair was headed, riding as fast as their horses could run. It occurred to Bill that they could get to the canyon, split up, and wait behind the boulders for him. They could catch him in a crossfire. Still, he couldn't abandon the chase.

"Keep going, feller. Keep those legs pumping."

Now the railroad crew was in sight. There were a string of wagons and about twenty men. One man was waving his arms and yelling something. With the wind whistling in his ears Bill couldn't hear. The two hooligans rode on past the railroad crew, spurring their horses into the canyon. Bill hadn't gained a step.

When he was close, he could hear the railroader yelling, but still couldn't understand. The man was jumping and waving his arms. Then Bill was close enough to understand.

"Stop. Stop. She's gonna blow."

Bringing his horse to a stop, Bill yelled, "What?"

"She's gonna blow, she's gonna blow."

Bill rode forward at a walk, close enough to talk without yelling. "What's gonna blow?"

"We put two boxes of Giant Powder Number Three in there. She's gonna blow off the top of that mountain."

"When?"

"Any second now. I tried to warn them two, but they didn't listen. They're gonna get buried."

"Aw for crying in the . . . any second, you say?"

"Yeah. We gave 'er enough fuse to get far away, but she's gonna blow up half the goddamn canyon any second now."

"Aw for . . ." Bill waited. Nothing happened. "You sure? You could have miscalculated or a fuse could have gone out."

"You're the sheriff, ain't you? Well, I'll tell you a fact, Sheriff, I ain't goin' in there to find out."

Bill got down from his winded horse and loosened the cinches. He waited. Other workmen were waiting too, eyes glued to the canyon. The two gunsels could be on the other end of the canyon by now. Or, not knowing about the danger, they could be hiding behind some big rocks waiting for the sheriff to ride into their gunsights. Bill wished there were a way to warn them, but like the railroader, he wasn't about to go into that canyon just now.

Then it blew.

The dynamite was buried deep enough that the sound was muffled, but it looked as if the whole top of the ridge jumped ten feet. Dirt and rocks shot hundreds of feet into the air. One wall of the canyon collapsed. The ground shook all the way to where Bill was standing with his horse. Men cheered and waved their hats. Rocks and dirt rained down.

A cloud of dust hung over the canyon for two or three minutes before it dissipated.

But no one moved.

"Wait," the railroader advised. "There's two boxes of powder. The second ain't gone off yet."

It went off. As before, debris shot high into the air and the ground rumbled. Another cheer went up.

"By God," the railroader said, smiling, "that ought to do 'er. We got tired of pickin' and shovelin' and drillin' and blastin' a little bit at a time. The rail crew's gettin' closer, and we got to get a way through that canyon. By God, that oughtta do 'er."

"That canyon will never be the same," Bill said.

"Nope. That's a fault canyon. That's what the engineers said. We're buildin' a bigger fault. A few more blasts like that and she'll be wide enough for a steam engine."

"Well," Bill said, "is it safe to go in there now?"

"Yup. Don't know as you can ride a horse, though. There'll be broken boulders ever'where, and you'll have to climb over 'em."

"Are you men going in?"

"Yup. It's gonna take a lot of manpower to clear the rocks."

"If you find the bodies of that pair or their horses, send word to Concha Lake, will you?"

"Yessir, Sheriff, we'll do 'er."

"I'm going around, through the notch, and see if I can pick up their trail on the other side. If they got that far."

Luke was coming to meet him. He'd saddled Bill's bay horse and was coming on a gallop. When he saw Bill, he pulled up and waited. "What in holy hell happened over there, Billy?"

"They planted two boxes of dynamite where they're building a railroad through the ridge."

"Jumpin' Jesus. Well, I reckon you didn't get kilt."

161

"Not this time. I should have, as dumb as I am."

"I couldn't see exactly what was happenin', but I heered shootin', and I guessed somebody was shootin' at you. Who was them sonsofbitches?"

Bill told him what had happened, and he described the pair. "Does that sound like the ones who robbed youall?"

"Could be. Like I said, they had flour sacks over their heads, but they was that size. Their horses was a brown and a bay, like I said."

"I'll bet they're the ones. I wish I'd . . . aw hell, I'm no lawman, Luke. I didn't want to arrest men who might be innocent, so I let a couple of robbers get away. What I have to find out now is how they got hold of some Double O horses and where they stole the steers from."

"You think they're dead?"

"Probably, but I'll go around the ridge and see if there's any sign of them."

Looking at the sky, Luke said, "You're gonna get wet."

Following his gaze, Bill saw dark clouds boiling overhead and obscuring the western horizon. "Sure as hell. You got a slicker I can borrow?"

"Ain't got a damn one. Maybe I can find a piece of canvas you can make a poncho out of, or something."

At the relay station, Luke produced a strip of canvas which Bill fashioned into a poncho by cutting a hole in the middle and putting it over his head. It was wide enough to cover his shoulders, but not his arms, and it was long enough to cover him down to his waist. He tied it in place with a short piece of rope. Mounted in his own saddle on his own horse, he picked up the reins of the county horse, said "Adios" to Luke, and rode over the notch. Now that the danger was over, the left side of his neck was throbbing like a war drum, and he rode at a slow trot, not wanting to aggravate it. The sky was boiling. Thunder growled. "No doubt about it," Bill muttered, "we're going to get wet."

Sure enough, lightning flashed and popped a shower of sparks off a granite boulder a hundred feet west of him. Thunder cracked like the whole world was splitting apart. Hail followed. It pounded down, stinging his arms and hands and drumming on his hat. Tree limbs could break the fall of the pea-sized hailstones, and there were a few big ponderosas nearby, but with lightning flashing that close, he didn't dare get under a tree. The horses were jumping, nervous.

"Whoa, boys. Whoa now." It was all Bill could do to keep his seat, hang on to the county horse, and control the bay horse. "We got to get down off this mountain, fellers. Let's lope." He slacked up on the reins and let the bay horse break into a gallop. The county horse was glad to keep up without pulling back.

Within two minutes the ground was white with hailstones and the footing was slippery. But with lightning popping and crackling off the granite, Bill gritted his teeth and let the horses run, hoping they stayed right side up. Down the road they went, down off the notch. The horses were in a full gallop now, splashing through puddles and hailstones. "Careful, boys, careful." The hail turned to rain, a cold high country rain.

Near the bottom of the notch, Bill slowed the horses to a dog trot again. His hat and the strip of canvas kept his head and shoulders dry, but his arms, hips, and legs were thoroughly wet. He shivered in the cold, and tried to keep his teeth from chattering. Rain poured down.

"Well," he reminded himself, "it ain't the first time I've been wet and cold. And if I live long enough, it won't be the last time. Come on, boys, we can't go home yet." He reined off the road, going north, keeping under Dynamite Ridge.

Soon the rain slacked off and gradually stopped. But then a cool breeze came up from the southwest. It cut right

163

through Bill's wet clothes and chilled his bones. Glancing at the sky, he silently wished the clouds would drift on and the sun would come out. It didn't happen.

Shivering, teeth chattering, neck throbbing, Sheriff Billy Walker rode on, looking for the narrow canyon that came out of the Dynamite Mountains.

23

It was useless. All he found when he got to the bottom of the fault was a stream of brown water running out, a stream that normally wasn't there. Hail and rain had soaked the ground and not a track of any kind could be seen. Bill rode a wide circle at the bottom of the mountain, looking for a sign of two horses, but found nothing. He rode a wider circle, hoping to cross some hard ground where tracks wouldn't be washed out. Still nothing. Finally, he turned toward town.

The first thing he wanted to do after unsaddling and feeding his horses was go to his room and change into some dry clothes. He might also build a fire in the cookstove and get warm. But first he had to check into his office. Eddie was there, and he had news.

"A couple of things, Bill," Eddie drawled. "First I had to break Silver Adams' right arm. Had to. He would of shot me. And Jeff Overton came to town an hour ago and said some more cattle was stole form the Circle J."

"Were the stolen cattle steers?"

"Yeah. Eight or ten of 'em."

"Does he know when they were stolen?"

"Sometime in the past five days. They was seen five days ago."

"Well, I know where they are. The two ranihans who stole them are probably dead."

The deputy's mouth dropped open. "The hell, you say."

Bill told him all about it, then asked, "How did you happen to tangle with Silver Adams?"

"About noon. Some cowboy from one of the outfits down

south said he cheated at poker. When I heard there was a ruckus, I went arunnin', and found that cowboy about to meet his maker. Old Adams had 'im in the sights of that nickel-plated pistol of his. I told 'im to drop the gun. He dared me to try to make 'im drop it. I got close enough to bust 'im one on the jaw and grab his gun arm. That gun is one a them double-action kind that don't have to be cocked, and it went off, but the bullet hit the floor and didn't do no harm. I broke Old Adams' arm gettin' the gun out of his hand. Dr. Hadley fixed 'im up. You should of heard 'im holler when the doctor pulled the bone back in place. He wrapped it with a couple yards of something or other and made a plaster cast out of wet starch."

Chuckling, Bill said, "Well, that'll put Silver Adams out of business for a while. He can't deal off the bottom with a busted arm."

"Ain't that a shame," Eddie said with a grin.

"I guess Old Hadley is a-better doctor than we gave him credit for. He fixed both of us up."

"Yeah, but I'd hate to let 'im cut on me the way his hands shake."

"You're right about that, but I'm glad he's here. Say, is Jeff Overton still in town?"

"I think he is. I seen 'im over at the store a while ago. Want me to go fetch 'im?"

"Yeah. I'm going around back and put on some dry clothes."

It wasn't until he was dry and warm that Bill remembered he'd missed his noon meal. He'd fed his horses but not himself. Rummaging through the room, he discovered he was out of coffee and bread. There was a little bacon that could be fried and a pot of beans that could be warmed up. He tasted the beans. Eddie must have cooked them. It seemed Eddie wasn't much of a cook, or he'd never tried to cook in the high country. Beans took a lot of simmering. At least five hours. Well hell, he didn't hire Eddie to cook.

The sun was shining low in the west, but dark clouds overhead sprinkled rain when Bill went to the mercantile. There he met the Widow Osborne and her oldest stepdaughter, Cissy.

"How is your wound, Mr. Walker?" Mary Osborne asked. She wore an ankle-length blue dress that was clean and neat, and she carried a covered basket by the handle. Her gray-streaked dark hair hung down her back, and her face, though showing work wrinkles, was pleasant and — yes — pleasing. A delicious smell came from the basket.

"Healing," Bill answered. "Has Daniel gone over to the Circle J?"

"He went this morning. His room in the barn is vacant if you ever need a place to stay."

"I appreciate that. How are you, Cissy?"

The child smiled. "Fine and dandy, Mr. Walker."

"Say, is that fresh bread you're carrying?"

"Yes it is. Mr. Jackson is buying bread from me now, and so is Mrs. Witter at the café. Cissy and I are keeping busy baking."

"Boy, it sure smells good."

"Well here." She lifted the cloth that covered the basket's contents and took out a loaf of bread. "It's still warm from the oven."

"Oh no, I can't take it."

"Sure you can."

"Well, all right." Bill dug into his pockets for some coins. "Here, I'll pay you more for that loaf of bread than anybody else in town."

"You don't have to pay me, Mr. Walker."

"Your husband called me Billy, not Mister. And yes, I want to pay you." He handed her the coins. "In fact I want to pay for the feed and care you gave me."

"Oh no. That I can't accept. I'll take ten cents for the bread, but that's all I'll take."

Bill bought a jar of apple butter and was headed back to his room to make a meal of it spread over some fresh bread, but he didn't get there. Jeff Overton caught up with him.

"What's this I hear about you findin' some of our rustled cattle?"

Bill repeated the story again. "I think one steer was shot. As cool as it is he'd do to butcher if you get to him soon enough."

"I ain't got a wagon handy, so I reckon he'll feed the coyotes and magpies. But we'll gather up the rest of 'em in a day or two."

A few minutes later, Bill was spreading apple butter on a thick slice of warm bread. "Now," he said to himself, "this is going to be good." Sitting at the table in his room, he took a bite, chewed. Umm. Good. He took another bite, chewed. But before he could swallow it, there came a knock on the door. *Aw-w-w.*

It was Angelina Peterson standing there in her big-brim hat, wool pants, checkered shirt, and leather vest. She had spurs on her boots and a pearl-handled pistol in a holster high on her right side. "Sheriff," she said, "there are two men in your office I think you ought to talk to."

Not wanting her to see the inside of his bachelor digs, Billy Walker stepped outside and shut the door behind him. "Who, Mrs. Peterson?"

"Two men we found in our territory on foot. They said their horses were killed in a rock slide on Dynamite Ridge, and they look like they'd been in a rock slide. They were beat up and half-drowned. When we rode up on them, they acted like they were going to shoot at us, but there were four of us and they changed their minds."

Excitement built up in Bill's chest. "Uh-huh. In my office, you say?"

"Yes. Three of my men and I put them on Circle J horses and brought them to town. We took their guns away from them until you have a chance to question them."

"Did you find them anywhere near that narrow canyon that comes out of Dynamite Ridge?"

"Yes. That's where the rock slide was supposed to be. They said they work for the Double O and they said they were lost, but we don't believe them."

"You bet I want to talk to them, Mrs. Peterson. I sure do." Bill took off at a fast walk around the corner of the building, heading for the street side. Angelina Peterson had to half run to keep up with him, but keep up with him she did. The spurs on her boots jangled.

168

They were standing against the bars of the jail door, guarded by Eddie and three Circle J cowboys, all armed. They looked up briefly when Bill and Anglina Peterson came in, then ducked their heads and looked down. Jenkins was bareheaded and his shirt was torn. Jones had a rip in his shirt and another in the right pant leg. Their faces were dirt-smeared.

Bill studied them a moment, then said quietly, "You must have been still in that fault when I tried to cut your sign, right after the rain."

They said nothing.

"Those steers were stolen from the Circle J, weren't they?"

Jenkins shuffled his feet and mumbled, "No, uh . . ."

Jones snapped a mean look at him and said quickly, "We ain't talkin'."

Eddie asked, "Are these the two, Bill?"

"Yeah," Bill said. "They're the ones."

Looking from the deputy to the sheriff, Angelina Peterson said, "Would you mind telling me what you're talking about?"

"I guess you haven't seen your foreman in the past few minutes, have you?" When she shook her head, Bill told the story again.

"Well I'll be darned. This is the first time any law officer has ever recovered any of our stolen cattle."

"There was some luck," Bill said. Grinning wryly, he added, "Yeah, there was a lot of luck."

Turning to the men against the jail door, Angelina Peterson snapped, "What are your names?" Neither man looked up.

"Jenkins and Jones," Bill said, "if you can believe them."

"Made-up names, no doubt." She snapped at them again, "Where were you selling stolen beef?"

Jones mumbled "We ain't talkin'."

"Damnit, Sheriff," Angelina Peterson said, "Isn't there some way to get some answers out of them?"

With a shrug, Bill said, "What do you think I ought to do, burn them at the stake?"

"There's got to be a way. If we can find out where they've been selling rustled cattle and shut down their market, and if we hang

169

these two, that will put a stop to the rustling going on around here."

"I think I know where some of the beef has been sold, and I've got a hunch about another market. If I ever get a chance, maybe I can go to Rosebud and find out for sure.

She turned her back on Jenkins and Jones, put her hands on her hips, and said, "I want them prosecuted and hung."

"It'll be up to the judge to pass sentence."

While they were talking, Jones bent over and rubbed his right lower leg. Looking up, he said, "I've got a bad cut here. I need a doctor."

"All right, we'll get Dr. Hadley. But first I'm arresting you on suspicion of cattle rustling and attempted murder."

"It's bad. It's bleedin' down my boot." Jones started to pull up his pant leg.

"Open the door, Eddie," Bill said. The deputy moved toward the cell door.

Angelina Peterson was between Bill, the Circle J cowboys, and the two prisoners. They all took their eyes off Jones for two seconds—two seconds too long. Jones straightened up fast. He had a gun in his right hand, a double-barreled derringer. In another second he had Angelina Peterson around the throat with his left arm. The gun was against her right temple.

Bill's hand went to the butt of the Navy Colt, but it was too late.

"Stand back," Jones snarled. "One wrong move from any of you and I'll blow her brains out."

"Oh no," Bill groaned. "Not again."

It was the same trick John Wicher had pulled in the relay station on the divide. The difference was that Jones had had a hideout gun in his boot. Bill silently cursed himself for letting it happen again. How could he be so dumb? Why did this woman do something so foolish as to stand between him and two desperate men? "Damn," Bill muttered between clenched teeth. "Goddamn." But there was another difference.

Angelina Peterson was no helpless female.

24

While Sheriff Billy Walker was desperately trying to find a way to save her, Angelina Peterson bent her knees, jumped, and bumped Jones in the face with her hat. The blow didn't hurt Jones, but it distracted him for a half-second. That's all it took for Bill to draw and cock the Navy Colt.

The shot blew off the top of Jones's head.

Like a sack of grain falling off the tailgate of a wagon, Jones dropped to the floor. Five guns covered his partner.

Jenkins's hands shot up as if they'd been jerked up on ropes. "Don't shoot," he said. "Don't . . . I . . . he . . ."

"Turn around," Bill barked. Jenkins spun around, hands still high. "Search him, Eddie. Make sure he ain't got a hideout."

While Eddie was searching the prisoner, Angelina Peterson reset her hat and stepped away from the dead man. "Well, that's one we won't get to hang. Good shooting, Sheriff."

Through clenched teeth, Bill said, "Yeah."

Blood from the dead man's head was spreading across the floor. Particles of flesh and brains dripped from the cell door. Angelina Peterson discovered a spot of blood on her left boot and coolly she bent down, pulled the dead man's shirt tail out of his pants, and wiped her boot with it. Standing upright again, she saw the disbelieving look on Bill's face.

"Sheriff," she said, "if you'd lost as much livestock to the thieves as I have, you'd feel nothing but the utmost contempt for this breed of man. For all we know, he's the one who murdered your former boss."

"Yeah."

Eddie pushed the still living prisoner inside the jail, slammed the door, and locked it. Bill finally let the hammer down on the Navy Colt and holstered it. "Well," he said, "there's a mop and a bucket in my room. I'll get it and clean up this mess."

"I'll get it, Bill," Eddie said.

"No, we'll . . . we'll both do it."

"So, what are you going to do with this one?" Angelina Peterson demanded.

"Get the district attorney to charge him. Maybe, after he sees what kind of trouble he's in, he'll talk to us."

With a shrug, she said, "I suppose that's the proper way. Too bad."

By the time Bill and his deputy had the mess cleaned up, the news was all over town. Curious men and a few women stopped in front of the sheriff's office and tried to look inside. Bill wanted to go to the mercantile and see if County Chairman Jackson recognized the men or knew anything about them at all, but he thought he'd never get through the crowd. He answered questions patiently, remembering the disgust he'd felt when lawmen had the attitude that what happened was police business and nobody else's. When finally he got to the store, Jackson wasn't there. He wasn't at his home either, and his housekeeper didn't know where he was. Probably at his Double O ranch, Bill concluded. Well, he'd catch him tomorrow.

At supper time, Bill took a plate of beef, beans, and fried potatoes to his prisoner and went back to the Home Café to eat. He and Eddie were the subject of stares and whispers, but they tried to ignore that and fill their stomachs. Irene Ringeley was too busy to be social, but she smiled at Eddie every chance she got.

Later, in their shared room, Eddie asked, "Do you think this gent's the last of the rustlers and thieves, Bill?"

"Naw. Too many things don't make sense."

"Like what?"

"Like the stage station robbery. I'd be willing to bet this pair did it. But if they did, they got enough money out of it to be living high in Denver. What in hell were they doing stealing a handful of cattle?"

After thinking it over, Eddie shrugged. "They was ridin' Dou-

172

ble O horses, and there was some Double O horses stole. But there was about twenty head of Double O beefs stole too. And they wasn't fresh-branded mavericks. If it was them two that done the stealin' on the Double O, what was they doin' with eight head of Circle J steers with burnt-over brands?"

"Headed for the railroad work camp, no doubt. The question is, where are the stolen Double O cattle?"

"There's too damn many questions. But one thing's sure, them two ain't the only ones stealin' and robbin'.'."

"Nope. Tell you, Eddie, we're going to have to do some riding over there under the Dynamite Mountains, south of the Notch Road. Ever been in that country?"

"No. I've heard Concha Creek turns south just under the hills and goes to hell and gone, plumb down to the Colorado or the Rio Grande or one of them rivers. That's big country over there, and somebody's hidin' stole cattle in it somewhere."

"There's got to be a place where they can hide out and change brands."

"Might take a lot of ridin' to find it. When do you want to start, Bill?"

"In the morning, I guess. I don't know what else to do."

"I'll be ready."

"No, on second thought, Eddie, you'd better stay here and try to keep the peace in town. I'll go. If I find something I can't handle by myself, I'll come back for you."

"I'll go if you want me to. I'll go by myself if you want me to."

"Naw. I'd feel better if you stay here."

"Whatever you say. Meantime, I'm goin' back to the café and wait for Irene to finish work," Eddie grinned sheepishly. "She likes for me to walk her home."

Chuckling, Bill said, "Why not? After all, you're supposed to protect the citizens."

He estimated it was around ten-thirty when Eddie came back. It was an hour later that a gunshot shook them both out of bed.

Bill got his pants and boots on and his gun belt buckled, but his shirt tail was flapping as he ran out the door and around the corner to the sheriff's office. His deputy was right behind him.

The office door was open, and Bill noticed at a glance that the padlock had been busted. Inside it was too dark to see until Bill located a lamp, struck a match, and lit it. The jail door was still locked, and the prisoner was still there, lying half on the bunk and half off it.

He wasn't moving.

"Aw for . . ." Bill muttered. "Eddie, go get the key. Run." Eddie ran all the way to their room and back, his boots clomping on the ground and plank walk. Breathless, he unlocked the jail door. Bill ducked inside.

"Is he dead?" Eddie asked.

"Yeah," Bill answered after a moment. "Shot through the heart."

"Well, that sure tears it."

"Yeah," Bill said, sourly. "Somebody was afraid he'd answer some of those questions we were talking about."

"Yep. Well, it answers one question, we know now that them two was only part of our troubles. There's more."

Sourly, Bill Walker muttered, "Yeah, there sure as hell is."

25

He rode out of town early, riding his good bay horse and leading a county horse which carried his canvas-wrapped bed, a skillet, ax, and some groceries. He followed the Notch Road, keeping Concha Creek in sight until the creek turned south under Dynamite Ridge. From there on, the going was rough. It took two hours to get to the trail he'd once seen from the Double O's Concha Creek camp. It was a steep climb from there.

In spite of the rain, there should have been some kind of impression on the trail left by cattle and horses. The tracks of that many big animals couldn't be wiped out entirely. Bill allowed the horses to travel at a slow walk, and stopped every few minutes to let them blow and to study the ground. Twice he got down and walked, leading the horses, taking a closer look at the ground. He found no sign of anything.

When he looked back, he could see Concha Creek away down there and the cattle camp. There was no sign of life at the camp, only the house, stock shelter, and pens. No animals and no humans. The ground was rocky up here, and the trail was barely visible in places. Tall spruce and ponderosas grew out of the hillside. Farther on, Bill rode through a stand of aspen, with their leaves shimmering in the breeze. Where there was a thick growth of aspen, there were a lot of downed trees. Aspen grew fast and died fast. The horses had to step over blow-downs and their hooves broke several, making cracking noises.

And that's where he saw the first sign of big animals. Something had stepped on some of the downed trees, breaking them.

Sure, Bill mused silently you couldn't push even a few cattle through here without them stepping on aspen sticks. Something had been through here recently.

But when he rode on and broke into the open, he was disappointed. Elk. Eight cows, four bulls, and four calves. Beautiful, with their light tan rumps and dark shaggy necks. They were grazing in a grassy park, and they watched him curiously, their heads up and ears fanned forward.

The trail was barely visible in the tall mountain grass and brushy cinquefoil, but what Bill could see of it went right through the herd of elk. He kept his horses on it. The elk watched him until he was within fifty feet of them, then turned and bounded away into the timber. All but one. A calf stayed behind, watching Bill, confused as to which animals it should follow. When Bill and his horses got ahead of it, it fell in behind them, chirping like a loud bird.

Bill grinned. "Go on. We're not your mama." A cow came back, crossing the trail behind the man and horses. She whistled repeatedly, crossed and recrossed the trail until the calf stopped, stared at her a moment, then went trotting to her. Cow and calf disappeared among the ponderosas.

Chuckling, Bill rode on, climbing steadily. It was pleasant, the wild animals, the tall grasses, and the cinquefoil with tiny yellow flowers. The pines smelled good and the cool breeze felt good. But he saw no other sign of big animals.

At the top of the Dynamite Mountains, he reined up and tried to study his backtrail, but tall timber obscured his view. Ahead was the vast high prairie where the trail disappeared in the tall prairie grasses.

Disappointment clouded Bill's face when he dismounted. He ate half a loaf of bread while his horses grazed. The stolen cattle had to have been driven up this trail. They had come up the mountain here or up the Notch Road, where they would have been seen or over Dynamite Ridge on Circle J land north of the road—unless there was another passage over the mountains somewhere south of here.

Looking south, he shook his head sadly. Rough country.

High steep pine-covered hills, castle-sized boulders, deep canyons. As far as he could see to the south, there was no break in the mountains. Mountains circled the prairie up here, and away to the south they rose even higher, with snow on the peaks and ridges.

Overhead a bald eagle soared on the breeze, floated, looking down, its white head and neck gleaming in the sunlight. That's what I need, Bill said to himself, wings like an eagle so I could fly up there and look around. Maybe I could see what I'm looking for from up there.

His meal over, he mounted and turned south. "Well hell, fellers," he said to the horses, "we'll go as far as we can and see what we can see."

After five hundred yards he reined up again. No use staying on the prairie, he decided. Rain and hail would have wiped out any tracks up here. Got to get down in those hills and hope to find a sign of cattle and horses. He rode on, looking for any kind of trail coming out of a canyon or over a hill. Another five hundred yards, and he found one. It was narrow, and it hadn't been used lately but it was definitely a path made by hoofed animals. He turned onto it and followed it downhill into a steep canyon. For an hour he rode around huge boulders on the side of a steep grassy hill where one slip of a horse's hoof could send them rolling a hundred feet to the bottom. After another half hour he knew he was wasting his time. Nobody could drive cattle over this trail. But now he was on a path that wound around boulders and was so narrow that he couldn't turn two horses around on it. To his right, the hill rose almost straight up, and to his left it fell off into the brushy bottom of the canyon.

"Goddamn," he muttered. "Got ourselves in a jackpot, didn't we fellers."

He dismounted on the off side of the horse, uphill. The bay horse didn't like being dismounted from the right, but it was smart enough to keep its feet still, knowing that one mistep could be its last. "Now, this is the tricky part," Bill said. "Be damned careful, boys, damned careful."

Moving cautiously, watching where he put each foot down, Bill went to the pack horse and backed it up a few steps to where the path was a few inches wider. "Now, got to turn around," he said. "Best to turn uphill. All right, let's do it." He got uphill and pulled on the lead rope. The horse got its forefeet up off the trail and turned. Its hind feet slipped downhill, but it kept its balance and scrambled, turning, until it faced the opposite direction.

"Whew. Atta boy. Now to get the other one turned around."

He repeated the process, backing the horse until it was on the wider spot, then pulling its head around. The bay horse's forefeet slid on the steep hill, and its hind feet slipped downhill. For a horrible second, Bill thought it was going to slip onto its back and roll. But the horse, with a combination of fear and determination, kept scrambling until finally it was on the path again, headed back the way they had come.

Exhausted with relief, Bill sat on the hill with his knees drawn up and his chin in his hands. "I apologize, boys," he said. "I should have known. Nothing but deer and goats can get over this trail. It sure as hell wasn't made by horses. I'll try not to make the same mistake again."

Finally, he got up and tied the saddle horse's reins to the tail of the pack horse, by using his hands to grab tufts of grass, he made his way up to the head of the pack horse. He couldn't get the saddle horse around the pack horse and he couldn't ride the pack horse, so he walked, leading the animals. As he walked, he cursed himself, and muttered, "Maybe someday, if I live long enough, I'll be smart enough to be a mountain man."

It was nearly dark when he climbed out of the canyon to the high prairie. He got his horses picketed on thirty-foot ropes, keeping them far enough apart that they wouldn't get the ropes crossed, then went about making a camp for himself. He had a canteen of water, which quenched his thirst, but wasn't enough to share with the horses. The first thing he'd have to do in the morning was look for water. He walked back to the edge of the prairie where the ponderosas grew and broke off some dead

178

limbs for a fire, then made his supper out of fried bacon, warmed-over beans, and bread.

Lying in his bed, listening to the night sounds—the breeze rustling the tall prairie grasses, his horses grazing—he guessed he was a good ten miles from the nearest human animal. He'd heard about rich Easterners who paid experienced Western outdoorsmen good money to take them on hunting and camping trips. Now he understood why. Here, all was peaceful. Nobody was yelling, "Sheriff, come arunnin'. Somebody's been shot." Or "Somebody robbed the stage." Or "Sheriff, somebody stole my pig." Or worse yet, "Sheriff, go out there and collect taxes."

And that got him to thinking about his job as sheriff of Concha County. Did he want to run for election? Naw. That would make him a politician, and politicians had to make speeches, kiss the asses of the big money boys, and evict honest folks from their homes. Nope, he wanted to go back to driving the six-ups—if he could get the job. Samuel Price would have to let some men go and sell some of his equipment when the railroad gets to Concha Lake, and there would be teamsters out of work. Maybe he couldn't get a job.

Aw hell, Billy Walker turned over on his side, bringing a sharp pain to the side of his neck. Goddamn. Have to lay on my goddamn back all the time.

Before sunup he was horseback again, riding along the rim of a deep canyon. Down below, the canyon was filled with willows, which was an indication that water was there too. Willows needed water. A spring, maybe, where water came out of the ground. He looked for a path going down, but found only another dim game trail. Sitting his saddle he studied the country. South were more canyons, a maze of them, canyons, ridges, steep hills, boulders as big as churches. A man could get lost in those canyons. This one, though, seemed to go down to a wide valley. About four miles down, he figured. Could a horse make it? Well, he decided, they'd try. If they couldn't make it, they could turn around and come back like they did yesterday. "Come on, old boys," he said aloud.

There were places where the trail traversed steep hills, where

179

it dipped across gulleys and where it wound behind huge boulders that stuck out of the hills. The trail had to have been made by deer and elk, but there were no tracks of any kind. "Lordy," Bill muttered, "I didn't think horses could travel on ground like this." At times his jaws tightened and at times he kicked his feet out of the stirrups in case his saddle horse slipped off the narrow path and fell. A rock chuck — some folks called them whistle pigs — sat on a boulder on its hind end and watched them pass, then chirped and ducked into a hole between two rocks. A raven overhead looked down on him and squawked. Was that squawk a warning?

"Careful, boys, careful."

Traversing a hill, the pack horse's hind feet slid off the path, and it scrambled wildly, trying to keep its footing. Its lead rope was wrapped around the saddle horn, and the saddle horse strained and pulled until the pack horse was back on the trail. Bill reached down and scratched the bay horse's neck. Thank God you've got the power to do it, feller." They dropped two feet from the top of a rock onto the valley floor, and they were in the willows.

"Whoo." Bill let his breath out with a rush. But traveling still wasn't easy. The ground in the willows was spongy, and the willows were so dense he couldn't see ten feet ahead. There was nowhere to go but through them. "Lordy," Bill said, "I'd hate like hell to have to turn around and go back now." He kept the horses moving.

Here, there was no trail. The horses sank in to their hocks and had to hump their backs and buck their way through. That had Bill hanging on to the saddle horn. He ducked his head and depended on his broad-brim hat to protect his face from the branches. Now the horses were too winded to go on, and they stopped. "Goddamn, can't stop here, fellers, you might sink in deeper. Come on." He kicked the bay horse with his bootheels, kicked hard. The horse grunted, heaved itself up, and took a couple more jump-steps. "Come on," Bill pleaded. "Can't stop now. Keep going."

These damn bushes didn't cover the whole world. There had

to be an end to them. If they could keep going, they'd come out of them somewhere. "Come on, fellers."

And then they were in a stream.

It was a narrow creek that came out of the ground somewhere behind them—narrow but running clear and gurgling happily. Not only that, there was a third-acre grassy park on the other side. Bill let the horses drink, then rode out of the creek and into the park. There, he unsaddled so the horses could rest better, and seated himself on a small boulder. On each side of the stream there was nothing but willows, and on each side of the willows were steep hills studded with boulders and tall pines. Downhill, nothing in sight but willows.

At least, Bill mused, the horses could walk in the creek, where water had washed the ground down to rocks and gravel. It would be slippery and tricky, but better than bucking through the bogs. After eating the rest of his bread, he saddled up and mounted the bay. "Well, boys, let's see what the rest of this day brings."

It took an hour and a half and the sun was making its final descent to the Wet Mountains when they finally got down to the valley Bill had seen from up on the rim. Down here the footing was good and it was a pleasure to be horseback and traveling. Bill reined up, twisted in his saddle, winced at the pain in his neck, and looked back. He shook his head with a wry grin. "Did we really come down that? From here, I wouldn't have thought it was possible."

It was decision time. Did he go back to town now, taking the easy way, or go on south a little farther. He'd been over a lot of country, rough country, and hadn't found a damn thing. How far was he from the Double O's Concha Creek camp? Not so far, he guessed, but it was only a guess. He really didn't know where the hell he was, though he was in no danger of getting lost. All he had to do was keep the Dynamite Mountains on the east and head north and he'd come to Concha Creek. But— glancing at the sky—he decided to go a little farther south. Hell, he mused, he couldn't get back to town before dark anyway so he might as well search a little farther.

He hadn't traveled more than a mile when he came to a cattle trail. A well-used trail. It came from the north, and from where Bill sat, it looked like it went up and over the Dynamite Mountains.

"Well now," Bill mused, "whatta you know about that."

26

It was everything Sheriff Billy Walker had hoped to find. The trail was washed clean of tracks, but it had been used recently. Cattle droppings weren't more than a week old, if that old, and there were horse droppings too. Like Samuel Price had once said when he was cleaning his barn, where there are horses there's horse manure. Bill followed the trail to the foot of the Dynamite Mountains, to where it split. One fork went uphill and the other into a canyon. Bill rode into the canyon.

Yep. This was the place. The canyon was about a hundred and fifty yards long, and the end and the sides rose almost straight up. It was all granite, shot through with cracks created millions of years earlier when this whole territory was under the floor of an ocean. And there was the remains of a fire. Yep. It would be easy to hold a bunch of cattle in here. This canyon was so well hidden, cattle could be branded and kept here for weeks. Well, not so well hidden. Bill had wasted his time climbing and descending game trails, but if he'd stayed on top of the Dynamite Mountains and kept going south he'd have seen where this trail topped out.

That meant it was no secret. It was probably on Double O land, and every Double O cowboy had to know about it. Well, that wasn't necessarily so either. Eddie Wilhoit had worked for Charlie Goodnight in New Mexico for nearly a year without seeing the entire ranch holdings. Double O cowboys could cover a lot of land without coming over this way. But somebody on the ranch knew about this canyon and this trail.

Somebody like Walt Hudson, the cowboy who held down the Double O's Concha Creek camp.

Bill rode out of the canyon and started up the other fork of the trail. "Well, boys," he said, "I hate to ask you to do this, but I've just got to see where this path goes."

It was hard work for the horses, climbing, but the footing was good. Like the game trails, this one wound around boulders, crossed a narrow stream several times, went through dense woods of spruce and pine, and finally came out on the high prairie south of the Notch Road. Away south.

The sun was going down over the Wet Mountains when the horses got their feet on prairie soil again. Bill was surprised to see a small creek up here. It came from the east and went southwest down the canyon where it no doubt joined Concha Creek. Bill couldn't even guess where it came from. Most streams on this side of the Continental Divide flowed southeast, not southwest. But water followed the route of least resistance, and this creek had to have branched off a bigger stream somewhere east.

Up here the trail disappeared, an indication that cattle were allowed to scatter and graze. This was another place where stolen cattle could be held until the thieves were ready to move them to market. In fact, though Bill was no cattleman, he knew this was damned good summer grazing land.

Men had camped here. Bill would camp here. And the next time cattle were stolen, he'd know where to find them.

At sunup he was mounted and following his own tracks back down off the Dynamite Mountains. No more long hills to climb, he promised his horses. Not today, anyway.

Staying on the trail at the foot of the mountains, Bill followed it about three miles to where it crossed the southern trail of Concha Creek. From there it divided into a half-dozen dim trails, which eventually disappeared altogether. When he saw cows and calves grazing along the creek he rode to them, as close as they would allow, which was close enough that he could read the brands. Double O. Old brands on the cows and fresh brands on the calves. Nothing unusual about that. Bill guessed that stolen cattle had been driven over country grazed on by other cattle, which would make their tracks hard to follow.

He rode on, keeping the mountains on his right, until he topped a low hill and saw the Concha Creek cow camp a mile or so ahead.

Reining up, Bill tried to estimate the distance between the cow camp and the trail made by stolen cattle. Six miles? No, probably eight. Yeah, eight or nine miles. Close enough that Walt Hudson knew about it. From where he sat his eyes picked up the closest route over Dynamite Ridge, the trail that Bill had followed two days ago, the trail that told him nothing.

All right, Bill said to himself, let's go have a talk with that jasper.

When he was closer, he stopped again and studied the camp. No human was in sight, and no horses were in the corrals. There were six horses grazing nearby, however. Two of them had collar marks on their necks. They had to be the team that pulled the buckboard parked near an open-sided stock pen. Bill touched bootheels to the bay horse and rode closer. Now he saw a curtain in the house part, then close again. Somebody was at home. "Hello," he yelled when he was still closer. The door opened and a woman came out, the woman he'd seen in the buckboard with Walt Hudson, heading for town. "Mrs. Hudson?"

"Yes," she said, shading her eyes with her right hand, "I'm Mrs. Hudson. You're Sheriff Walker, ain't you?"

"Yes, ma'am. Is your husband at home?"

"No, he ain't, Sheriff. He went over west to look at the grass and maybe move some cows over there."

"The rain helped the grass, didn't it?" Bill said, trying to make conversation. He stayed on his horse, but hoped she'd invite him to get down.

"Yes. That rain helped, but we need more of it."

She was pleasant enough. Thin, with a wrinkled face and a long skinny neck. Did she know anything about cattle rustling?

Maybe. Maybe not. No use asking her. It was her husband that Bill wanted to talk to.

"Uh, Mrs. Hudson, I reckon you cook for whatever Double O crew that happens to be working around here."

"Yes, I do."

"Have you had to cook for very many this summer?"

"Only a few at a time since the calf roundup."

"Do you mean like two or three?"

Her eyes narrowed. Now she was wondering why the sheriff was asking questions. "Well, yes."

"Were they always the same two or three?"

"No. They came and went."

"Uh, did you happen to see the two men who were shot after they robbed the sawmill payroll?"

"What do you mean?" Her voice had taken on a hard edge.

"I mean the bodies. I don't reckon you saw their bodies."

"Of course not. Why?"

"Did your husband happen to take a look at them?"

"No. We didn't even hear about the robbery and all for a week after it happened."

"Who told you about it?"

An exasperated sigh came out of her. "Why are you asking all these questions, Sheriff?"

He decided to be frank. "I just wondered if they were two of the men you cooked for."

"Well, I don't think so. The men I cooked for are cowboys, but gentlemen."

Either she knew nothing about who had been doing the rustling or she was a damned good actress. No use asking any more questions of her. "Any idea when your husband will get back, Mrs. Hudson?"

"It'll be late. He took some biscuits with him for his dinner."

"Well, I got to be going. Tell your husband hello for me." He touched bootheels to the bay and rode out of the yard, leading the pack horse.

Instead of following Concha Creek, he stayed on the wagon road, crossed the creek, and kept going north until he came to the Notch Road. What would Walt Hudson do? Pack up and quit the country? For that matter, what would Billy Walker do? He had cause for suspicion—strong suspicion—but no proof. Nothing he could take to the district attorney. About all he could do was go to Rosebud, find the gent who'd been buying stolen cattle, and get him to admit it. Then arrest Walt Hudson and get the buyer to identify him. But, aw hell, nobody was going to admit anything. And who all was mixed up in this scheme anyway? If Walt Hudson was, then somebody else on the Double O had to know about it. Was the whole outfit a pack of thieves? Come to think of it, he didn't know who was foreman on the Double O. He'd probably seen him in town a time or two, but didn't know who he was. He'd have to meet that gentleman face to face. Yeah, that was something to work on.

Anyway, Bill thought wryly, they would know now that he was wise to them, and that ought to put a stop to the cattle rustling. It was a mistake questioning Mrs. Hudson. He didn't learn a damned thing from her and all he did was tip his hand. Then another thought came to his mind, a thought that made his heart beat faster and his pulse quicken.

They'd murdered Sheriff Koen and they'd tried twice to murder him. Now they'd try again. They'd have to.

27

Eddie Wilhoit had been busy. A brawl in the Pink Lady had left one man with a bullet in the stomach and another in jail. The wounded man wasn't expected to live. "It's a couple of them carpenters," Eddie reported when Bill dropped into his desk chair. "They got tanked up on that Taos Lightning and remembered they had a grudge agin' each other. One packin' iron." In still another saloon brawl two men had made the fur fly with their fists, but the only damage was a bloody nose and a cut lip. They weren't arrested.

Bill grinned. "Well, we can't lock up everybody who swaps a few punches. If we did, we'd have the jail full all the time. Does Dr. Hadley have any hope at all for the shooting victim?"

"Not much. He said the slug was still in 'im, and he wanted me to put 'im on the stage and take 'im to the hospital in Rosebud, then he didn't, then he did. By the time he made up his mind, the stage was gone." Eddie parked one hip on the edge of the desk and faced Bill. "Know what I think? I think Old Hadley is scared. He wanted to dig the lead out, but his hands was shakin' so bad he couldn't hardly get a whiskey glass to his face."

"That's his trouble. He's a boozer. I don't suppose you were able to identify the two dead cattle rustlers."

"Naw. I got a bunch of folks to go look at 'em, but nobody ever saw 'em before."

"How about Hiram Jackson?"

"Him, I ain't seen. I heard, though, that he got on the stage

188

and went to Rosebud day before yesterday, the day you left. I don't think he's been back."

While they were talking, Dr. Hadley came in. He smelled of liquor and his long sad face was even longer and sadder. "I'm sorry to report," he said, slurring his words, "that Mr. Slaughter has expired. Fortunately, he said he has—had—no family. I'm—I'm sorry. I, uh . . ." He turned and slumped out.

"Goddamn," said Eddie Wilhoit, standing, "the graveyard is growin' ever' day, and nobody is dyin' of natural causes."

Bill told Eddie of his plan to go out to the Double O headquarters next morning, hunt up the foreman, see what kind of man he was, and throw a few questions at him. Eddie wanted to go along, and at first Bill balked, believing the deputy might be needed in town. But after mulling it over, Bill agreed. A man alone would be easy. Two men were not an army, but anybody thinking about backshooting might think twice. "It's a hell of a note, Eddie. But the fact is two shots could wipe out all the law enforcement in Concha County."

"Yeah, and I got a hunch somedamnbody wants to do that."

Grinning crookedly, Bill said, "You watch behind us and I'll watch in front of us. Until this hole in my neck heals, I can't see too good behind."

They left town just as the stage from the east was pulling in. "Was that Hiram Jackson in there?" Bill asked. "Looked like him," Eddie said. "Him and four other men." Bill was riding a county horse and Eddie was riding his own. "I want to talk to him," Bill said, "but it can wait."

The Double O headquarters was big. It was built beside another creek that came out of the Wet Mountains, and it was built to last. The main house sprawled over a quarter acre, with a wide front porch, two chimneys, and a big glass window overlooking a green meadow. There was a big barn built of rough lumber, a smaller barn, a three-sided shed, four corrals, a log bunkhouse, and a cattle chute made of heavy planks. Two shaggy dogs barked as they rode up but wagged their tails.

The two lawmen expected somebody to come out and see what the dogs were barking at, but no one did. "There ought to be somebody here," Bill said. He yelled, "Hello. Hello. Anybody here?" When he got no answer, he rode up to the front door of the big house and yelled again. Finally the wide door opened and a bald man with a dirty white apron around his middle came out, squinting at them.

"I'm Sheriff Bill Walker and this is Deputy Eddie Wilhoit. Can you tell me who the foreman is here?"

"Tanner," the man said. "His name is Tanner."

"I don't suppose he's anywhere around?"

"No, he ain't. Him and the boys rode out two-three hours ago."

"Any idea where they went?"

"Said somethin' about goin' over to the Concha Creek camp. Got somethin' to do over there."

"How many men are there here?"

"Four now. Five includin' me."

"Did you lose some men lately?"

"They come and go but we ain't had none quit lately."

"Thanks."

"Well, Eddie," Bill said after the Double O cook had gone back inside, "think we can find the Concha Creek camp from here?"

"Easy. We can cut cross country. All we have to do is keep the Dynamite Mountains ahead of us and look for Concha Creek."

"Well, it's probably a waste of time, we might not find them, but hell, let's go."

It was noon when they got to the cow camp. Nobody was in sight. One horse was in a corral, and the others grazed nearby. The wagon was gone and so were the two harness horses. "If anybody's here, it isn't anybody we want to see," Bill said.

"Looks like they took a trip to town."

"Tell you what, while we're over this way I'll show you the trail they've been taking stolen cattle over, just so you'll know where it is."

As they approached the box canyon where cattle had been held and branded, Bill said, "Keep your eyes peeled. They

190

might be in there." But no one was there and no one had been there recently. "Goddamn. The Double O crew and their foreman could be anywhere in a hundred thousand acres."

"This ain't our lucky day, Bill."

"Wish we'd brought some biscuits or jerked beef or something."

"Yeah, my stomach is gettin' mad at me."

"Tell you what, let's go on up to the top and if we don't find anything interesting, we can go over to Samuel Price's relay pens and maybe Old Luke'll find something for us to eat."

"My guts've been mad at me before."

The sun was on its way down and dark clouds were gathering when they topped out on the high prairie. They dismounted, loosened their cinches, and let their horses rest a few minutes. Then they mounted again and turned north toward the Notch Road. Lightning flashed over west and thunder rumbled. Glancing up at the darkening sky, Bill commented, "Think it'll rain?"

"If it don't, it's gonna miss a hell of a good chance."

They were surprised to see a Concord coach in front of the house. The front end was jacked up and the front axle and wheels were standing beside it. Two men were working under it and three well-dressed men stood nearby and watched.

"Busted axle, I'll bet," Bill said.

"Yep. Must be the westbound."

When they rode up, Bill could see he had guessed wrong. "Its' the couplin' pole," Luke allowed, shaking his head sadly. "Had to take the whole damned front end off to fix it."

"Where'd she break?"

"Just behind the front axle. Lucky it was long enough that we could saw 'er off at the tail end and fit 'er back."

Charley, the teamster, crawled out from under the front end of the jacked-up coach. "Heard 'er pop 'bout six mile up the road. Had to come back, and I mean to tell you I didn't know if the fifth wheel was agonna stay put."

The two riders could see what a job it had been to jack up the coach. They'd had to use a corral pole for a pry bar and drag a wooden water tank over for a fulcrum. Then it had to have taken every man on the place to push down the end of the pole and raise the front end of the coach. They'd pushed another wooden trough under it to hold it up.

Charley and the shotgun messenger had taken out the king pin, unstacked the rocking bolster, pried up the fifth wheel — the two flat iron plates which make it possible to turn the front axle — then removed the broken coupling pole. The coupling pole kept the front and rear axles exactly the proper distance apart, and with it broken, the front end was next to impossible to control. A teamster with less skill than Charley couldn't have done it. By sawing off the rear end of the coupling pole they had enough pole left to replace the broken stub.

But it had taken hours. The stage wouldn't get to Rosebud that day. To make matters worse, it was rapidly turning dark, and the lightning and thunder were coming closer.

Charley crawled from under. "Let's git this front axle back in here." Four pairs of strong hands rolled the wheels and axle assembly under the wagon, jockeying it into place. Charley and the shotgun guard went to work with heavy wrenches. "I'll git some light," Luke said, hurrying to the house. The three well-dressed passengers could do nothing but stand and watch.

Working by lantern light, the two men under the coach got everything back together and crawled out. Then every hand pushed down on the corral pole pry bar and within minutes the coach was ready to travel.

"Bring up them horses, Luke."

Lightning cut a jagged streak across the sky. Thunder cracked.

And from somewhere a rifle cracked.

28

Nobody saw where the shot came from. Charley grabbed his stomach with both hands, fell onto his knees, then fell over on his side. He groaned, "Godamighty, godamighty."

Bill's six-gun was in his hand and he looked around wildly for something to shoot back at, ignoring the pain in his neck. Eddie Wilhoit yelled, "Over yonder, back of the house."

Another rifle shot. Bill felt the heat of the bullet as it went past his cheek and thudded into the side of the stagecoach. He snapped a shot at the gunflash. Eddie was shooting too. Luke was running to the house to get his shotgun.

The stage guard's shotgun boomed in Bill's ear, and the guard cursed, "Goddamn it, can't see."

"Hit the ground, everybody," Bill yelled. The three passengers were already on the ground. One had a pistol in his hand. Two more shots came from behind the house, and Bill started running toward them.

Another flash of lightning illuminated the house for a second, and Bill saw the rifleman. He fired, but not soon enough. The rifle cracked again and the rifleman disappeared.

Eddie spun half around, doubled over, and clamped his left hand against his right side. "Damnit," he cried. "Damnit, damnit, damnit."

Bill got to the front of the house at the same time Luke ran out with his shotgun. "He's behind the house, Luke. I'll go this way." Bill stayed against the wall, and walked with quick steps to the rear. The night was black.

Silently, Billy Walker swore, Got to get that sonofabitch. Got to get him. Come on, show yourself, you goddamn trigger-happy, blood-thirsty sonofabitch. When he got to the corner, he stopped, listened. Then, keeping his back to the wall he inched forward, the Navy Colt ready. Thunder exploded and lightning zigzagged across the sky.

For a second Bill could see around the corner. Nothing but blackness. He waited, listened.

Then the rain came. Only a few fat drops at first, but within seconds it was pouring. Thunder pounded Bill's eardrums. Lightning lit up the world. There was no one behind the house. No one but Luke. Luke stopped short when he saw Bill, and Bill yelled, "It's me, Luke."

"Where'd he go, Billy?"

"Don't know. Can't see him."

Another flash of lightning, and Bill saw him. Two of them. Carrying rifles. Running onto the prairie behind the house. Bill took aim and fired, but he was shooting into the dark. Luke's shotgun roared. "Hold your fire, Luke." Bill ran after them, hoping he could see them in the lightning flashes. But the flashes were too far apart, and when he heard hoofbeats he knew he'd lost them. "Luke?" From near the back of the house, Luke answered. Yeah?"

"They're horseback. I'm going after them." Bill ran back to the house, around in front of it, yelling, "Eddie, get mounted, they're heading south."

A man's voice said, "Eddie can't."

"What?" Bill slid to a stop, almost fell, regained his balance.

"He's hit." A man was kneeling beside Eddie, holding a lantern.

"Oh God," Bill said, dropping to his knees. "How bad, Eddie?"

The deputy's face was screwed up in pain, but he managed a crooked grin. "Why it's just a little bee sting, Bill. Soon's I get my wind, I'm gonna get up." Rain drummed down on his face, but Eddie didn't notice.

"No, don't. Stay down." Bending closer, Bill saw the bullet

194

hole in the deputy's right side between the lower ribs and the hip bone. He yelled, "Luke, get the horses."

"Charley's down too. He's hit bad."

Bill stood and went to Charley who was lying on his back, still holding his stomach. "I've got my dose, Billy. I'm done for."

"Not yet, Charley. Hang on, pardner. We're gonna get you down to Dr. Hadley."

One of the passengers said, "The horses are coming." Another passenger cried, "What is this? What's happening? Why were we shot at?" Another passenger growled, "Shut your trap, and maybe we'll get out of here alive."

Luke was driving the six-horse team while the shotgun guard led the leaders. Bill helped them hitch the horses to the singletrees. "Who's gonna handle them lines?" the guard asked. "Me, I ain't ever drove that many horses."

"Billy can do it," Luke said. "She ain't gonna be easy, Billy. Gittin' through that notch in the daytime is bad enough, and this black mare in the lead is kinda boogerish."

"Let's get the wounded inside. Give them plenty of room. Then the rest of you get in."

They propped Charley up on one seat, helped Eddie climb in beside him, and let the three passengers crowd onto the other seat. "She's gonna be a wild ride, folks," Luke warned. "Old Billy here is in a hurry, and he ain't gonna spare nobody or nothin'." Bill climbed up onto the high seat, sitting on the right where he could work the brake handle. The shotgun guard sat beside him with a long snake whip. Six horses meant six driving lines, which Bill laced between his fingers. The lines and his voice were the only communication between him and the horses. He tested the lines, making certain he could communicate with the lead team, then barked at the guard, "Go."

The long whip snaked out over the horses with a pop, Bill yelled, "Hit in there," and the coach lurched forward.

Even before they got onto the Notch Road, Bill knew he was going to have trouble with the leader. In the dark he couldn't see the lead team, but he could feel the black mare on the off side lunging in her collar, pulling on the bit in her mouth. The wheel team seemed to be steady, but the off swing horse, behind the lead mare, was catching some of the mare's nervousness.

"Goddamn." Bill worked the lines, trying to hold the lead mare back without pulling on the others. On the road where the traveling was easy, he yelled at the horses and got them into a gallop. The lead mare was still lunging, wanting to stampede. All that held her back was her partner in the lead, a twelve-year-old bay gelding that had been pulling coaches for over seven years. Silently, Bill thanked the gelding. When they started up the long grade to the notch, he worked the horses down to a trot, and then where the road was the steepest, he let them walk.

He had a terrible sense of urgency, but he knew he'd get to town no faster by wearing down the horses. "How's Eddie doing?" he asked the guard. The guard leaned over and hollered back into the coach, "How's everybody?"

"The deputy's still alive," a passenger yelled back. "I'm not so sure about the other man." Another passenger was holding a lighted lantern near Eddie's face.

Teeth clenched, Bill muttered, "Goddamn."

The storm had passed now and the sky was clearing. A half-moon slid out from behind a cloud, casting a dim light over the horses. The road was still invisible.

Then came the notch.

"I can light this here lantern and get out there in front," the guard said. "Mebbe that'll help."

"No, I don't want to stop. I think I can see. The team can see, and that bay gelding in the lead knows where to go."

"That black mare's a bitch. Old Luke was plannin' to put her on the wheels, but a lead horse went lame and he had to put her up front."

"She needs experience," Bill said, "but she'll be all right. Pulling this hill might settle her down."

"Right here is where it gets ticklish. These damn coaches wasn't made for sharp turns."

196

"Easy, boys and girls," Bill said. "Easy now." He could feel the lines slacken when the lead team reached the notch, then felt the lead mare's line jerk. She was fighting. "Whoa. Whoa, now." Bill kept his voice calm, trying to keep the horses calm. The lead team was so far away that he had little control over them. "Easy, now."

The guard pleaded, "We gotta unhitch 'em, Billy. Them leaders're gonna run away. Let me get down and unhitch 'em 'till you get around the notch."

"Can't do 'er. We've got two wounded men in here. Can't take the time. Whoa, now."

Then the mare's line jerked, jerked twice, and went slack. She was trying to turn back.

"Oh Christ," the guard said, "she's comin' back up the tongue. She's atryin' to turn herself inside out."

"Whoa, fellers." Bill manipulated the lines, hoping the lead gelding stayed in his traces, hoping the off swing horse kept looking ahead. The coach's front wheels turned sharply.

"Oh Christ, she's agonna tip over."

"Whoa." Bill hauled back on all the lines, trying to stop the team. "Whoa, whoa there." Everything came to a stop. Bill could see the mare was standing still now, but turned sideways. He could feel in the lines that she was trembling. A passenger yelled, "What's going on? Are we gonna turn over?"

Without answering, Bill manipulated the lines, holding the horses steady until, in the dim moonlight, he could see the lead mare facing ahead again. "All right. Get up. But easy, now. The worst is coming." He couldn't be sure in the semidarkness, but he believed the mare was still in her traces. "Let's go, boys and girls, straight ahead. Easy."

The horses moved, the wheels straightened. But then came the sharp curve.

"This's gonna be hairy."

"It's gonna be all right," Bill said through clenched teeth. "It's gonna be all right—be all right." The mare was nervous, lunging. "Come on, fellers, slow. Slow now."

The guard had put his shotgun in the boot under his feet and was hanging on to the seat with both hands. A passenger yelled, "What's going on? Where are we?"

The lead gelding had been over the notch before, and he was on the near side, the side where the road dropped off. He knew what to do. But the mare was crowding him, pushing. "Easy, girl," Bill said. "Nothing to be scared of. Let your partner show you how to do it. Slow now."

It occurred to Bill that he was making a mistake. Sure, he had to get two wounded men to a doctor, but he had three other passengers too. It wasn't smart to risk their lives, trying to save the lives of Eddie and Charley. He ought to stop the team and let them get out and walk. But as soon as it occurred to him, it was too late. They were on the curve. One side of the road went straight up and the other side went straight down. The passengers couldn't get out.

"Slow, fellers." He pleaded. "Slow and easy. Please."

Up ahead the lead gelding was pushing back, leaning with all his strength against his partner. The coach inched along. With the lines laced through his fingers, Bill managed to keep the black mare's head away from her partner, keep her going.

Trace chains and singletrees rattled. The coach moved. The front axle turned on its fifth wheel. "Whoa." Bill got the horses stopped, kept them still until the lead mare was quiet, then got them moving again. The coach turned sharply to the right. The shotgun guard was correct, the coach wasn't made for sharp turns. One wrong move from any of the horses could tip it over and send it crashing off the road.

"Oh Christ," the guard said.

20

Through clenched teeth, Billy Walker repeated, half under his breath, "It's gonna be all right, be all right, be all right. Easy, fellers." With his hands he kept in communication with each horse. The lead mare was prancing, but looking ahead, staying in position.

Then they were around the curve, and the road ahead was straight. Downhill, but straight.

"Man oh man." The guard let his breath out with a whoosh. "I didn't think we was gonna make it. Good work, Billy. You can let 'em run now."

"Heeyup," Bill yelled. "Heeyup there." The team broke into a gallop, but Bill kept control, kept in communication. The road was steep here and an out-of-control team would cause a bad wreck. He slammed his right foot on the brake handle and pushed, slowing the coach wheels.

The horses ran. The coach bounced and rocked.

Not until they were off Dynamite Ridge did Bill take his foot off the brake handle. Now he, too, let his breath out with a whoosh. It was a straight run on into Concha Lake. "How's everybody in there?" he asked.

Leaning over, the guard yelled, "How's ever'body doin'?"

"We're still here," a man yelled back. "The deputy's still alive."

"We're over the notch now," the guard yelled. "We're agonna hit town on the run."

Twenty-four shod hooves thundered down the hard-packed

street in Concha Lake. The coach rattled. Dogs barked. Men in the dark street watched with a mixture of surprise and curiosity on their faces. Six badly winded horses brought the stage to a stop in front of Samuel Price's barn, and stood, heads down, nostrils flared. Samuel Price himself came running out of the barn, carrying a lantern.

"That you, Billy? What the holy hell happened?"

Bill yelled, "Get Dr. Hadley. Run, somebody. We've got two men shot." A man said, "I know where he lives. I'll fetch 'im." A pair of boots took off at a lope.

Townsmen came running up, wanting to know what happened. They all pitched in to help with what had to be done. While two men unhitched the horses, strong hands carried Charley out of the coach and laid him on the ground. "I don't think he's breathin'," someone said. Eddie had to be helped out, and he was too weak to stand. He tried to joke: "My get-along ain't gettin' too good."

"Let's get him over to my room," Bill said. "We'll carry him." Four pairs of strong hands picked Eddie up and, half-running, carried him to Bill's room behind the jail. Bill told Samuel Price what had happened, and the businessman swore. "Goddamnit, why'd anybody wanta do that?"

"They were after us," Bill said. "It's Eddie and me they want. Where in hell is that doctor?"

Eddie was on his back on his bed. His breathing was heavy, labored. He groaned. Bill pulled Eddie's shirttail out and took a close look at the wound. It was bleeding and Eddie's shirt and pants were soaked in blood. "The doctor's coming, Eddie. Hang on, partner."

Then Dr. Hadley was there, his nightshirt tucked inside his pants, which were held up with suspenders. His high-top shoes were unlaced. He took one look at the wounded man and said, "Need more light. Bring more light." There were only two lamps in the room. Someone said, "I'll fetch some more."

Eddie's eyes were only half-open, but he spoke. "I heard

200

somebody say Charley Lupkin was shot too. He needs you worse than I do, doctor."

"Charley's dead," a man said. "We put 'im on a cot in the barn, and he ain't breathin'."

The deputy's eyes squinched tight and he groaned, "Oh God."

Dr. Hadley looked around at all the curious faces, and said, "Will you all leave, please? Everybody except you, Sheriff, and maybe one more. Build a fire in the stove. Heat some water. Hurry."

More lamps were lighted, and the room was ablaze with light. The doctor opened his leather satchel, then looked down at Eddie. "Help me get his clothes off. Find something to cover him with. A clean sheet, if you please."

Soon the deputy was naked from the waist down. Bill jerked a bed sheet off his own bed and covered him with it. The doctor unbuttoned Eddie's shirt, but Eddie complained, "I ain't shot up here and I'll be damned if I wanta lay here plumb nekked." The shirt was pulled up around Eddie's shoulders but left on.

"Where's the hot water?" Doctor Hadley asked. "Got to wash my hand. And, oh yes, I had better boil some horse-hair."

"It's heating."

"Very well. Hmmm." The doctor examined the wound. "Missed the lung. Missed the vital organs. But it's still in there. Bleeding. Got to get it out and tie off some blood vessels. Got to open it up for drainage. Got to . . ." He held his hands in front of his face. His hands trembled. "Lord help me. I . . . Lord help me."

"What's wrong, doctor?" Bill asked.

Dr. Hadley was on the verge of tears. "I can't do it. My hands won't function. I swore once I'd never operate again. I . . . I'm sorry. So very sorry."

The door opened and Irene Ringeley came in. Her face was white with fear and her voice was high, excited. "I heard Eddie was shot. I . . . Eddie." With quick steps she was at the bed. "Eddie, are you. . . ?" She turned to the doctor, "How is he? Is it bad?"

Bill answered, "It's bad, Miss Ringeley. The doctor thinks he can't operate."

"Oh my. Eddie, can I do anything? Eddie, please don't leave me."

A weak grin spread across the deputy's face. "Irene, you couldn't chase me away with a stick." The grin disappeared and his face screwed up in pain.

"All right," Bill said, "if you can't do it, doctor, I'll do it. Tell me what to do."

Dr. Hadley shook his head. "You—your hands are too big, too callused. You don't have the sensitivity."

"Do what?" Irene Ringeley's eyes were wild. "Do what?"

Bill answered, "Get the bullet out and whatever else needs doing. The doctor's hands are shaking too bad."

"Then I'll do it."

"Miss Ringeley, it's a bloody mess. I don't think you can—"

She cut him off, "Yes I can." To the doctor she said, "Tell me what to do."

The doctor wiped his face with a white handkerchief. "Are you sure, miss? You have to cut human flesh."

Her face blanched, but quickly she regained her composure. "I can do it. Just tell me what to do."

Looking at Bill, the doctor said, "Is the water hot?"

"Yeah. It's about to boil."

"Very well." He was in control of himself again. "Now, here's the situation. I can give him a hypodermic of morphia, but that takes about an hour to take effect. I have some chloroform that will put him to sleep within minutes, but I don't have an inhaler. I'll have to apply it to the face and it sometimes burns the skin."

"Look, doctor, I think he's about out of it now." Eddie's eyes were closed and his breathing was shallow. But his muscles were tight, his body tense.

Dr. Hadley put his stethoscope to the deputy's chest and felt the pulse in his left wrist. Looking up, he said, "His heart is strong, but we have no time to waste. Is the water boiling? Are you sure you want to do this, miss?"

"I'm sure."

"Once we start, we'll have to finish. You have to be sure you are up to it."

Irene Ringeley's features twisted in consternation. "I'll do whatever you tell me to do. He's the man I love."

"I see. Very well." The doctor produced a large wad of cotton from his satchel and a bottle of chloroform. He poured some of the liquid onto the cotton and held it over Eddie's face. "Bring some hot water and soap."

Miss Ringeley's glance went from Eddie to the doctor to Bill and back to Eddie. She murmured, "Oh please, God." Soon the deputy's muscles relaxed. The cotton was removed. Dr. Hadley slapped the deputy's face and got no reaction. "Wash your hands, miss. Thoroughly. I wish I had some surgeon's gloves, but I have not. Thoroughly, now. Scrub your nails." The young woman did as she was told. She was handed a scalpel.

"We have to open the wound, enlarge it. Cut here." His fingers traced a short line along the deputy's side, a line that crossed the bullet hole.

"Uh—uh," Her voice trembled, and her hand shook as she took the scalpel.

The doctor snapped, "You have to be steady. Can you do it?"

Her jaws tightened, her shoulders straightened. She took a deep breath and cut where the doctor's fingers had traced. Blood welled out of the cut.

"Deeper. A little deeper."

Bill stood on the other side of the bed, holding a lamp as close to the wound as he could. He glanced at the young woman. Her face was set, determined. She cut deeper.

"That's good. Now we have to get the projectile out. Put

your finger in the wound and try to find it. Your finger is the best probe."

She hesitated a few seconds, then did as told.

"Can you feel it?"

"I feel something hard."

"That's it. There is no bone there. Here." He handed her some long handled forceps. We can't waste time. He'll come out of it soon. Be careful, but try to get hold of it with the forceps. Steady now."

Sweat beaded her forehead. She blinked the sweat out of her eyes, as she pushed the forceps into the wound. The doctor said, "It's like tweezers. Just try to get hold of it."

"Uh—uh, I think I've got it, doctor."

"Carefully pull it out. Careful now."

"I, uh, I can't see."

"Hold the lamp closer." Bill held the lamp next to the young woman's face. She said, "I—I'm sweating so bad, I . . ." The doctor wiped sweat off her forehead with a rag. "Pull carefully, but pull it out."

Then it was out, an ugly misshapen piece of lead. She dropped it on the floor.

"Very well. Now here's where we need steady hands. Are you all right, young lady?"

Bill asked, "What's left to do, doctor?"

"We have to tie off one—two—three blood vessels to stop the bleeding. We'll use horsehair as I have no cotton or silk thread. Boiling the horsehair sterilizes it and makes it pliable and elastic. Look here, miss. Look closely now."

She bent over the wound, still blinking sweat out of her eyes. "See there. Here's where small hands are necessary. Steady hands." He handed her a length of hair from a horse's tail. "Tie this around that vessel there. See it? Just tie a simple knot."

Irene Ringeley straightened up, closed her eyes a moment in silent prayer, then bent to her task. In two minutes it was

204

done. Her hands were bloody and she washed them in the pan of water.

"Not a bad job," the doctor said. "Now we'll cleanse it with carbolic soap and sew him up. Bring another pan of hot water."

The young woman's work was not over. She had to do the sewing. When finally she was finished, she collapsed in a chair, her hands folding and unfolding in her lap. Tears ran down her face, and her shoulders shook as she sobbed quietly. Bill put a hand on her shoulder. "You did a fine job, Miss Ringeley. You're a brave girl. Eddie's going to be proud of you."

"Will he . . . will he live, doctor? Oh, please God, I hope I didn't hurt him."

"Yes, barring complications, I think he will recover. He'll be sick and unable to move for a time. Perhaps a long time." Then the doctor got down on his knees in front of her, his face below hers. "Miss—and Sheriff Walker—I apologize to you both. I'd like to explain something." He paused a moment, then went on in a halting voice. "I . . . I won't bore you with a long story. Once upon a time I was a fine surgeon. I performed more than twenty-five operations in the Memorial Hospital of Kansas City. But I made a mistake and a patient died. A strong young man. I couldn't deal with it. I took to the bottle." His head drooped and his voice was barely audible. "Now I'm worthless."

Irene Ringeley touched his face with her fingertips. "You knew what to do, doctor. No one else in this whole territory knew what to do. You're worth everything."

A groan brought their attention back to the patient. Eddie's eyes were open, roving around the room. "Irene," he said, "what are you doin' here? What's happenin'?"

She went to him, knelt beside the bed, took his hand, forced a smile. "Oh, I just thought I'd stop by and see how you're getting on."

30

The doctor and Irene Ringeley stayed until daylight. Eddie slept sporadically. Around midnight Bill answered a knock on the door and found Carl Ringeley standing there. He was a tall man with black straight hair and a black moustache. "I'm looking for my daughter," he said. "Someone told me she might be here."

"Come in, Mr. Ringeley," Bill said, standing back. When Irene's father was told what had happened, he put his arm around the young woman's shoulders and hugged her. "I'm proud of you. Your mother will be proud of you. I'll have to go back and tell her where you are. She's worried."

Before the doctor left, he advised Bill and Irene that Eddie would be bedfast for some time and would have to use a bedpan. Bill said he would take care of that. Irene would see that the patient was well fed. The few times that Eddie awakened, he was in pain, and Bill and Irene were relieved when he drifted to sleep again. Once, when the deputy awakened, he looked down at himself, saw that the lower half of his body was covered only with a sheet, and said, "Irene, did you . . . ?"

With another forced smile, she said, "Get used to it, Eddie. Husbands and wives see each other all the time."

"Husbands and wives? Do you mean . . . ?"

"Yes. How does that suit you?"

A smile spread across his face. "That just tickles me plumb to . . . it tickles the heck out of me."

Shortly after daylight, Bill went over to Samuel Price's barn and was surprised to see one of the well-dressed passengers just getting dressed. "Morning," Bill said. "I guess you don't live in Concha Lake. I expect you'll be on the eastbound stage this morning."

"Indeed I will. This time I hope we get all the way to Rosebud before anything goes wrong." He had gray mutton-chop whiskers and needed a shave.

"Would you mind," Bill said while the man laced his shoes, "if I asked your name?"

"Scott. Thomas J Scott."

"You're a visitor in our fair city," Bill said, "and I can't help wondering why. It's probably none of my business, but would you mind telling me?"

"A business matter. I had business to discuss with Mr. Hiram Jackson."

"Oh, I see. Hmm." Bill absorbed that, and said, "Others have come here to discuss business with Hiram Jackson and they all stayed in his house instead of sleeping in this barn. I apologize, but I'm curious as to why you aren't a guest in his home."

"It's a private matter, Sheriff."

"I see. Hmm. Would you mind telling me what business you're in?"

With a hint of impatience Thomas Scott said, "I'm in the banking business. I am on the board of directors of the Mountain National Bank of Rosebud, Colorado."

That was something else Bill had to absorb. "Well, there's a Mr. Vincent Rutledge who I was told is chairman of the board. I can't help wondering why you're here instead of him."

Standing, buttoning a brocaded vest, the banker said, "Mr. Rutledge is no longer a member of the board of directors."

"Well," Bill said, his mind working as he talked, "I can't help wondering why."

"That is a private matter."

"I see. Hmm." He looked down at his boots, going over it in his mind. Then he said, "What this sounds like to me is Mr. Rutledge had a falling out with the other members of the board, and you came here to see what you could see about the bank's investments."

"There again, Sheriff, I must decline to comment."

"Uh-huh. And it also sounds like you had a disagreement with Hiram Jackson, and are not welcome in his house." A pause, then, "And that sounds like some of the investments you are interested in are investments in Hiram Jackson's enterprises, his new hotel, his store, his ranch."

"I am sorry, Sheriff, but all this is private business."

"Uh-huh. Well, I'm thinking that you will have to tell somebody about it. Maybe the district attorney — or in court. You can be subpoenaed, you know."

The banker's shoulders slumped. He was suddenly weary. "You could be correct. But as of now, it's a private matter."

"Uh-huh. Well, Mr. Scott, you told me a lot whether you intended to or not. Can I do anything to make you more comfortable until the stage leaves? Buy you some breakfast?"

"Thank you, no."

"Here's wishing you a good trip home, Mr. Scott."

Bill went into Samuel Price's office, sat at his desk, and wrote a note. Addressed to Geoffrey Rodeman, it read: "Come to Concha Lake as soon as possible. You will have legal work to do here. I am going to make some arrests today. This is urgent." When Samuel Price came in, Bill handed the folded note to him. "Will you see that this is delivered to the district attorney's office today?"

"Shore, Billy."

Then, after doing what he could to make his deputy comfortable, Bill went to his office and took down the rifle. It was one of Marlin's first lever-action repeating rifles, a .45

208

caliber with a long octagonal barrel. He checked the magazine to be sure it was fully loaded, put a box of shells in his shirt pocket, then checked the cylinder on his Navy Colt. Carrying the rifle, he went to the corral behind the mercantile and saddled a county horse with the county saddle. He rode out of town, going east on the Notch Road. The rifle was in a boot under his right leg.

He rode past the homesteads, seeing no one, then followed the dim wagon road across Boulder Creek and on east. He could feel the tenseness in his shoulders, throat, and stomach. It was what he'd felt in the war a long time ago, a nameless nervous tingling that went through every soldier's body when a battle was at hand. A night without sleep meant nothing. The light breakfast he'd fixed for himself and Eddie was not important. All that mattered in the whole wide world right now was what lay ahead. As soon as he was in sight of the cowcamp, he stopped.

They were there. Three horses stood in the corral munching hay, and the light wagon was parked about fifty feet in front of the house. From where he was he couldn't read the brands on the horses, but he could see that one was branded on the right hip. Double O horses were branded on the left shoulder. No human was in sight.

Three men and a woman were in the house and at least two of the men were killers.

He hoped he could circle the house, see where all the doors and windows were, without being seen, but he knew that was unlikely. The cover was sparse, no trees, no brush. Nothing but a few gulleys where a man on foot could kneel and keep out of sight of the house, but where a man on a horse would be in plain view. All right, so they'd see him. There was nothing he could do about that. He reined the county horse south, staying far enough away from the house that a rifle bullet would have to be aimed exceptionally well to hit him. Yep, there was a window in back and another on the south side. Another window was on the front, near the door. Three windows and a door. No way one man could cover the house.

Staying wide, Bill rode around to the east side where the corrals and loafing shed were. As he approached, he kept his eyes glued to the door and the window beside it. Any movement there would have him dropping off the horse and making himself as small as possible on the ground. Still no sign of human life.

Dismounting, he tied the county horse to a corral post on the far side of the corral. From there he tried to figure out what to do.

There was no doubt now that he had been seen. They were staying far enough away from the window that he couldn't see them, but he was being watched. Any second now they could poke a rifle barrel through the window.

The bold thing to do was to walk up to the door and knock. That would be bold but stupid. While he was talking to whoever answered his knock, the others could slip out the back window and come at him from around the house. They could come at him from each side, catch him in the middle. Shaking his head, Bill muttered, "That won't do a-tall."

Let's see. The wagon was standing broadside to the house and could be used for protection. The sides were made of thick planks. One side of the wagon wouldn't stop a rifle bullet, but the two sides probably would. But that would leave his feet and legs exposed under the wagon. Let's see. There was a water barrel next to the corral gate. If nobody shot at him, he could tip it over and roll it to the wagon. That was a big *if*. Maybe the best thing to do was just run to the wagon and get behind the rear wheels. With two wheels between him and the house, it would take a well-placed shot to hit him. The thick round spokes would deflect a bullet. But if they fired enough shots, one would find its way between the spokes.

All this went through Bill's mind. He couldn't just stand there behind the corral. He had to do something. Gripping the rifle, he ran for the wagon.

31

Sheriff Billy Walker ran in a zigzag pattern, making himself a moving target. When he got behind the wagon, he felt a little foolish. Nobody had shot at him. Was it possible that nobody was at home? Or maybe only the woman, Mrs. Hudson, was in there. From his position he could see the brands on the horses in the corral. One Double O. The other two were something else, a Rocking R and something he couldn't read. All right, so maybe he had run like a rabbit for nothing. This playing Indian might look silly to the woman if she was watching from the window. But those horses were ridden here by somebody other than Double O cowboys. They were ridden here last night from Rosebud. That was the only explanation. Well, he'd find out.

Standing, showing only his head and shoulders, keeping an eye on the window, Bill yelled, "Hudson! Walt Hudson! This is Sheriff Walker. Come out. I want to talk to you!"

No answer. He yelled again. Quiet. Aw for crying in the beer, what were they waiting for? For him to go to the door? Yeah, that's what they wanted. Get him between them. Damned if he would. He yelled again.

When no one answered, he pointed the rifle skyward and fired a shot in the air. A curtain in the window moved. Some damned body was watching him. He yelled again, "Mrs. Hudson! This is Sheriff Walker. Come out. I'm not after you. Come out here!"

The door opened and Mrs. Hudson came out, wringing her hands. "Is that you, Sheriff?"

"It's me. Send your husband out too."

"He's not to home."

"Don't lie to me, Mrs. Hudson. I'm not here to arrest you, but if you lie to me, I will."

She glanced at the house and turned fearful eyes back at Bill. "They, uh . . ." She was scared and undecided.

"Come over here, Mrs. Hudson."

"But my husband, he . . ."

"All right, tell him to come out too."

Still undecided, she looked from Bill to the house, back to Bill. "I . . . I don't know what to do. Walt, he . . . he's not a bad man, Sheriff."

"Tell him to come out."

Turning to the house, she pleaded, "Walt. Walter, come outside. Walter, please come out." She was wringing her hands and crying. "Walter, please."

The door opened and Walt Hudson stood in it. He yelled, "Maggie didn't do nothin' wrong, Sheriff."

"Come out here," Bill yelled.

"I can't. I . . ." Then Walt Hudson moved fast. Bending low he ran, ran at the wagon, ran as fast as he could. He grabbed his wife by the hand and pulled her along. Bill saw the window curtain move, saw a rifle barrel. He threw the Marlin to his shoulder and fired at the window, saw the bullet poke a hole in the curtain. Quickly, he jacked another round into the firing chamber and fired another shot through the window, then a shot through the door. He was ready to fire again when Walt Hudson and his wife ran around the wagon and squatted behind the front wheels.

Now the door was wide open, and two quick shots came from inside. One tore through the far side of the wagon and thudded into the near side. Another screamed off a wheel spoke. Bill answered by firing into the open door. The Marlin kicked back against his shoulder, but the gun had a good solid recoil. Then the firing stopped.

Glancing at Walt Hudson, Bill saw he was carrying a wal-

213

nut-handled pistol in a holster, but hadn't drawn it. "How many are in there, Walt?"

"Two, Sheriff." The skinny man was cowed, his eyes downcast. "Give me your gun, Walt." The cowboy handed it over, butt first.

Bill stuck the gun in his belt, and keeping his eyes on the house asked, "Did they come in from Rosebud last night."

"Yeah. That's what they said."

"Did they say Hiram Jackson hired them?"

"Yeah."

Mrs. Hudson spoke. "Walt didn't do nothin' bad, Sheriff. He only done what he was told."

"I'm afraid he's gonna have to answer a lot of questions about that. Did they tell you what happened at the relay station last night?"

"No," Hudson answered. "What happened?"

"Two men were shot from ambush. One died."

"Aw-w-w. I didn't even know about it."

"Did they tell you their names?"

"Yeah, uh . . ."

"Let me guess. Theodore Magill and Shelby Swasso."

"How'd you know Sheriff?"

"They work for Hiram Jackson and they're from Rosebud. And the owner of the Double O could use more of the land along Boulder Creek, homesteaders' land, and he tried to use this pair to get it. Now, the question is, how do I arrest them?"

"You can't. Not by yourself."

Sheriff Billy Walker worried about that. The two weren't going to be arrested without a fight. They could be out the back window by now and running away. Running where? Their horses were here in a corral, and they would have to shoot the sheriff to get to them. The sheriff was somewhat fortified behind a wagon. If they were running, they were afoot. Where would they go?

No shots had come from the house for a while. They would go either to the Double O headquarters or to the Notch Road, where they might stick a gun in some travelers' faces and take their horses and wagon. Or they might go to one of the homesteads and take some horses at gunpoint. They would kill if necessary. They might kill even if it wasn't necessary.

How to stop them?

Try as he would, Bill could think of no way. He said to Walt Hudson, "They probably slipped out the back window, but I can't be sure. I'll have to find out." He paused, thinking, then said, "I'm going to take a look. If anything goes wrong, you and your missus get to town and tell Samuel Price what happened. Will you do that?"

"Yeah, Sheriff."

Reloading the rifle, Bill doubted he could trust Walt Hudson, but it didn't matter. He had the cowboy's gun, and he wouldn't be shot in the back when he approached the house. Standing, he fired two shots through the window and two more through the open door. Then, rifle in his left hand and six-gun in his right, cocked, ready to fire, he stepped out from behind the wagon and started walking.

Sheriff Billy Walker was afraid to blink. His eyes moved constantly from the window to the door and back to the window. His pulse pounded, his legs were a little weak. Could he shoot fast enough and accurate enough?

The light was bad in the house, and he couldn't see more than a few feet inside the door and window. He watched for movement, eyes wide, walking straight at the door.

Something moved near the door. He fired two shots from the Navy Colt. The window curtain moved, and he fired two shots through the window. He saw more movement near the door and fired at the same instant a rifle cracked. The bullet burned the air near Bill's head. He fired again through the open door, then realized he wasn't going at this right. He had to get to the door fast.

He ran. Again, he zigzagged, Indian fashion. No shots came at him.

When he reached the door, he flattened himself against the outside wall next to the door. He listened, finger on the trigger of the six-gun. Then two thoughts came to his mind: the Navy Colt had no more live bullets in it, and the two men could come around each side of the house. He holstered the Colt and held the rifle ready.

Or they could be inside, hidden in the other rooms, one in each room, peering around the door jambs, waiting for him.

He wished the six-gun were fully loaded. He could aim and shoot faster with a pistol. But he didn't dare reload it now. Had to keep his eyes peeled. Had to listen. Nothing happened. Waited. Watched. Listened.

He had to get in the house, and there was only one way to do it. Rifle ready to fire from the hip, he jumped through the open door, then immediately stepped aside against a wall, out of the doorway. Eyes searching, he waited, heart pounding. He was in the kitchen, and there were two doors to the other rooms, both open.

With his back against a wall, Bill moved toward an open connecting door, moved slowly, carefully, as quietly as he could. When he reached the door, he paused a moment, wishing his heart would slow down, then stepped quickly into the room.

Two cots, a scarred dresser, a wire stretched across one corner to hang clothes from, a steamer trunk at the foot of the bed. Nothing human.

By now Bill suspected the two had climbed out the window of the other room and were running away. But he wasn't sure. Moving slowly, carefully, he made his way to the third room. One double bed, a handmade wooden armoire, a dresser. That was all.

Bill went to the open window and looked out. They had climbed out, no doubt about that. They had run and were out of sight, hidden in one of the gulleys. Going after them

216

would be even more dangerous than searching the house. Out there he would be a perfect target. And if the pair knew their business, they'd be far enough apart that he couldn't see them both. One could show himself just long enough to draw his attention, then duck, while the other took aim.

Or—and when the thought popped into Bill's mind he immediately ran back through the house and out the door—they could have waited until he was in the house then sneaked out to the corral and the horses.

Bill's eyes tried to take in everything at a glance. He saw Walt Hudson standing behind the wagon, looking at him. Bill yelled. "Did they come this way?"

"No!" Hudson yelled back.

Could Bill trust him? Was it a trick? He tried to see everything. The horses were standing quietly in the corral. If anyone was in there with them, they didn't show it. Rifle ready, eyes searching, he walked back to the wagon. "Did you see them? Are you telling me the truth?"

"Honest, Sheriff, I'm done lyin' to you. They didn't come this way."

"Then they're running west. They're afoot. Here's what I want you to do. Harness your team and hitch up the wagon. Go to town. Wait for me there. If I don't show, go to Samuel Price and tell him everything. And I mean everything."

"Yessir, Sheriff. I'll do that."

"Listen to me now." Bill tried a lie. "He already knows about you and your part in all this. You're already in trouble. If you hightail it, you'll be in more trouble. Don't make that mistake."

Mrs. Hudson answered, "We're gonna do what you said, Sheriff. We're both sick and tired of all this."

Bill stood watch with the Marlin while Hudson and his wife caught and harnessed the team. While they were hitching the horses to the wagon, he asked, "How did you get into this jackpot, anyway?"

Again, it was Mrs. Hudson who answered, "He got in a

fight in Denver and shot a man. The man didn't die, but the laws was gonna put Walt in jail. We snuck out of town. Mr. Jackson found out about it some way—prob'ly from one of his hired hoodlums—and he used that as a club over Walt's head."

Hudson said, "It was a saloon fight. I shouldn't of shot 'im, but he was bigger'n me."

"Get in your wagon and get going."

Bill watched the wagon rattle out of the yard, then opened the corral gate and let the remaining three horses out. The horses were happy to be free and left on a run. Bill's county horse wanted to go with them, but was tied to a corral post. Now it was decision time again. Should he get on the horse and go after the two killers, or search for them on foot? On a horse he would be a good target. On foot he would be a good target. He reloaded the Navy Colt, trying to decide what to do. At the same time he was puzzled. Why did they quit the house and run on foot? They were well forted up in there. Did they think Walt Hudson had turned on them and would help the sheriff? Or did they think the sheriff had help coming from town and they would be trapped in the house? Whatever, they were desperate. Then another thought popped into Bill's mind:

They could waylay the Hudsons and take their horses and wagon.

32

That settled it. Bill went on a run to where the county horse was tied and stepped into the saddle. He'd dropped Walt Hudson's gun back there in the yard somewhere, and the cowboy was unarmed. He couldn't send an unarmed man anywhere near two well-armed killers.

He rode at a lope, carrying the Marlin across the saddle in front of him until the wagon was in sight, then hung back, watching. Where would they strike? Would they jump up out of a gulley or would they be hiding behind the trees along the creek? He didn't have to wonder long.

The wagon was nearing the creek crossing, the horses traveling at a trot. A man suddenly appeared—just appeared—with a rifle in his hand. Reining up, Bill aimed and fired from the saddle. And suddenly he had a rodeo on his hands.

The county horse broke in two and pitched wildly. Bill hit the ground on his left shoulder. Air left his lungs with a whoosh, and for some crazy reason he remembered an old saying among big game hunters: You can shoot a gun off any horse—once. The horse was still pitching, the empty stirrups were flapping. The Marlin was near Bill's hands. He scrambled to his knees, grabbed the gun, and tried to see what was happening at the wagon. A man was aiming a rifle at him, aiming carefully. Then suddenly he had trouble too. Walt Hudson jumped from the wagon onto the man's back, wrapped his arms around the man's head. Mrs. Hudson screamed. "Sheriff. Hurry. Hurry."

Bill got up and ran.

He got to the wagon just as Walt Hudson was losing the fight. The thin cowboy was being shaken off, was losing his hold. But he got there in time to slam the butt of the Marlin against the side of a killer's head. The fight was over. So it seemed. Both killers were down.

Winded from running, Bill said, "What . . . how. . . ?"

"They just jumped up from somewhere," Mrs. Hudson answered. "Your shot knocked that 'un down, but this 'un thought he had you dead to rights."

"He darned . . . near did."

"Look out, Sheriff!"

The man Bill had hit was rolling onto his back with a rifle in his hands. He fired from the hip at the same instant the Navy Colt jumped into Bill's hand. The killer was on his back. His shot missed.

Sheriff Billy Walker's shot did not miss.

33

Geoffrey Rodeman was a happy, happy young man. He leaned back in the sheriff's chair, put his feet on the sheriff's desk, and smiled to himself. This was just dandy. The murderers, armed robbers, cattle rustlers were all dead. But the big fish were still very much alive and in his—the deputy DA's—grasp. He'd do it in a professional, legal manner. Go back to Rosebud, get an arrest warrant. Make sure the *Rosebud Herald* knew about it, make sure they got his name spelled correctly. Then come back, perhaps with a reporter, and serve the warrant himself. Personally.

Hiram Jackson wasn't going anywhere. Neither was Vincent Rutledge. And with that cowboy, Walter Hudson, more than willing to testify, they were as good as convicted. Geoffrey Rodeman could see his name in the headlines now. There would be a story about the arrest, another about the formal charges, and more about the trial. The deputy DA's name would be in the lead of every story. He would soon be *the* DA of the sixth judicial district. And from there . . . who knows?

Oh, the sheriff would get some credit too. He was the one who pieced it together. How Mr. Jackson borrowed too heavily from the Mountain National Bank and was in danger of losing everything through foreclosure. How the chairman of the bank's board of directors offered a deal whereby Mr. Jackson would slip him a bribe under the table as payment for postponing foreclosure. How Mr. Jackson had a contract to sell beef to the railroad work crews, but to raise money he sold stolen beef rather than his own. How Mr. Jackson hired toughs from the saloons of Rosebud to do the stealing. How he reported cattle stolen from his own ranch to divert suspicion. Yes, with cooperation from the railroad purchasing agent the evidence was there.

And, oh yes, how the toughs weren't satisfied with stealing a few head of cattle now and then and stole bigger herds, and worse, took to murder and robbery. How they murdered poor Sheriff Koen. But how the law caught up with them when they robbed the sawmill payroll, and how Mr. Jackson merely went to Rosebud and hired more toughs. How he'd replaced his pair of toughs twice. The sheriff and his deputy would be in the news too, but when the trial started, they would be forgotten. As for Vincent Rutledge, a very important man, the hard-fighting deputy DA would charge him with a crime too. He'd have to do some reading of the law, but he'd find something to charge him with. And when the publicity subsided, he'd investigate the slaughterhouse in Rosebud and uncover more crime. Yes sir, Deputy DA Geoffrey Rodeman would personally put a stop to the corruption in the sixth district. It was going to be grand.

The only sour note in all this was having to share a room with a sick wounded man or sleep in the detestable barn.

Sheriff Billy Walker wasn't so happy. Sitting in his room, watching his deputy sleep, he couldn't help thinking about it all. He'd killed five men since he'd pinned on this badge. Three innocent men had been killed, and his deputy had damn near died. A few lines from an old Confederate war song came to his mind: *Though their corpses strew the earth/ that smiled upon their birth/and blood pollutes each hearthstone forever.* He had to decide whether he wanted to continue being sheriff. Samuel Price was now the chairman of the county board, and he'd promised to hire a county clerk to do the tax collecting if Bill would run for election in the fall. After all that had happened and after the way it had turned out, the job would be easier. The sheriff of Concha County had a reputation that would keep the hardcases away. But Billy Walker was no politician. And he didn't want a tough reputation.

Wearily, he stood and poured himself another cup of coffee. He wished that dandy lawyer would get out of his office and out of town. He wished . . . aw hell, he didn't know what he wished. Well, maybe he did.

He envied Eddie. Eddie had Irene. He had nobody. There were times when a man needed somebody.

A tapping on the door brought him out of his thoughts, and when he opened the door, he was astonished. The woman standing there had chestnut hair curling down to her shoulders. She wore a blue dress with white lace around the collar and down the front. A little lacy hat was perched on top of her head. She was beautiful.

Billy Walker stammered like a bashful child, "Why, why, Mrs. Peterson, I almost didn't recognize you."

Her smile was dazzling. "I thought I'd come to town in a buggy for a change, Sheriff Walker, and I just had to stop by and thank you for everything. A young man in your office said he thought you were back here. Forgive me for bothering you in your living quarters."

"Why, that's, uh, that's all right, Mrs. Peterson." But he kept his back to the door to block her view of the inside.

"Call me Angelina, would you. Or Angie. May I call you Billy? It seems all your friends do, and I hope I'm one of your friends."

"Why, sure."

"And that brings up another subject. I would very much like you to come to the Circle J for supper. You can stay overnight. We have extra rooms in the house. That way you can take your time leaving."

"Why, I'd, uh . . ."

"I don't want to pin you down, but let's set a date. How about Saturday?"

"Well, uh, all right."

223

"Wonderful. We'll see you Saturday then. Good day, Billy."

He watched her walk away, holding her skirt off the ground with both hands. There was one damned fine-looking woman. But when he went back inside and finished his coffee he realized something. He wasn't over feeling lonely.

Finally, he picked himself up. He had another chore to do, but this one would be easy. He would go out to the homesteads and inform the farmers that they no longer had to worry about two gents named Magill and Swasso taking over their properties. But he would advise them to get to the land office as fast as they could and sign all the papers.

It was four hours later when he rode back to town. The sun had just gone down behind the Wet Mountains. Its light reflected off the clouds hanging over the horizon, turning them several spectacular shades of red and blue. This really was a pretty valley, a good place to live. The sheriff was feeling better now.

He had a good meal under his belt, and he'd just made some arrangements. He would take his meals at the Widow Osborne's and move into the vacant room in her barn. He would pay her, of course. It would be a good deal for both of them.

Angelina Peterson didn't want to pin him down, she'd said. But she'd pinned him down.

Mary Osborne, with her round pleasant face and her well-mannered kids, they were the kind of people he needed.

When Sheriff Billy Walker rode into Concha Lake that evening, he was smiling.